Until September

CHRIS SCULLY

RIPTIDE
PUBLISHING

Riptide Publishing
PO Box 1537
Burnsville, NC 28714
www.riptidepublishing.com

Until September
Copyright © 2016 by Chris Scully

Cover art: Lou Harper, louharper.com/design.html
Editor: Carole-ann Galloway
Layout: L.C. Chase, lcchase.com/design.htm

ISBN: 978-1-62649-356-8

First edition
February, 2016

Also available in ebook:
ISBN: 978-1-62649-355-1

Until September

CHRIS SCULLY

RIPTIDE
PUBLISHING

For anyone who ever felt they weren't good enough—you are.

Table of Contents

Chapter 1

Twenty Years Ago

I hope you rot in hell, you sick motherfuck.

Sixteen-year-old Archie Noblesse took a long, defiant drag on his cigarette. He was hidden by the dumpster behind the community center but getting caught was the last thing on his mind at the moment. No one cared what he got up to. His grandfather would have smacked him upside the head—it had never taken much to get his *moosum* going—but he'd passed on years ago, so Archie stubbornly puffed away.

A good chunk of the one thousand-strong band was inside the center for his uncle's wake, but Archie hadn't been able to pretend for another minute. He shuddered at the thought of enduring it all again tomorrow for the funeral. *If only they knew you like I did, you fucking pervert.* Maybe they had. The reservation was full of buried secrets; you only had to scratch the surface. But no one ever did. No one wanted to.

He felt ready to shatter at any minute. The anger he usually kept in check was churning in his gut like molten lava in a volcano's crater. It was pushing at his chest, ready to spew from his lips. The thought of his uncle's saggy gut and sour breath made him shudder; the limp dick that, thank God, he couldn't get up half the time. Although that had never stopped him from trying. Or making Archie try.

A door opened. The gentle Cree hymns, all too familiar on the reservation, poured out.

"I thought you'd be here," said his sister Marguerite as she peered around the edge of the dumpster. Technically, she was his half sister, although he never thought of her that way. They had different fathers, both anonymous strangers, but Margie had gotten lucky—given her much lighter-colored skin and narrow face, hers had obviously been white.

As a child, Archie used to dream that his father had been a white businessman from the east who had come through Winnipeg, but he was a whole lot wiser now. Rich, white men used a better class of prostitute than their mother. And the mirror didn't lie; Archie hated his almond-shaped eyes and round face for marking him pure Cree as much as his tanned skin. His father was probably some drunk from the reservation. Sonia had never told him who it was, and as he had gotten older, he'd figured that she probably didn't even know.

Sometimes Archie was jealous of Margie for her light skin. He didn't want dumb Indian blood. But he kept his secret to himself. It wasn't her fault, and most of the time he loved her, loved her like he'd never loved anyone else on this earth.

Margie plucked the cigarette from his fingers and crushed it beneath her scuffed shoe. "Smoking's bad for you."

"So's this place." It was his favorite saying.

"*Kookum* says you should be inside."

"*Gran* can kiss my ass. I'm not spending another minute with that fucker."

Margie leaned her slight weight against his side, and Archie wrapped his arm around her narrow shoulders, noticing how the fabric of her secondhand dress pulled tight. At thirteen years old, she kept outgrowing her thrift-store clothes.

He would do it all again, make the same sacrifices, if it meant Margie was safe. He'd been her protector since birth, keeping her quiet while Sonia entertained in the next room, or on the nights she never came back to the apartment at all. He'd shoplifted formula from the store when there wasn't enough money for food, so Margie wouldn't go hungry. When Sonia made the mistake of leaving them alone in their rented-by-the-month motel room for three days, and the CFS finally caught up with them again, he'd thought it would be different than all the other times; *this* time they were being sent to live with family and now they'd be safe. But on the isolated northern Manitoba reservation Archie had found himself in a different kind of hell. Sure they had food on the table, and a roof over their heads, but there were new dangers.

While Margie had adjusted to life on the reservation quickly, making new friends as she always did, it had been more difficult for Archie.

Grandma Betty, *Kookum* as she insisted on being called, had her own problems, like an abusive alcoholic husband and a drug-addicted son with a fondness for little kids. She couldn't protect herself, let alone Archie and Marguerite. Uncle Russ had been the only person to take an interest in him. At first, he'd been fun—when he wasn't high that is. He'd show up every few weeks, hang around for a couple of days—long enough to score some drugs, or when he couldn't afford that, a bag of paint thinner or glue to sniff—and then disappear again. He treated Archie like a grown-up: taught him how to shoot a pellet gun and smoke a cigarette. But then one night he drove Archie out to the middle of nowhere, and what little hope and faith Archie had left in the world had died.

Afterward, when his uncle had zipped up his pants and boasted that no one would believe Archie if he told, Archie had known, with a sinking heart, it was true. The local RCMP detachment was half an hour's drive, and folks around here would never help him. He was an outsider. And what if they sent him away? Split him and Margie up? So he'd stayed quiet, and after a while it hadn't been so bad. At least it had kept Margie safe.

Archie was tainted goods—he accepted that now. But Margie still had a chance.

At least their sick, drug-addled fuck of an uncle had croaked before he could get to her—finally OD'd on a bad batch of heroin. Just in time too, because with summer coming there would be no hiding her budding breasts under layers of clothes like they had been all winter. Archie wouldn't have been able to keep his uncle away from a temptation like that for much longer. Even if he was small for his age, he was getting too old for the pedophile's taste.

There was a tiny part of him that did feel a bit sorry for his gran, losing first her husband four years ago and now her son, with her daughter swallowed up by the city. No wonder she'd never noticed what was going on in her own house. But loss was a way of life around here.

"I'm leaving tomorrow," he said abruptly, his mind made up. "While everyone's at the funeral."

"You can't," Margie cried. "Why? He's gone. We're safe."

"For now. But we need to get outta this place. And we need money, more money than I've got, to do it. You have to go to college, and I'm not waiting around here for the pushers to get to me. I don't wanna croak before I hit forty like Uncle Russ."

"But you're only sixteen, Archie. Where will you go?"

"I have enough for the bus ticket to Winnipeg. And from there . . .?" He shrugged as if it wasn't a big deal, as if fear wasn't a giant boulder in the pit of his stomach. Margie didn't know about the money tucked away under his mattress in their run-down double-wide trailer. Five hundred dollars. It was enough to get away if not exactly a windfall. It wasn't like he could have walked down the street and gotten a job at the local fast-food hangout—there wasn't one—so he'd spent a lot of time on his knees to earn that dough over the years, even in the winter, giving blowjobs behind the school for twenty dollars a pop, twenty-five if they wanted to come in his mouth. Sometimes it even turned him on—especially in those last few minutes when he was working them good, and he held all the power. They begged him then, especially the macho married ones who kept their eyes closed and pretended it was a woman's mouth wrapped around their dick. His uncle had taught him one useful skill at least.

But it was dangerous. He held a lot of secrets.

If he stayed, it was only a matter of time before this place got to him and he gave in to the addictions that ran in his family. Or worse, killed himself like the two kids in his class had last spring. And that was if he was lucky. If he wasn't, if word got out what he'd been doing, he wouldn't stand a chance. He was too small and scrawny to fight back.

He could feel the badness in his blood waiting to escape. He had to get away before it spilled over to Marguerite. He had to protect her.

"What about school?"

Archie snorted. "You're the smart one, not me. I've learned all I need to know, thanks."

"But what if mom comes back for us? How will we find you?"

"She won't come back," Archie said bluntly. Marguerite, so good and pure, had never given up hope that Sonia would return one day, but Archie knew the truth. They hadn't heard from her since the day, seven years ago, when Grandma Betty and Grandpa Tom drove all the way to Winnipeg to pick them up from foster care. The last memory Archie had of his mother—he hated calling her that—was of her asking them if they had any money they could lend her. No, their mother—not that she'd ever really been their mother—was either dead or would be soon. That's what happened to junkie whores in Winnipeg's notorious North End.

Margie pursed her lips. "What will you do?"

"Whatever it takes," Archie replied with false bravado. His chances were slim, but they were a hell of a lot slimmer if he stayed here.

He had to get away. It was the only option. Once he made it to the city, he would bus tables, do dishes. If he had to, he'd turn tricks. The key was to stay away from the drugs and alcohol or else he'd end up like so many other Indian kids. He'd seen how slippery that slope could be.

When she grew silent, he knew Margie was thinking about Sonia too—the needle tracks running up her arm and the bottle of cheap wine always within reach. "Don't worry, I'll be safe. I won't end up like her. Once I make enough money, I'll get you out too. You'll be able to go to any college you want."

"I don't care about college."

She was lying. Margie was the smartest girl in her grade. She would do something good with her life and make him proud. "Yes, you do," Archie insisted. "You don't want to stay here and pop out babies."

"Don't leave me, Archie," Margie sobbed, clutching at his arms. Gran had plaited her long, dark hair in two braids, and it made her look so young. For one brief moment, Archie's eyes stung, but he wouldn't let the tears spill. He had to be strong. He would take all the bad as long as Margie got the good. "Please."

"You'll be okay now, Margie. Just stay in school. Stay away from the drugs. And boys. Whatever you do, don't get knocked up. It'll only be a few years at most. Promise me." He shook her by the shoulders, hard enough to drive his point home. "You have to be strong. We have to be strong."

"I promise."

Archie hugged his sister, the last good thing in his life, tight. When Gran found them a few minutes later they were both crying, wrapped in each other's arms.

Chapter 2

Present Day

*A*rcher Noble toyed with the buttons of his charcoal-gray Armani suit as he waited for the makeup lady to finish blotting the forehead of the panel show's host and the cameras to start rolling. Unable to shake the feeling that his good fortune might disappear at any second, he caressed the expensive fabric. He may have taken a white man's name, changed his haircut and his clothes, but there were times when he could almost smell the weary stench of the reservation clinging to him. It was in his pores, in the color of his skin. No matter how he tried, he would never be able to completely mask it.

The suit, the only designer one he owned, was reserved for public appearances like this. He changed it up by varying the brightly colored silk ties and pocket squares so that he never appeared to wear the same outfit twice in a row. The money he'd spent on the jacket alone would have fed his family for months growing up. On his feet, his sole pair of dress shoes, buffed to a high shine, were a long way from the secondhand sneakers he'd grown up with. If he had finally learned one thing in thirty-six years of clawing his way out of the muck, it was that appearances were important. People tended to think twice about shitting on you if you looked—and acted—like you had money. And *nobody* shit on Archer Noble, not since he'd left poor, dumb Archie Noblesse behind.

He glanced around the vast studio, blinking under the bright lights, and tried not to let his awe show. After years of scrounging freelance writing and speaking gigs, and the occasional appearance on PROUDtv, his sacrifices were finally paying off.

Sales of his latest book, *I Don't: The Truth About the Gay Marriage Agenda*, had surpassed his expectations. In fact, the whole same-sex marriage issue had been one big cash cow for him and his publisher as everyone scrambled to voice their opinion on the debate. Now, after six weeks of making the rounds on the public access cable and local radio circuit, an op-ed in the *Huffington Post*, and a two-second sound bite on CNN, he had finally hit the big time. A national network with a live, syndicated talk show. Kim, the publicist his agent had set him up with, was a miracle worker.

He glanced over at her. She stood in the shadows next to the floor director. Behind her, the small studio audience was filing into the seats. Kim gave him a nod and a thumbs-up. She had done her part. Now he had to do his.

Who would ever have thought poor, scrawny Archie Noblesse, who grew up without a TV set and never finished high school, would make it all the way to Los Angeles, television capital of the world?

This was the final stop on his North American book tour. With the initial controversy over his book dying down, and the US Supreme Court decision on same-sex marriage come and gone, the networks were starting to lose interest—their focus had moved back to the crisis in the Middle East—and the pressure to stay on top was eating at him.

Archer's phone vibrated in his pocket. The area code indicated a Toronto number, but one he didn't recognize. It wasn't Marguerite's. The thought of his sister reminded him he hadn't spoken to her in weeks. He made a mental note to call her later tonight. Right now though, he didn't want to be disturbed. He switched the phone off and tucked it back away.

"So, where are you from?" asked the middle-aged, well-dressed woman seated to his left as they waited to begin. They had been introduced in the green room, but Archer couldn't remember her name. Something innocuous and appropriately suburban: Patty or Debbie. She wore a navy-blue skirt and matching blazer and, yes, even a string of pearls around her neck. She was part of some family-values organization. He didn't recall which; they were all the same anyway. On her other side sat a dour-looking pastor from an evangelical church he had never heard of. This was a conservative panel for a conservative talk show, and they certainly had all the usual bases covered—religion and family morals. *One of these things does not belong*, thought Archer, who only two days ago had guested alongside a drag queen and gay porn star, and then fucked said porn star in the restroom afterward.

"Canada," Archer replied. He knew where this conversation was going.

She gave him a patronizing smile. "I meant originally. Hawaii? You look a bit Hawaiian."

"And originally, I'm still from Canada." Archer loved screwing with people who tried to figure out his ethnicity. Aboriginal people were something of a novelty in American media. Hispanic was usually people's first guess, followed by Filipino. Hawaiian was new. "I'm First Nations Cree."

She frowned, but then the lights went down and Glenn Smith, the host, took his place behind the curving desk with a practiced smile. Archer straightened his tie and savored the surge of anticipation coursing through his veins.

"Three, two, one, and . . . we're on."

"Friends, today we are discussing a serious topic that is having repercussions throughout this country: same-sex marriage." Glenn Smith's cherubic face squinted into the camera, lips tightening to reflect how serious he was. "My guests are Pastor Gordon Sinclair of Holy Light Church, Mrs. Penny MacDonald from the American Family Association and leading member of One Million Moms, and Archer Noble, controversial blogger and author of *I Don't: The Truth About the Gay Marriage Agenda.*"

Glenn turned to the weasel-faced pastor and began the discussion. Archer listened with half an ear. Not that it mattered anyway. The arguments were always the same. *Blah, blah, destroying the fabric of society. Blah, blah, sanctity of marriage.* You'd think someone could come up with an idea that hadn't already been beaten to death.

Was this show being broadcast up in Toronto where Margie would see it? He would send her a link if it went online. She hated his alter ego but still faithfully sought out his every appearance, saved every article, with all the devotion of a younger sister.

Archer made eye contact with the PA he'd been flirting with earlier. The man was younger than he preferred and a shade too Abercrombie & Fitch for his taste, but the production assistant was clearly interested, and Archer's flight back to Vancouver didn't leave until morning.

"What about you, Mr. Noble?" Glenn asked, finally swiveling in his direction. "You are a practicing homosexual who doesn't believe same-sex couples should marry or raise children, correct?" Archer heard Penny's swift intake of breath, as if learning she'd been seated next to Satan himself. *Yes, that's right, lady. Betcha never saw that one coming.*

"Oh, I'm practicing, Glenn." Archer leaned forward in his chair with a wink to the camera. Bastard obviously hadn't even read the book. "Actually, Glenn, I've never said we *shouldn't* be allowed to marry—that's a civil-rights issue, and the lawyers are welcome to argue over it—they have to earn their keep, don't they? My book is about why on earth we would want to in the first place.

"The gay establishment doesn't speak for all of us. Yeah, gay marriage is a threat, but not to your families or straight marriage." Here he deliberately paused. "It's a threat to *my* sexual freedom. It's one more way to make us more socially acceptable, to oppress our sexual freedom by forcing us to conform to antiquated notions of religion and monogamy. And making us feel worse about ourselves if we don't."

Glenn's nostrils flared. His stare hardened and then narrowed in on a point behind Archer. Seeking guidance from his producers perhaps? Archer sped up.

"Gays want to be accepted by society. Isn't that what you hear all the time? But why aren't we demanding acceptance as we are? Civil unions weren't enough? In pushing for traditional legal marriage we're not asking for acceptance, we're trying to *mimic* heterosexuals. And why would we want to be just like heterosexuals? I thought we were loud and proud. You can't be both."

"But—" sputtered the pastor.

Archer kept going. "You've got this whole fairy-tale fantasy thing taking hold now, a generation of upper-middle-class white lesbians and gays obsessed with the idea of marriage and happily ever after.

The notion that marriage and, by extension, monogamy is the ideal is laughable. Monogamy doesn't even work for straight people. The sexual freedom we've spent years fighting for is being eroded from within. Instead of being liberated, we're being brainwashed into thinking anonymous, promiscuous sex is bad. But you know what? That will never go away; it will only go underground and we'll stop being able to have open, healthy relationships because we're living off a rom-com script that was never written to fit us."

Glenn's eyes bulged. His face was red with rage. Still, Archer had done his research on the host. He would have to push harder to get the explosion he wanted. "Thank you for your opinion, Mr. Noble, now—"

"If you ask me, these demands for same-sex 'marriage' are simply slowing chances for real progress," Archer continued as if Glenn had never spoken. "The only people winning here are the lawyers and wedding planners."

"What about equality?" Glenn's eyes narrowed as though he saw a way to trap Archer. "I thought you people were all about equality. Are you saying you don't want that?"

Archer flashed a quick smile. "Do I think I'm as good as you? Certainly. Do I deserve the same rights? Of course. But don't mistake that for thinking we're the same. We're not the same. Unless you like sucking dick, Glenn."

Chaos erupted in the back of the studio. A roar of outrage emerged from the shadowed audience. *Cha-Ching.* Archer could practically see the dollar signs now.

Out of the corner of his eye Archer caught the producer frantically signaling, and Kim doing her best not to laugh. Glenn smiled tightly to the camera. "We'll be back in a minute, folks, with more of our show after this commercial break."

As soon as the red light on the camera winked out, Glenn jumped to his feet. "Get this faggot off my set," he shouted and stalked away.

Archer calmly stripped off his mic and stood. "Guess that's it for me. Very nice to meet you," he said to his companions, who were still gaping in shock.

Kim grabbed his arm as he left the stage. "Oh my God, the social media frenzy is going to be awesome. This will be on YouTube by tonight. And on all the networks tomorrow. Way to go out with a bang."

Archer looked over to where Glenn was arguing with his producer. "What if it's not? What if they somehow lock it down?"

Kim waved her smartphone at Archer. "One way or another it will be on YouTube tonight. I've got the whole thing here."

"Are all publicists so evil, or did I just get lucky?"

The cute PA he'd flirted with was glaring at him from the sidelines. Kim nudged his elbow. "Speaking of getting lucky . . . I think you blew your chances."

Archer shrugged. Looked like he would have to change his plans. Too bad. He felt like celebrating. "Oh well, that's what the internet is for."

"Let's get out of here before they lynch us." Kim hurried him out of the studio without incident, and they jumped into the car she had waiting. "I'm heading back to New York tonight, but I'll give you a call in a day or so. Sooner if this goes viral. We'll figure out our next steps."

"Sounds good. Thanks, Kim."

"Better get ready for all the hate mail."

"I'm already used to that." He rolled his eyes. "I'm not exactly on the GLAAD Christmas-card list, you know. I'm a traitor, I've betrayed the queer community . . . yadda, yadda, yadda."

"Yeah, but now we're talking the right wing."

Archer snorted. His armor was impenetrable. "As long as it rakes up sales, I say 'bring it on.'"

"Oh, I've also got a couple of organizations that want to book you."

"Nonprofit?"

"I think so."

"I'm not interested."

"Could be good exposure."

Archer shook his head. "I can't stand all that self-help, do-gooding crap." As the car weaved through stop-and-go LA traffic, he turned his cell phone back on and saw five voice messages in his inbox. They were all from the Toronto area code but different numbers. What the hell was going on? "Shit."

"What is it?" Kim asked.

"I don't know." The only person he knew in Toronto who would call was Margie.

Just as he was about to listen to the first message, the phone rang in his hand.

"Hello?" he answered with dread in his stomach.

"Is this Archie?" It was a man's voice.

"Yes." The feeling deepened. Only Marguerite called him by that name.

"I'm calling from the Toronto Police Service. Do you know a Marguerite Leblanc?"

"She's my sister."

"We found your number on her phone." Pause. "I'm sorry to inform you there's been an accident."

The rush of white noise in Archer's head drowned out the cop's next words.

Chapter 3

"No answer again?" Ryan Eriksson asked when his principal, Susan Taylor, hung up the phone.

"Left another message." She sighed and lowered her large frame into the chair behind her desk. "I hope we're not going to have to call Children's Aid."

Ryan glanced over his shoulder at the two tired children seated on the wooden bench outside the school office. For a five- and seven-year-old, they sat surprisingly still, as if they knew something was wrong. "Can't we wait a bit longer? I'm sure Marguerite will be here any minute." He gave her his best pleading look.

"Kill the puppy-dog eyes, will you? You know the policy, but I'll wait another half an hour. You don't need to stick around though. Go start your summer vacation."

Ryan shook his head. His overlong bangs fell into his eyes, and he brushed them off his forehead. "I'll stay."

"I wish all my teachers were half as dedicated as you. Most of them were outta here as soon as the bell rang."

"I want to make sure they're all right." Ryan watched the two dark-haired youngsters with a tight chest. He'd given them each a notepad and some markers from his stash to keep them occupied as they waited to be picked up. That had been almost an hour ago when school let out, and there was still no word from their mother. He and Susan had called every number Marguerite had listed on file, only to leave multiple messages at all of them. Ryan had even sent a couple of texts directly to Marguerite's cell but received no response. He had to admit he was worried. "I could take them home with me. Wait there," Ryan said suddenly.

"I can't allow that, Ryan. Even if you are friends with the family, I can't let you take them without permission."

"But she gave me permission," he blurted, hit with the memory of a conversation that had taken place several months ago, back when he was still happily deluded and dreaming of a future that would never happen. He had run into Marguerite after school one day, and stopped to watch the kids playing on the jungle gym and update her on his adoption plans. She had smiled and told him he was going to be an amazing father, and then she had asked him for a favor.

"I signed a paper and everything."

Susan frowned. "What?"

"Marguerite made me a temporary guardian in case of an accident. She had it notarized too. She was supposed to leave a copy with the school."

"Let's not panic yet. She's probably having car trouble."

"And not call?" That wasn't like her. He'd gotten to know Marguerite Leblanc well over the last year; initially because Dillon was in his second-grade class, but they had also hit it off immediately when she joined the Parent-Teacher Association. She was like the older sister Ryan had always wanted. And as a recent widow, she seemed like she needed all the friends she could get. He'd never met her husband, Jackson—he'd passed away two years ago, before Ryan met Marguerite—but from the way she often spoke of him, he had the sense he would have liked the man too. To lose a husband so young was such a tragedy. Whenever he'd been invited to the house, the happy, smiling family photos lining the walls had touched something inside him.

"Do you have any plans for the summer?" Susan asked, wrenching his thoughts away from Marguerite's unusual absence. She continued to clean up her office, putting anything she wanted to take home for the summer into a cardboard box.

Ryan hesitated. He'd had plans, big plans, but only Marguerite had known about those. Now they were gone. In a way it was a godsend that he hadn't blabbed to more people, so he didn't have to deal with the inevitable looks of pity. The two months loomed ahead of him, long and empty, with nothing to do except dwell on what he didn't have anymore. "I put my name on the substitute list for summer school."

"You're a glutton for punishment, aren't you? I thought you were planning to visit your parents up north."

"I can do that in August. A week with Arne and Karen is about all I can take anyway."

"As someone who's been around, can I give you some words of wisdom? You're an amazing teacher, but this job can burn you out if you're not careful. You need to have a life beyond the classroom."

Ryan didn't need another reminder about his lack of a social life. He got that enough from his roommate, Jill. "Thanks for the advice, Susan."

"Hey, I'm being selfish here. You're our most popular teacher so I want to keep you around. Have you seen the waiting list to get into your class for September? I've already had three parents try to bribe me to get bumped to the top of the list."

Ryan gave her a wan smile, but inside he was still focused on Marguerite. He chewed off the lip balm he'd just reapplied his lower lip. Marguerite would never be late in picking up her children, especially on the last day of school. She lived for those kids. And she would never be out of reach for so long. Something was wrong.

"I still can't believe Archer Noble is their uncle," Ryan marveled. He'd been shocked to discover the brother Marguerite spoke of in such glowing terms, and whom she had listed as an emergency contact, was the polarizing author.

"Why, who is Archer Noble?" Susan asked absently.

"Only the man who is single-handedly setting the gay-marriage debate back a generation."

"I thought it was legal here."

"It is. Has been for more than a decade. That's why it's so awful he's Canadian. He's a discredit to gay men everywhere. Marriage is bad; indiscriminate sex is good."

"Don't knock indiscriminate sex."

Ryan snorted. "He writes gay travel guides, with chapters on the best parks for cruising and the top-ten places for public sex."

"Is he hot?"

"It's not all about being hot, Susan."

"At your age, hon, it should be," she replied with a twist to her lips. Ryan felt the blood rush to his cheeks and cursed his fair skin. So maybe he had been intrigued by Archer Noble's tan-colored skin and the dark eyes gazing out at him from the photo on the book jacket. Intrigued enough to subscribe to his YouTube channel anyway. And maybe he *had* visited the man's blog, more than once. Too bad the man stood against everything Ryan believed in and longed for.

"I'm going to check on the kids," he said and left the office before Susan could tease him any more.

"Where's Mommy?" asked Emma when he approached.

"Don't know, sweetheart. We're trying to find her."

"Is she lost?"

"Why can't we wait at home?" Dillon demanded. "Mrs. Benning has a key. Mommy gave it to her just in case. After Emma locked her out one time."

Emma pouted. "I didn't."

"Yes, you did," Dillon retorted. "You were little. You don't remember."

Ryan folded his lanky six-foot-two frame onto the bench between them. Emma immediately cuddled against his side. He was usually more cautious about things like that, but there was no one left in the building save for Susan and himself, so he savored the innocent gesture and he slipped his arm around her shoulders. Teachers weren't supposed to have favorites, but he couldn't help it—these two were his. His heart swelled with love that was all too bittersweet. If he was ever lucky enough . . .

A familiar pang of regret soured his stomach, and he tried to push it away. He'd been so close to having this for himself that he couldn't bear to think about it. "So what are you guys doing this summer?" he asked instead. "Did your mom sign you up for camp?"

Dillon shook his head but didn't take his eyes off his drawing.

"Why not? I thought you were looking forward to soccer camp."

"We couldn't ford it," Emma chirped.

"She means 'afford,'" Dillon interjected.

Ryan frowned. He knew Marguerite had recently taken on a second, part-time secretarial job in addition to the bookkeeping she did from home, but he had no idea things were so tight. If only she'd come to him, he would have lent her the money. Dillon had been going on about soccer camp for months, and he hated to see the boy disappointed like that. Maybe it wasn't too late. He would talk to her about it when she arrived.

Emma turned her round face up to him. "Did you like our present, Mr. Eriksson?"

"I *loved* your present." He had been assailed by end-of-the-year gifts from his students—everything from boxes of chocolates to gift cards for dinners out and a bottle of chardonnay he couldn't wait to get home to open. But it had been the Leblancs' homemade popsicle-stick picture frame, with its glued-on rhinestones and feathers that had made him tear up. The photo inside was one of him and the kids that Marguerite had taken at last year's Christmas party.

"Mommy even let me use the glue gun. Because I'm almost six," boasted Emma.

"It was stupid," Dillon grumbled. "Everybody else bought you something."

Dillon had been uncharacteristically sullen all day while the rest of the class had been bursting with last-day excitement. Is that what had been bothering him? "Your gift came from the heart, and that's what makes it special—not how much it cost. I can have lots of chocolates, but I will only have one picture frame made by Dillon and Emma."

"We can make you another." Emma smiled sweetly, making Ryan laugh.

"I especially liked the feathers," he added with a wink.

Dillon brightened. "Really? Those were my idea."

Ryan bit the inside of his cheek to keep from grinning. Dillon was such a sweet, fanciful boy, shy and sensitive. A daydreamer like Ryan had been as a child. He'd known immediately that the white feathers had been Dillon's contribution.

"I'm hungry," Emma whimpered.

"You're always hungry," Dillon snapped.

Ryan rooted around in his backpack, and found an unopened granola bar, which he split carefully down the middle and handed them each half. "What's going on buddy?" he asked. "You don't seem too happy. It's summer vacation."

"Why do I have to be in Miss Bogie's class next year?"

"You wanted Mr. Nelson?"

"No, I want to be in *your* class."

Ryan smiled. "You already were in my class."

"But why can't I stay in second grade?" Dillon demanded.

"Because that's not how it works. You don't want to stay in second grade forever."

"Will I be in your class?" Emma piped up.

"Not for another year, sweetie." Ryan tugged gently on her long, silky ponytail. He paused, an idea suddenly coming to him. The Leblancs only lived a few blocks away from the school. He'd been there a couple of times. He could ride over on his bike and see if anyone was home. Or if not, the neighbors might have heard something. Maybe Marguerite had had some sort of accident and couldn't make it to the phone. Why hadn't he thought of it before?

But as he got to his feet, the massive oak doors of the main entrance swung open, flooding the foyer with afternoon light and silhouetting the two figures who stood there.

"Mommy?" Emma cried excitedly as she jumped up from the bench.

But it wasn't Marguerite.

An icy chill swept up Ryan's spine, as if the strangers had brought a blast of arctic air with them. The doors closed with a heavy boom, and he got his first good look at the pair. The man's bearing screamed police officer, despite the lack of uniform. He tucked a pair of sunglasses in the front pocket of his sport coat, and when the fabric parted, Ryan caught a glimpse of the badge attached to his belt. The woman at his side, dressed in an ill-fitting pantsuit and carrying a clipboard, was young but already had the unmistakably jaded air of a public servant. Susan dashed out of her office. The color drained from her face.

She visibly collected herself and stepped forward to greet the strangers. They spoke softly, glancing over repeatedly to where Ryan stood with the two children. He gripped them close to his sides.

"Ow," Dillon protested, and Ryan loosened his hold. "Who are those people?"

Ryan couldn't answer. Without a word, Susan led the pair into her office and shut the door. The look she gave him in passing told him everything he needed to know.

His knees buckled, and he dropped onto the bench.

"What's wrong, Mr. Eriksson?" Emma asked.

Ryan peeked over his shoulder, through the window of the outer office where the secretary usually sat. Susan had closed the door to her personal sanctum, but through the sidelight he saw her gesturing angrily at the cop and the woman.

"Wait here, guys," he instructed, trying to sound casual. The hole in his stomach grew larger as he neared the office and heard Susan's strident tone. He entered without knocking.

"Ryan." Susan sighed but didn't order him to leave. Her face was still pale, and she looked a decade older than she had only moments ago. "This is Detective Pickering and Mrs. Scott from Children's Aid."

Ryan hesitated. "What's happened? Is she . . . is she okay?"

"No." It was the cop who spoke. His tone was gentle but matter-of-fact. "There was an accident on the Gardiner Expressway this morning."

"What hospital is she in? I can get the kids over—"

The detective shook his head. "Mrs. Leblanc died of her injuries about an hour ago at St. Mike's."

The world seemed to slip away from him. It wasn't possible. The blood pumped so hard between his ears it was all he could hear. It had to be a mistake. He had talked to Marguerite only this morning when she dropped off cupcakes for the class to celebrate the last day of school. They had discussed getting together over the summer now that he was free. She couldn't be gone. For a second he thought he was going to be sick and clamped a hand over his mouth just in case.

"No," he repeated weakly. "It's not possible. Wait. This morning? And you're only here now?"

The cop bristled. "It's taken some time to track down next of kin and the children."

Susan laid a cautionary hand on Ryan's arm. "Mrs. Scott is here to take Emma and Dillon into foster care until Marguerite's brother arrives. Apparently he's out of the country."

Shocked, Ryan glanced back and forth between them. "You can't."

"It's standard procedure in cases like these," the social worker offered. "Until we can determine legal guardianship." She held out a plain white business card with her name on it: Annabelle Scott. Funny, she didn't look like an Annabelle.

"I don't fucking care about standard procedure." He sounded hysterical. He *felt* hysterical. "I'm not letting those kids spend the night in some institutional office, or worse, with strangers. That's the last thing they need."

"We don't have a choice, Ryan," Susan murmured.

"The file," he croaked, his throat rough as sandpaper. "My temporary guardianship. Did she leave a copy with you?"

Susan flew to her desk. The rest of that strange conversation flooded back into Ryan's mind and made him shiver. Much as he had that day.

"Do you believe in dreams, Ryan?" Marguerite asked, her beautiful brown eyes turning dark with uncharacteristic worry.

"As in prophesies?" He laughed. "No."

"My grandmother used to say dreams were the way we communicated with the spiritual world. I dreamed of my mother last night. I never really knew her—she left us when I was five . . ." Marguerite crossed her arms over her chest and hugged herself tight, as though frozen from the inside out. She turned imploring eyes to him. "If something were to happen to me, I don't want the kids in foster care. I've been in the system, Ryan. I don't want them to go through that."

"They won't," he said simply, naively. "Because nothing's going to happen to you."

"Here it is," Susan exclaimed, jerking him out of his trance. She handed the paper to Mrs. Scott, whose lips thinned as she read the short document.

Ryan's heart dropped to his stomach. When Marguerite had made her proposal, he'd never imagined this. He'd thought she'd been overreacting, that he'd only be called upon if she had to stay late at work, but now he had to wonder. Had Marguerite truly sensed this day would come? Or having had her own experiences in foster care, had she just wanted to be prepared?

Oh God. He turned and found Dillon and Emma with their noses pressed to the glass of the outer office as they made funny faces at him. They blurred in front of his eyes.

"Well," he snapped, swinging back to Mrs. Scott. He squared his shoulders, standing tall. His stomach flipped, but he was not going to back down.

"There is no legal weight to this, I'm afraid," she replied. "There's no law in this province governing emergency guardianship."

"Don't her wishes count for anything? Please," he begged, voice thick with unshed tears. "What more do you need? Run a background check. I'll give you all my information. You can check up on me whenever you like . . ."

Annabelle Scott's hard face softened, and he saw how young she really was. Probably no older than him. "I'm not a monster—"

The phone on Susan's desk rang. All four of them stared at it uneasily, before Susan answered.

"Hello? Mr. Noble," she sighed. "I'm so sorry—"

Ryan's hope flickered back to life; Marguerite's brother had returned their call. "What if he agrees too?" he asked the social worker.

Susan's gaze flicked to Detective Pickering and Mrs. Scott as she spoke into the phone. "Yes, they're here now. The police and Children's Aid."

Ryan heard the voice on the other end of the line grow louder. He couldn't blame the man. He couldn't bear to see Emma and Dillon carted off with some stranger either.

He motioned for the phone. "Let me talk to him." Susan handed him the receiver. Ryan gripped it in a sweaty palm. "This is Ryan Eriksson. I'm Dillon's teacher." He quickly apprised Archer Noble of the situation and what he wanted to do. "I can take them home and wait with them until you get there. Apparently the neighbor has a key."

At first there was only silence on the other end of the line. Then a deep sigh filled with the weight and weariness of a much older man. "Thank you. I'm . . . I'm still in LA. I'm booked on the next flight to Toronto, but it won't get in until after midnight."

Ryan had heard Archer Noble speak on a number of occasions, mostly YouTube clips, but the deep timbre of the man's voice managed to startle him. He suppressed a shiver and focused on the matter at hand. "What do you . . . Do you want me to tell the kids?"

"I don't know." The man sounded lost. "I don't have the faintest clue what to do right now."

Ryan was equally adrift. But Dillon and Emma were the priority. He gathered his thoughts. "Okay, we'll figure it out when you get here. Let me give you my number in case you get delayed." After they exchanged information, he handed the phone to Mrs. Scott with shaking hands. She finished up her conversation while Ryan tried to get himself under control.

"So?" he asked when she was done.

"Are you sure this is what you want?"

"Of course I'm sure. I can handle it."

"All right, Mr. Eriksson. Believe it or not, I'm only looking out for those children. And I agree with you—it's in their best interest to be with people who care about them."

Ryan felt light-headed at the reprieve. "Can we go then?"

"You can go," she agreed, with a relieved sigh. "I'll need a copy of this for the case file. And identification."

"Anything." He scrambled to make the necessary photocopies in the outer office before she could change her mind. There was a brief second, as the bright beam of the scanner blinded him, where he almost crumpled. *Keep it together. They're depending on you.* He took a deep breath, pasted a smile on his face, and stepped back into the hallway. Detective Pickering had obviously decided he was no longer needed and had left, but Mrs. Scott was crouched in front of Emma and Dillon, her face soft and friendly as Dillon chattered.

"...and Amy wouldn't come down from her chair until Henrietta was back in her cage. She thought she was a rat," he finished, recounting the tale of last week's classroom chaos when Henrietta the Hamster escaped from her cage. The social worker laughed along with Dillon. "And where is Henrietta now?"

"Spending the summer with another teacher," Ryan answered. "My roommate has a cat."

Dillon looked up at him, his eyes wide with worry. "It's okay to talk to her, isn't it?" he asked in a loud whisper they all could hear. "I know she's a stranger, but Mrs. Taylor is right there."

"Yes, Dillon," Ryan assured him, combing his fingers through the boy's fine hair. The last thing Ryan wanted to do was alarm the kids. "It's okay. Are you guys ready to go home?"

"Is Mommy coming?" Emma asked.

The innocent question felt like a punch to his gut. "No, *I'm* going to take you home instead." He threw Mrs. Scott a challenging look.

"You are?" Dillon's face lit up for the first time that day. It made Ryan want to cry. They were so innocent. And all that was about to change. To lose both parents so young . . . What would happen to them now? "Are you going to stay for dinner? Was that her on the phone?"

"Yes to dinner," Ryan managed to say with a reassuring smile. It sat forced and tight on his lips. "Something's come up. We'll talk about it later. So you get me tonight. The arrangements are all made. Put your stuff away and we can go. If we're lucky, Mrs. Benning still has your house key."

"I'll take care of everything here," Susan said, wrapping him in a big hug. "Get them home. Call me as soon as you know more."

"I will," he promised, squeezing her just as tightly. He pulled back with a sniffle and turned away, pretending to be busy gathering up his things until he could focus again. He had to be strong. Dillon and Emma needed him right now.

Ryan slung his backpack over his shoulders, fastened the buckle of his bicycle helmet around the straps, and then took Emma's hand. He'd told Annabelle Scott he could handle this. But how? How did you explain death to a child? He knew how to teach, but no one had trained him on how to deal with loss and grief. *Could anyone ever really deal with it?*

He would leave things until their uncle arrived, let them be happy a little while longer. But it would take Archer Noble hours to get here. What if they had questions? How would he manage? For once, Ryan didn't have any answers.

Chapter 4

*C*rcher was numb. Paralyzed. He stood on the sidewalk outside Marguerite's modest house, suitcase at his side, and watched the taxi's taillights drive off. He wished he could call it back, throw his bag in the trunk, and drive, drive until he was far enough away to pretend this wasn't real, wasn't happening. Maybe if he stayed out here forever he wouldn't have to deal with it.

The street was quiet except for the gentle rustle of trees in the late June breeze. It was well after midnight and the neighborhood was dark, the leafy canopy blocking out the moonlight. Marguerite's was the only house on the block still lit up.

She had chosen a good neighborhood, centrally located with lots of young families, but a lot had changed since he'd last been here. Even in the shadows he could see that many of the older bungalows, which had made the street so charming, had been torn down and replaced with new, larger château-style houses. A BMW or Lexus— sometimes both—sat in every driveway except for Marguerite's. The only thing in her driveway at the moment was a dark oil stain that in the shadows appeared as deep and dark as a black hole. Jackson's well-used Honda, or what was left of it, currently sat in some police impound lot. From what Archer had been told, it would be good only for scrap.

Marguerite's was the smallest house on the block, a thirty-year-old split-level that had been showing signs of wear two years ago, when he'd last visited, and even more now. The windows were old and flaked with layers of paint, the eaves' trough sagged in the corner. But there were flowers in the planter and he saw a homemade wreath on the front door as he approached.

Everything appeared so normal that for a moment Archer had the crazy thought the police had been wrong and Margie was home safe after all. His heart leaped.

But the shadow that moved behind the blinds was too tall to be hers. The slats parted, and someone peered out. Archer had been seen. No choice now but to move forward.

The inside door opened before Archer reached the stairs, but he didn't get a good look at the stranger until he reached the top and a young man leaned out to take Archer's small suitcase.

Dillon's teacher was tall and lean, gangly almost, with delicate features and blond, baby-fine hair that fell in his eyes. A feminine bow mouth and smooth pale cheeks completed the angelic impression. Dressed in a rumpled button-down shirt and khakis, he was clean-cut and preppy, like he'd stepped out of a Gap ad. "Come in," he said with a gentle hitch to his voice. *Gay*, Archer thought as he followed him into the foyer. And quite obviously *gay* gay too.

In the weak light he saw that the teacher's large hazel eyes were red-rimmed and puffy. His lashes were pale like the rest of him, and clumped together. "I guess you're Uncle Archie." He hesitated, seeming ill at ease. "Do you prefer Archie or Archer?"

"Archer. Only Margie still calls me Archie."

"Okay. I'm Ryan." The younger man held out his hand cautiously. Archer took it briefly, noting the long, slim fingers and soft skin. That lilting, faintly effeminate voice had sounded comforting over the phone, but grated on his nerves now. Could he be any more of a stereotype? Archer tried to hide his distaste as he set down his bag and looked past Ryan's shoulders into the house.

The last time he'd visited had been for Jackson's funeral, and even then he had only stayed an obligatory three days before escaping as fast as he could. Seeing Marguerite's pain had been his undoing.

But not much had changed in the interval. The décor was dated but homey, cluttered but clean. Although the house was small, it was still a far cry from the tobacco-stained, crammed quarters of the double-wide trailer they'd lived in on the reservation, and a world away from the roach-infested apartment in Winnipeg.

He should have come at Christmas like they'd planned, but at the last minute he had turned down the invite in order to spend the holidays in Mexico with an artist he'd just met. Actually, he'd leapt at the excuse to stay away. Now, he felt sick with the thought that he couldn't remember the guy's name.

"The kids are asleep," Ryan said quietly from behind him.

"Did you . . .?"

"No. All I said was Mommy couldn't make it home. They didn't ask too many questions. I kept them busy playing board games."

Shit. Archer had been hoping Ryan would save him the trouble and do the dirty work for him. Now he had to tell two children he barely knew that their mother, their only parent, was never coming home.

"It was on the late news. A truck tire flew off on the highway. There wasn't time for her to react. They didn't release names, but I recognized the car . . . what was left of it." For a panicked moment Archer thought the man was going to cry right in front of him. But he turned away, wiped at his eyes. "Sorry. I was holding it together until I saw that. Do you want a drink? I've got some wine left, but that's it I'm afraid. There's nothing harder in the house."

"That's my Margie," Archer murmured.

"I'm sorry?"

"We come from a long line of alcoholics. Never touch the stuff."

"Oh." Ryan blushed and glanced at the coffee table where a wineglass sat empty. He moved to snatch it up, leaving the faint scent of vanilla in his wake, as though he'd been baking.

"Don't let me stop you, though. I don't have a problem with other people drinking."

"I—I'm very sorry. I considered Marguerite a friend. I really can't believe it." Ryan headed into the small galley kitchen. Archer slowly followed. Sometimes he longed to be like everyone else and enjoy the oblivion alcohol would bring, but he couldn't risk giving in to temptation. One would lead to another and another. It always did. That's how it got you. Right now he needed to be strong. Marguerite would want him to be strong.

"You must be tired," Ryan said, his back turned as he rinsed his glass at the sink. "If you want I can change the sheets on the bed in the master . . . Or there's a guest bedroom in the basement."

Archer shook his head. He felt ancient. Bed sounded heavenly, but even if he could sleep, there was no time. "I slept a bit on the plane. Besides, there's so much to do. I have to meet with the cops in the morning. And find a funeral director to arrange for the body to be transferred..."

"Are you sure?" Ryan asked, his expression soft and concerned.

"I'm fine," Archer snapped. Having to constantly look up at Ryan, who was a good four or five inches taller, was beginning to irritate him. He hauled his laptop out of the bag, set it on the kitchen table, and grabbed the nearest chair. "Is there wi-fi here?"

"Yes, but I don't know the password. You might be better off using the computer in the office downstairs." Ryan fidgeted. "I-I took the liberty of going through her filing cabinets. I found a copy of her will. And I pulled anything else I thought you might need." He gestured to a stack of documents at the far end of the table.

Archer frowned. What kind of person did that? Was he trying to be helpful or just snooping? He turned to Ryan with narrowed eyes. "Are you always this organized?"

"I needed to keep busy."

Now that Archer looked closely, he noticed how immaculately clean the kitchen was. Recently washed dishes sat in the drain board, the bare counters gleamed. Had Ryan done that? Marguerite had been a decent housekeeper, but she had never worried about the clutter of family life.

Ryan was clearly fighting back tears again. At a time like this, Archer knew how it must look that he could not do the same.

"Thank you," he said grudgingly. "For everything. I'm sorry if I came off like an asshole."

"It's okay. It's a lot to process, I know." Ryan heaved a sigh. He put the clean dishes back in the cupboard, wiped down the already sparkling counters, and then, clearly at a loss for what to do next, stood there with his arms wrapped around himself and watched Archer with a strange mix of curiosity and wariness.

Archer sensed he was being judged.

Finally, the lanky young man swung out a chair and sat down next to him. "Have you thought about what we should tell them?"

"'We'?" Archer flinched at the foreign word.

"Oh." Ryan's fair skin turned a rosy pink as he studied the scarred surface of the table. "I guess I should—"

"Are you—?"

The teacher's lips curled ever so slightly in amusement. "You first."

"So, Margie named you guardian, huh?"

"Temporarily. In the event of an emergency."

Archer's laugh was hard and bitter. He raked a hand through his hair, wanting to tear it out by the very roots just to feel *something*. "I'd say this fucking qualifies as an emergency, wouldn't you?"

Ryan blinked. He swallowed, and his Adam's apple bobbed in his long, thin neck. "Now that you're here . . . There's enough food in the house for breakfast, but you'll need to go shopping soon. There's juice and cereal for breakfast. Dillon likes soy milk with his cereal, but Emma eats hers dry."

Archer felt a surge of irrational anger toward this stranger who knew more about his sister's family than he did. Margie was *his* sister. Who did he think he was? What was he to Marguerite?

"Will you let me know about the funeral arrangements?" Ryan rose to his feet. "Marguerite has—I mean had—a lot of friends, and I'll pass on the information."

Was he leaving? Mention of the funeral made Archer's stomach lurch. The last one he'd been to had been Jackson's, and before that, his uncle's twenty years ago. He hadn't even gone to his gran's funeral. Now, stronger than Archer's jealousy, was his fear of being left alone with his niece and nephew. Of being left alone in this house with his dead sister's memory.

"Wait," he called. The younger man froze, his hand fluttering nervously to his face and brushing aside the hair that kept falling into his eyes. "Do you even have a car? I didn't see one in the driveway."

"I chained my bike in the back."

Archer saw his opportunity. He could use someone like Ryan. Hell, he *needed* someone like Ryan. He glanced at his reflection in the dark windows of the patio doors that led to the backyard. "It's late. And you've been drinking. Why not stay until morning? The kids would probably feel better seeing a familiar face too. I mean, unless you have a family of your own waiting."

Oddly, Ryan seemed relieved. He smiled tremulously. "No, no, there's no one. I guess I can stay. If you need me."

Archer opened his eyes to sunlight dancing across the ceiling. His gaze followed the bouncing beams, drifting along twisting hairline cracks in the plaster, noting an unfamiliar cobweb in one corner. This wasn't the LA Hilton. Then his mind clicked, the pieces falling back into place, and he remembered. Marguerite. And . . . oh God, the kids. The pain that sliced through him was sharp—intense. He forced it aside and drew a deep breath, flinching when his hand grazed the will still resting in his lap. He must have fallen asleep on the couch while going through paperwork. What the hell had she been thinking to name him as legal guardian? *Him*. Even if he liked children—which he didn't—he didn't have the first clue about parenting. He wanted to scream at the unfairness of it. *How could you do this to me, Margie?*

Thank God she'd had the foresight to name a backup.

With a groan, Archer turned his head and then blinked in surprise at the slight, dark-haired boy in Spider-Man pajamas who stood staring at him. This had to be Dillon. He'd grown a foot taller since Archer had seen him last. "Who are you?" the boy asked.

Archer slowly sat up, wincing at the stiffness in his muscles. "I'm your Uncle Archie. Don't you remember? I sent you that baseball glove for Christmas."

Dillon's forehead creased. "I don't play baseball. I play soccer."

"Oh, I didn't know that." Archer rubbed at his grainy eyes. Hell, he didn't know a lot of things.

"Where's Mom?"

Shit, he wasn't ready for this. He wished again that Ryan had taken care of it last night. "Come and sit down." Archer reached for the boy's arm, but Dillon started and ran away.

"Ryan," he screamed. The young teacher dashed out of the kitchen, and Dillon flung his arms around Ryan's waist.

Archer shot to his feet. "I didn't do anything, I swear."

"Of course you didn't," Ryan said with a quizzical expression. His eyes were bloodshot, his fine, blond hair lank. He looked like hell. "What's the matter, Dillon, don't you recognize your Uncle Archie? He's come a long way to be with you and Emma."

"Why? Where's Mom?"

Archer panicked. *What do I do?*

Ryan gave him a sad smile over the top of Dillon's head. "Let's have breakfast first, all of us, and then we'll talk. I know I sure could use some coffee." He clasped Dillon by the shoulders. "Why don't you see if your sister is awake?"

Dillon gave Archer one last uncertain, baleful scowl before darting upstairs. Archer trailed Ryan into the kitchen where he breathed in the scent of freshly brewed coffee. He could do with a jolt of caffeine himself.

"They call you by your first name?" he asked, his curiosity piqued by Dillon's obvious affection for the other man. Ryan was nothing like the angry, weary teachers he'd grown up with. Archer's classmates would have eaten him alive.

"Only since last night. I thought it was more appropriate. School's out and it seemed silly for them to keep calling me 'Mr. Eriksson' given the circumstances."

Ryan poured them each a generous mug. Archer accepted it gratefully, declining the cream and sugar, and letting the bitter brew burn his throat in an effort to get the blood pumping through his sluggish veins again. Mornings were never his best time.

"I finished the list while you were sleeping," Ryan said, plucking a notepad off the counter and handing it to him. Archer's eyes widened at the carefully laid-out notes. Talk about thorough. Ryan was an organizational guru. While Archer had been combing through the will last night, Ryan had leapt into action, sorting through the files and putting together a detailed to-do list, complete with contacts: lawyer, insurance, mortgage company, bank. Jesus, this guy could come in handy.

Archer set the list aside and stared into his mug. The thunder of feet overhead cut his thoughts short and sent chills down his spine. "I don't know what to say," he finally confessed. Ryan seemed to have the answer to everything; maybe he would know what to do. "I've never been in this position before."

"Me neither," Ryan murmured. "I think the only thing to do is tell them the truth. But gently."

Gently, Archer remembered later as they all sat on the couch, Ryan with a kid hugging each side of him. They clung to him with unquestioning trust. They clearly sensed something was wrong—at least Dillon did—had been full of questions over breakfast, and now they stared at Archer warily, with wide, dark eyes reminiscent of Margie's. More than ever, Archer felt like the outsider. He supposed he was as much of a stranger to them as they were to him.

How the hell did you break news like this gently? Archer wasn't a gentle man; he wasn't soft and cuddly like Ryan. He was hard because he'd needed to be hard, because life had been hard, and now that he needed to be comforting, he didn't have the first clue where to begin. No one had worried about frightening him and Margie, or shielding them from the harsh realities of life. At Dillon's age, Archer had been taking care of his sister full-time. There had been no Spider-Man pajamas or hugs for *him*.

He cleared his throat. "There . . . there was an accident."

"With Mom? Is she in the hospital? Can we go see her?" Dillon clamored. He looked to Ryan for answers, not Archer.

"No, Dillon," he replied softly. "She's gone."

"Where'd she go?" Emma asked innocently.

Archer grimaced. He didn't believe in sugarcoating things, or wrapping the hard truth up in pointless platitudes like Ryan. Best to get it over with. Pull the bandage off quickly so the wound could scab over and heal. "Your mom was hurt very badly," he said. "She died." When Dillon and Emma regarded him blankly, Archer grew worried. "Do you understand what that means?"

"It means she went to Heaven," Emma pronounced. "She's an angel. Like Daddy."

Archer cringed. Who had filled their heads with such nonsense? There was no God, no angels or fucking useless spirit Ancestors watching over them from above. He didn't believe in anything other than survival of the fittest. He'd thought his sister felt the same.

"No stupid-head," Dillon spat with a shove at Emma. "Angels aren't real."

"Hey, don't yell at your sister," Ryan cautioned, doing his best to keep them apart as Emma hit back. Dillon fought free from his hold.

"It's not true," he shouted. "It's not. Mom? Mommy?" He ran to the front door and pulled it open as though he expected her to be on the other side. "Where's the car?" he asked of no one in particular. "It's gone. Where is she?"

Archer was frozen to the spot. It was Ryan who went to the boy's side and clasped him in his arms. Dillon pounded his fists against Ryan's chest. "You lied to us. You said she was okay."

Ryan's face crumpled at the accusation. "I'm sorry, Dilly. I'm so sorry."

"You lied," Dillon repeated, this time in a smaller voice. The boy's lip quivered, and then his eyes began to overflow with tears. He buried his face against Ryan's chest, his quiet sobs tearing at Archer's heart and reminding him of the day he ran away from the reservation. The day he knew he was on his own.

How much worse must it be for Dillon and Emma? They had known safety and love. They'd had two adoring parents and now both were gone. How could Archer ever hope to give them that again? His chest tight, he sought Ryan's guidance. The man's nod of encouragement eased something inside of him.

Emma began to sob, but Archer couldn't tell if it was because she actually understood what was going on or because her brother was crying too. She dashed to Ryan's side, and he patiently wiped their wet faces and blew runny noses. A good thing too, because there was no way Archer wanted to touch those.

He looked at Ryan, cuddling the two exhausted children, and had the start of an idea.

Ryan had been in the will too, listed as an alternate guardian in the event Archer couldn't, or wouldn't, assume the responsibility. *Does he know?* Archer wondered now. *Is that why he was so quick to stay?* Archer would need to talk to the lawyer, but the solution seemed obvious to him. He couldn't raise two children. Never mind his career and lifestyle—it simply wasn't in him. But Ryan Eriksson, on the other hand, seemed born to the task.

No matter what, he needed to keep the young teacher around for a little longer.

"I want Mommy," Emma wailed. Archer couldn't have agreed more. Why would Margie do this to him?

"You can't have her," Dillon shouted. "She's gone. She's gone, and she's not ever coming back." He broke free of Ryan's arms and ran from the room. Emma's earsplitting shriek made Archer's head pound. A few seconds later, a door slammed shut upstairs.

If only he could run away as easily.

Chapter 5

"*A*re you sure this is wise?" asked Jill as she hefted yet another bag out of the trunk of her car and handed it over.

"How much did you bring?" Ryan muttered. "I only asked for a change of clothes."

"When you called and said you were staying, I didn't know how long you were planning on. Plus, I thought you might want your laptop and some books. God knows your toiletries alone take up one whole bag. On the upside, there's a ton of room in the bathroom."

Ryan smiled faintly. Jill knew him well. She should; they'd been housemates in college. And now she was once again sharing a space with him, having taken over the second bedroom in his small apartment so he wouldn't be alone after Kenny moved out.

They piled his bags in the foyer. Later he would take them down to the basement guest bedroom where he would be sleeping.

"So, how are the kids doing?" she asked quietly.

"As well as can be expected, I guess. They're upstairs, watching TV in their mom's bed. I thought it would be okay. I don't really know what to do in this situation." Ryan's throat tightened up again. He was dangerously close to losing it. But he needed to keep it together for Dillon and Emma's sake.

"Oh, sweetie." Jill pulled him into a hug and rubbed his back. "You're doing fine. The most important thing is for them to know they're still loved and protected. And if they need some grief counseling later, I can give you a few recommendations." Jill was starting her PhD in child psychology in the fall, and he often went to her with questions. "I snuck in a couple of books you might want to read."

"Thanks, Jill. It all seems so unreal, you know?"

Ryan had spent the morning making calls to friends and acquaintances he and Marguerite shared, building a list of other people who would need to be contacted. He'd broken the news to Mrs. Benning last night when he picked up the keys and by late morning word had spread through the neighborhood. Several neighbors had already stopped by to offer their condolences. Archer had ducked out after a quick shower and change of clothes to begin the long, arduous process of making arrangements, leaving Ryan to handle both the kids and the visitors. Ryan didn't know which of them had the worst end of the deal. Fortunately, he knew many of the neighbors from the school or from gatherings he'd been to at Marguerite's house, but every time the doorbell or the phone rang, and he had to go over it all again, another piece of him died inside.

"Want some iced tea?" Ryan asked, bolting into the kitchen without waiting for Jill's response. He needed to keep busy or else he'd break down and never get back up. "I made it this morning."

"I know how fond you were of Marguerite . . ." Jill began as she trailed after him.

"I hated being an only child, you know. I always wanted a sister. Marguerite was the closest I ever got to having one."

"Uh, hello? What am I?"

"I meant *older* sister," he quickly amended.

"I'm older."

"By six months. That doesn't count." Ryan hoped he'd covered his gaff. He adored Jill. She was his best friend. But he'd never felt the same immediate connection with her that he'd felt with Marguerite.

Carrying two glasses into the adjoining dining room—alcove really—Ryan sat down at the table. He stared vacantly back toward the kitchen. There was a yellow flyer for soccer camp posted on the fridge—the camp Dillon wanted to attend.

Ryan started when Jill reached across the wooden table and touched the back of his hand. "I still can't believe she's gone," he murmured. "I keep thinking she's going to walk through that door any minute."

"Ryan." Jill squeezed his fingers. "You staying here might not be the best thing . . ."

"Why not? School's out. I have no plans for summer vacation now, other than visiting my folks up at the lake in August. And believe me, I wasn't looking forward to that. You don't need to worry—I'll still pay my half of the rent."

"That's not what I meant," Jill said with a pointed stare. "I know you, Ryan. I know how you get with kids. The one thing you've always wanted is a family of your own. And with everything that's happened . . . I'm worried you're going to get too close."

"I can't help it, Jill. They need me." Ryan paused, remembering how Archer's fathomless dark eyes had pleaded with him this morning as he haltingly suggested Ryan stay with them a bit longer. The man had seemed so lost. "It's only until Archer gets on his feet. There's so many arrangements to be made, and he can't do that with Dillon and Emma underfoot. Plus they need to keep some sort of routine right now."

"Uh-huh. Let me ask you something: did he ask you to stay, or did you volunteer?"

Ryan frowned. Now that he thought about it, Archer hadn't actually come out and asked—it was more like he'd hinted. "What does that matter?"

"Because I don't want him to take advantage of you. Have you forgotten this is Archer Noble you're talking about? Your nemesis. What was it you called him? The Manwhore of Manitoba."

Ryan cringed. "He's Marguerite's brother. She would want me to help him."

"And it has absolutely nothing to do with your little crush?"

"I do not have a crush. The man is the antithesis of everything I believe in."

"So I heard. Repeatedly. For the first month after you read that book he was all you talked about, remember?"

"Ranted," Ryan corrected. "He made me furious."

"Furious enough to subscribe to his blog and follow him on Twitter?"

Ryan blew his bangs off his forehead, looked away from Jill's assessing gaze. Sometimes being best friends with a psychologist was no fun.

"So how is he? The manwhore?"

"Different from what I expected." He didn't quite know what to make of Archer Noble yet. He was more attractive in person than in photos, but he came across as serious, reserved, nothing like the outrageous, sarcastic character his online presence indicated. Behind those impenetrable eyes, Ryan sensed a carefully banked anger. And pain. So much pain. "He seems a bit cold, unemotional."

"Everyone handles grief their own way."

"I know."

"And you still plan to stay." Jill's lips thinned with apprehension.

Ryan nodded. "Until I know they're going to be safe. Archer doesn't know the first thing about kids."

"No shit. But he has custody, right?"

"Yeah." Ryan closed his eyes against the pain that pierced his chest. What would happen to those two beautiful children? Would Archer take them away? Somehow he couldn't picture Archer Noble checking out the latest hot spots with two kids in tow. That was no way to raise a child. His stomach turned over. They deserved better than that.

"I don't know why Marguerite would do this," he began. "I know he's family, but—"

"You mean why she wouldn't leave them to you, permanently?" Jill demanded with an edge to her voice. "Maybe because that's a big imposition when you've only known someone a year. And it's a lot of responsibility for a twenty-five-year-old to handle."

Ryan stiffened, and Jill blew out a heavy sigh. "I'm sorry, Ryan. That came out wrong." She began rubbing his back. "What about her husband's family? Maybe there's someone who can take them if he doesn't?"

"I don't think so. She never talked about anyone." But he was finding it hard to focus—the disdainful words Archer had thrown about in his book were flooding back to him. Yes, Archer was Marguerite's brother, but he was practically the spokesperson for the stereotypical self absorbed gay man. Hadn't she known that?

Ryan had to look out for Emma and Dillon. He'd do his best to honor Marguerite's wishes, but in the back of his mind he knew if it came down to it, the kids were all that mattered.

Jill was still worried—he saw it in her face. "Either way, they need me now. Look, with me staying here, you and Alex will have more privacy in the apartment. Maybe he'll finally pop the question."

"You don't think we're trying to get rid of you, do you?"

"No, of course not."

She must have heard something in his voice because Jill narrowed her eyes. "This isn't about Kenny is it?"

Ryan shook his head and stared out the patio doors. The sun sparkled on the turquoise water of the pool in the backyard. The beautiful day seemed like such a mockery. He couldn't talk about this with her anymore. It only made her angry because he wasn't moving on fast enough.

"It is," she gasped. "After everything—" She caught herself, held up her hands in surrender. Then she reached out and squeezed his fingers, and when she spoke again, she was calmer. "Kenny was an idiot. You'll find someone who wants the same things as you."

"Yeah, in ten years when they've all grown up," Ryan muttered with a roll of his eyes. He carried their empty glasses to the sink. None of the guys his age seemed to be interested in settling down. Like Kenny, who had said he wanted to get married but apparently not enough to stave off the cold feet. "*Later*," he'd kept saying. "*Later*."

He heaved a sigh. It seemed wrong to think about this now while Marguerite's death was so raw.

"So, you'll be okay?" Jill asked.

While he appreciated her concern, he was beginning to get annoyed. He didn't need a babysitter. "I've got it under control."

"Of course you do. Taking care of everyone is what you do best."

"What's that supposed to mean?"

"It's like you want people to walk all over you. You took care of Kenny during law school, only to have him bail when it was finally your turn to want something. And now you're going to do it again. I swear sometimes I want to strangle you."

"This is different," Ryan insisted. "This isn't a relationship."

"Remind me of that when you're crying on the couch with a gallon of rocky road ice cream in your lap."

Ryan's cheeks burned. Jill sighed and hugged him. "Okay, okay. I'm sorry. I know you can handle it. You'll call me if you need anything else?"

"I promise."

"And let me know what's happening?"

"Yes, ma'am," he replied obediently. She swatted his arm, the gesture so familiar he might have laughed if his cell phone hadn't rung. It was Archer.

"Don't worry," Jill said with a wave. "I'll let myself out."

Thank you, Ryan mouthed as he answered the call. His stomach clenched.

"I don't know what to do," Archer said without preamble.

"About what? Where are you?"

"I'm about to strangle this guy. They keep pushing a funeral service, but Margie's not religious. All I want is for things to be wrapped up as quickly as possible."

Archer's slip made Ryan smile. How long before reality set in and they started thinking of Marguerite in the past tense? "It doesn't have to be religious, does it?"

"I don't see the need for a service," Archer insisted. "She's . . . well, she's being cremated. Like Jackson." His voice was hollow, empty. If it had been anyone else but Archer Noble, Ryan would have offered some words of comfort. But he had a feeling they would only be thrown right back in his face.

"What about a memorial service?" Ryan suggested instead. "We could find a few photographs to display. The neighbors would come, and lots of people from the school."

"What's the point?"

Could Archer really be that hard-hearted? "The *point* is to say good-bye. Marguerite was well liked."

There was a long pause on the other end of the line. "You think so?"

"Yeah, I do."

Archer sighed. "I fucking hate funerals."

"It's not a funeral. It'll be a celebration."

"Because there's so much to celebrate," he returned scathingly.

Ryan bit down on the inside of his cheek. "The kids need the closure, Archer." *And so do you.*

Silence.

"Fine," Archer said abruptly, sounding anything but, and then hung up.

Ryan shook his head. The man was a jerk. Then again, when had death ever brought out the best in someone? He had to remember that he was here for Emma and Dillon, not Archer Noble. Archer could take care of himself.

Ryan took the short staircase to the upper level to check on the kids and hesitated outside the open door of Marguerite's bedroom. It was quiet except for the low murmur of the television. He felt like an intruder trespassing on a private space as he entered, noting with bittersweet sorrow the pair of cast-off sandals lying in front of the closet, a paperback splayed on the nightstand—all waiting for a return that would never happen.

The kids were buried beneath the covers even though it was terribly stuffy in the room. The air smelled faintly of Marguerite's perfume. Ryan crossed to the window, opened it a crack, and the cheerful song of the birds outside seeped into the room.

Emma was asleep, thumb between her lips, one arm curled around a well-loved stuffed toy. A jumble of emotions swirled in Ryan's chest. The pang of longing for the daughter he might have had was so strong that for a second he couldn't breathe. He hadn't allowed himself to think of her in months. For good reason. If they had finished the adoption process, they might have been parents by now. Ryan pushed aside those treacherous thoughts and focused on the two children in front of him. Their world had been turned upside down.

Dillon lay beside Emma, awake. He was humming softly to himself, his attention fixed on the television. The simple melody was haunting. Dillon was in the junior choir at school and loved to sing. He didn't seem to notice when Ryan turned the television off and sat down cautiously on the edge of the mattress next to him.

"Hi," he said softly, hoping that he was forgiven for this morning. Dillon blinked and stopped humming. "What's that song you were singing?"

"Something Mom used to sing to us."

"Well, it's very pretty." Ryan fought the urge to pull the boy into a hug. He settled for stroking Dillon's fine, dark hair instead.

"Sam likes it when I sing to him," Dillon announced.

"Yeah? Who's Sam?"

"My friend."

"Well he has good taste. I like to hear you sing too." Ryan mentally sifted through all the kids in his class this year. Not a Sam among them. Nor in the other second-grade class. "Do I know Sam? Does he go to our school?"

"He's new."

"Want to come downstairs and help me make lunch?"

Dillon shook his head. "We want to stay here."

"Okay, but only for a little while longer." It probably wasn't good for them to spend too much time alone.

Dillon peered up at him with wounded eyes. "What happens to us now? Are we orphans?"

This had to be the scariest part for them. Not knowing what came next. But Ryan couldn't give them an answer when he didn't have one himself. "We'll have to talk about that with your uncle."

Alarm flashed across his face. "Do we have to live with him? Like Harry Potter?"

"I don't know, Dilly."

"We don't like him."

"You don't really know him. Give him a chance. Everybody deserves a chance, right?"

"I guess," Dillon admitted reluctantly.

"I'm going to stay for a little while if that's okay. To help you and Uncle Archie get settled." The hope in Dillon's eyes was so transparent that Ryan's chest tightened. "Only for a few days," he emphasized, as much for Dillon as for himself. The last thing he wanted was to hear Jill say, "I told you so."

Chapter 6

"*I*'m not going. And you can't make me." Dillon sat cross-legged on his bed. His arms were folded across his chest, and he was naked except for his briefs.

"Get. Dressed," Archer barked through clenched teeth.

"You're not my daddy." He kicked the clothes laid out for him onto the floor.

Archer's temper rose another notch. "I'm in charge for now. And if I have to go, so do you."

He took a step forward but froze when Dillon cowered. Jesus, was he that much of a monster that his own nephew was afraid of him? A headache blossomed behind his eyes. This was all Ryan's fault for insisting on a service. For the kids, he said. And now the goddamn kid didn't even want to go.

"What's going on in here?" Ryan asked calmly from the doorway. Emma hung back, peeking out from behind Ryan. Today, all dressed up in a pretty spring dress and her hair in two shining braids, she resembled Marguerite so much that Archer had to avert his eyes because it hurt too much to look at her. He swallowed the lump in his throat.

Ryan gave Archer's shoulder a comforting squeeze as he slipped past and sat on the edge of Dillon's bed. "What's wrong, kiddo?"

"I don't want to go. Neither does Sam."

"Sam?" Archer repeated, impatient to get this day over with. "Who the h—heck is Sam?"

"Oh dear," Ryan murmured.

"What?" Archer demanded. He got no response.

Ryan stroked the top of Dillon's head. "Is Sam here now?"

"Of course. He's my friend."

Archer groaned and turned his back. Christ, the kid had an imaginary friend. That was all he needed.

Ryan ignored him. "Why don't you and Sam want to go?" he asked like Dillon's phantom friend was right there.

"What are you doing?" Archer demanded as he spun around. "Don't encourage—" Ryan's frown told him to shut up.

"We don't want to see her," Dillon whispered, the fear clear on his face.

Archer felt as though he'd been sucker punched. He thought back to his first funeral on the reservation, how he and Margie had stared in horror at the open casket and gripped each other's hands. His anger evaporated. At least he could spare the kids that trauma. "You won't have to."

Tears bloomed in Dillon's brown eyes. "Tommy McPherson went to his grandma's funeral. He said they had to look at her in the box. I don't wanna see Mommy like that."

Ryan shot Archer a horrified glance. Archer gingerly sat down on the other side of Dillon, doing his best not to frighten him this time. "There's no casket, I promise. Don't you remember your daddy's funeral?"

Dillon shook his head. "Only that there were lots of people."

Archer sighed. They had been pretty young, and Marguerite had tried to spare them most of it. Dillon probably hadn't understood much of what was happening.

"This is only for friends and family, Dillon," Ryan supplied. "It's a bit like a grown-up party. Your mommy had lots of friends, and right now they want to be together. Remember those photographs we picked out? That's all that's going to be there. Pictures." Dillon still looked unconvinced. "And then afterward we'll go to the cemetery to say good-bye."

Oh God, please don't let them ask me about that, Archer thought. *I'm not equipped to explain cremation to a child.*

"Uncle Archie needs you. And Emma. You guys have to stick together. You're a family now," Ryan insisted. Archer's gut churned with guilt, and the pounding in his head worsened. His eyes slid away from Ryan's warm gaze. He just wanted to make it through the afternoon, and they could deal with everything else later.

"But we don't have a mommy and daddy," Emma pointed out. She leaned her head on Ryan's knee.

"A family doesn't always have to be a mommy and a daddy. A family is people who love each other. Remember Allison and her two moms?"

"Will you be there?" Dillon asked Ryan, with such hope in his eyes that an unexpected stab of jealousy tore through Archer's heart. Why should he care if the kids liked Ryan better? Who wouldn't? The man was soft and loving, a natural at parenting. In only a few days Archer had seen that. Ryan cooked like a pro, took care of the house, entertained the kids. The question was, why hadn't Margie named him guardian to begin with? It would be the ideal solution for them all; the kids would have a devoted parent and more importantly, Archer would be free to go back to living his life as he pleased. Thanks to his antics with Glenn Smith, he'd already fielded two calls from PROUDtv for a new development project. He'd be crazy to let that opportunity escape.

"Of course I'm coming with you, silly Dilly," Ryan teased with a beatific smile.

Dillon looked to Archer and then back to Ryan. "Because you're family?"

Ryan's eyes grew suspiciously moist, but he managed to hold the tears back. "Because I'm your friend," he said hoarsely.

"Okay." Dillon abruptly slid off the bed to pick up his clothes. "Sam says we can go."

Yep, Ryan was definitely the perfect solution.

They drove in silence to the funeral home, squished into the compact car Archer had rented earlier in the week. Neither he nor Ryan owned a car, but until he finalized his plans, he hadn't wanted to make the commitment of buying one outright. Unfortunately child car seats had been the farthest thing from his mind when he grabbed the first vehicle off the lot. He also hadn't counted on a six-foot-tall giant with legs that went on forever riding in the passenger seat.

At Ryan's urging, he had compromised on a simple reception at the funeral home. No service, no eulogy, no Elders, no hymns. Simply a chance for friends to gather over tea and coffee and tasteless white-bread finger sandwiches. And Margie had a lot of friends he realized as they filed into the small parlor. More than Archer could have imagined. Ryan had been right. His sister had been well liked. The knowledge did little to ease the ache in his chest.

He recognized a few of the neighbors since they had been quick to offer up their condolences the second he set foot outside the house, but the rest were strangers to him. Ryan stood at his side, like they were a couple, and whispered names in his ear. Many of them seemed to be other parents from the school, but a number of Jackson's former coworkers from the factory were here too, looking distinctly working class and out of place amongst the well-heeled mourners. Archer barely paid attention. What was the point? As soon as he got things settled, he'd be out of here, back to his wandering lifestyle.

Archer let Ryan do the talking, while he plastered on the fake smile he was so good at and nodded as strangers told him what he already knew: it was a tragedy; Margie was so lovely; what were the children going to do? First their father, and now their mother.

His gaze wandered. The reception room was long and narrow, designed to be homey, with sprays of silk flowers and overstuffed furniture. The effect was far too formal to feel like home though.

Ryan and the kids had found some photographs of Marguerite—with Jackson in a number of them too—and arranged them on side tables throughout the bland space. There had been hundreds to go through, most from the last decade, as if Margie, having nothing from her early years, had decided to capture each and every waking moment of her life once she was free to do so. Archer had viewed them too, many for the first time, lending his approval or disapproval, and staring with mounting regret at all the moments of his sister's life he had missed by staying away.

He should be crying. They expected him to cry. Like Ryan, who every so often discreetly wiped at his eyes and sniffled. But Archer Noble didn't cry. Archer was smooth and confident and polished, and knew that tears never accomplished anything. Poor Archie Noblesse, on the other hand, would have bawled his little heart out if he hadn't already been empty inside. He'd shed all his tears as a child, wishing for things he could never have. Now he had none left. It was a void he always carried with him—had grown accustomed to—except for that one small corner Marguerite had inhabited. And no matter the distance between them, even though they'd seen each other less and less over the years, even though he'd stayed on the other side of the country, she had always been there. He had always felt her there. Until now.

And that's when it finally hit him. She was gone. His beautiful, laughing sister, who never had a bad word to say about anyone, was gone. Reduced to ashes in a cardboard box. Everything he'd done, everything he'd sacrificed—it was all a waste. It should have been him. Why couldn't it have been him instead? She was loved and needed, and he was neither.

And now he was supposed to be responsible for two children he didn't know the first thing about. God, he'd never been so terrified in his life. *What the fuck, Marguerite*, he wanted to howl. *What the fuck?*

He glanced around the room for Dillon and Emma. "They're with Susan," Ryan said, as if he'd read Archer's thoughts. Archer found the kids sitting on a floral-patterned sofa, plates balanced in their lap as if they were at some fancy party, and talking with a statuesque older woman Ryan had introduced to him earlier as the principal of their school. She was the one he'd spoken with on the day he'd gotten the news.

What did all these people think when they saw him standing next to the perfect white boy? Sure he was wearing his Armani suit, but one good look and they would see the dirt beneath it. Archer's well-practiced veneer cracked a little as he imagined the room staring at him, the mournful faces turning to sneers of disdain. Did they wonder why Marguerite would give her children to this messed-up queer, this high school dropout who'd sucked more cock than a West Hollywood hooker?

The urge to laugh stirred in his chest. Him, a parent? He tried to picture the playdates and school recitals Margie had always talked about, but all he saw was his mother passed out on the bed while he and Margie fended for themselves. The pressure built inside him. He knew this much: if he stayed, he would have to protect them, and make sure they went to school, and that Emma didn't get pregnant, and Dillon didn't fuck around with drugs. His life wouldn't be his own; it would be theirs. He would have to give up everything he'd worked for. His vision dimmed. It was too much. He couldn't do it.

Wait. He didn't have to. Ryan could be their guardian. As executor of Margie's estate, all Archer had to do was make sure they were provided for—had a roof over their heads, money when they needed it. Hell, his own mother hadn't done that much. They were already way better off than he'd been at their age, and he had survived. Ryan would do the rest, and Archer could still live his life the way he wanted to.

The serene piped-in music began to grate on Archer's nerves. His heartbeat surged between his ears and a scream built in his chest, rising up his throat and threatening to burst free. Then his numb fingers were enveloped in warmth, and utter calm stole over him. He looked down to find Ryan holding his hand.

"I got you," Ryan whispered. "It's okay."

Archer blinked, startled by how much he craved that simple touch, never wanted it to end. Margie had always held his hand as a child, clinging to him for comfort, letting him know he wasn't alone. The two of them against the world. And now here he was, depending on a near-stranger for the same thing. He didn't deserve it. He attempted to pull away, but Ryan tightened his grip and refused to let him go. After a while, Archer stopped trying.

He made it through one more hour before it all became unbearable again. One more hour of murmured voices, tearful condolences, and uncomfortable hugs from people he didn't know. *How long is this going to go on?* He had to get out of here.

Ryan was talking quietly to one of the neighbors on the other side of the room with Dillon glued to his side. Now and then he glanced in Archer's direction, as if afraid he might bolt. Ryan would be right—Archer had already scoped out the closest exit. As he was debating whether to make his escape now, his eyes lit on an older woman standing alone watching him.

The high slash of her cheekbones and the strong nose proclaimed her Native ancestry. She stood out amongst the mourners—some were even staring—but she didn't seem the least bit self-conscious as she wove her way toward him. Archer's stomach clenched automatically. He tensed. When she stopped in front of him, he politely extended his hand, which she took in a strong grip between her own much smaller hands. Her forearms were covered in bangles which jingled when she moved.

"I'm Alyssa Sky," she said in a gentle, surprisingly deep voice. "A friend of your sister's. I'm so sorry about your loss. But I imagine you've been hearing that a lot today." She glanced around the room with curious eyes. "I take it you decided against a wake?"

Like many Aboriginal Peoples, the Cree had a strong sense of spirituality. His gran had taught him that life was an endless circle, and that although the body may age and die, the spirit remained unchanged. The wake was the ceremony for delivering the body back to Mother Earth, and was usually filled with singing and prayers. He'd attended far too many on the reservation; to Archer it was all mumbo jumbo and one more reminder of a time he'd rather forget. The bitter taste of bile filled his mouth. He couldn't bear to associate Margie with that.

"I didn't know Marguerite that well," the woman continued, "but I could tell she was special. She had such a loving heart."

Archer's attention returned to Alyssa Sky. What was she talking about? "I'm sorry, *how* did you know Marguerite?"

"I'm from the Native Women's Association. Marguerite initially came to us for help in finding your mother."

Archer reeled as if slapped. Margie had gotten involved in some Native political organization? "Our mother's dead," he said dispassionately.

"Most likely, yes," she returned equally bluntly. "There are nearly twelve hundred dead or missing Aboriginal women in this country— in the last three decades alone. It's an epidemic. Marguerite wanted to learn if there had been any update on the case, or if a body had ever been recovered, and she had no idea where to start."

Betrayal knifed him in the gut. He'd done so much to get Margie away from that place, away from that life. Why couldn't she leave it alone? Of course their mother was dead. That's what happened to drug-addicted prostitutes from North Winnipeg. He didn't need confirmation. Why should she? Then again, Margie had always been softhearted, always held out hope for some fairy-tale reunion. But why hadn't she said anything to him about what she was up to? Had she been afraid he would be angry? That he would try to discourage her? He sure as hell would have.

"Look," he began, intending to tell this woman he had absolutely no interest in following Margie's lead, when he felt a tug on his suit jacket and glanced down to find Emma peering up at him.

"I have to go pee, Uncle Archie," she said.

He grimaced. "Well, go. The restrooms are over there."

"I'm not supposed to go by myself."

Archer saw his chance. "Kids," he said with a shrug, hoping Alyssa would get the hint and excuse him. How could she be offended by a man taking care of his orphaned niece?

She smiled fondly at them both. "Let me give you my card. In case you want to know more or continue Marguerite's work. Or if you'd like to drop by the Native Centre—we're starting up some children's programming you might be interested in." Rather than argue, Archer took the card and blindly dropped it into his suit pocket. He excused himself, leaving Alyssa staring after him. He could feel her deep-set, dark eyes boring into his back as he led Emma around the corner to the restrooms.

"Who was that lady?"

"No one," Archer said. He stopped now that they were out of sight.

"What are you waiting for? I have to go," Emma whined.

Relief rushed through him as he spotted an exit sign at the end of the hallway. He dropped Emma's hand and headed toward it. "Find Ryan," he called over his shoulder. "He'll take you."

Without a backward glance, Archer slipped out the fire door and emerged in the parking lot, eyes stinging at the brightness of the summer sun after the dim interior. He pulled a pair of Ray-Bans from his inside pocket and slipped them on. The craving was strong today, stronger than it had ever been—just a little drink, just a small hit of coke—that brief respite everyone but him seemed entitled to. He shook it off. He didn't dare take that first step. He'd made Marguerite a promise, and he couldn't break that, not today of all days. But he needed something . . .

If only he hadn't been so quick to give up smoking. Turning thirty a few years ago had put him on a health kick, determined to break his genetic legacy and make it past sixty. But fuck, he would kill for a cigarette right now. Or better yet . . .

With the blood rushing beneath his skin and his heart thundering, Archer grabbed his smartphone, logged in to Grindr, and in a few minutes found exactly what he needed. His next step was calling a cab.

"Hey, here you are," Ryan said a short time later, coming up behind him as he was waiting for the cab to arrive. "I wondered where you'd disappeared to. A little overwhelming, eh?"

"Yeah." Archer swung around to face the younger man. "Are you okay to take the kids home? You do have a driver's license, right?"

"Yes. But where—?"

Archer tossed the car keys at Ryan. "I need some time to myself."

"Now?" Ryan's hazel eyes filled with confusion and, if Archer wasn't mistaken, a healthy dose of ire. "What about the cemetery?"

Oh, hell no. He couldn't handle that. "It's not like she'll know if I'm there or not."

"The kids will."

"Yeah, well, they'll get over it." Archer sighed in relief as he saw the cab pull into the parking lot. He stalked toward it with Ryan on his heels.

"You *are* an asshole. Do you ever think of anyone but yourself?"

"Not if I can help it," Archer threw back as he reached the safety of the cab. He yanked open the door.

"What do I tell everyone?"

"Don't care what the fuck you tell them." He jumped in the backseat, gave the driver the address, and didn't look back.

"Oh, yeah. Harder. Fuck me harder," howled the burly man quivering on all fours in front of Archer as he nailed him with enough force to make the cheap IKEA bed rattle. His partner—Gary? Or was it Garrett?—wailed louder. Archer pressed down on the man's broad, meaty back with both hands, pushing Gary/Garrett's face into the mattress as he thrust with a ferocity that surprised him. He squeezed his eyes shut. Clenched his jaw as his hips hammered home. He fucked mindlessly, like an animal. But the usual escape eluded him. He tried to recapture that feeling of peace he'd had earlier when Ryan held his hand, but even as his balls drew tight, it remained out of reach. Still, at least Gary/Garrett sounded as though he was loving it.

Archer came quickly. It was almost anticlimactic. A release of the body, but nothing else. There was a brief second of forgetfulness, and then that restless, smothered feeling was back. This time topped with a healthy dose of self-disgust.

He pulled out of the ginger giant and tore off the used condom. The big man flopped to his back, fingering his ass. "Wow, you weren't kidding about being tense."

"Want me to get you off?" Archer asked, zipping up his slacks and hoping the guy would turn him down. Now that he'd come, he only wanted to leave.

His partner, whose name he still couldn't recall, grasped the base of his softening dick in invitation. "Blow me?"

Archer's throat seized unexpectedly. Normally he loved giving head, and this guy was exactly his type, but today he just wasn't into it. He forced himself to relax. He'd done this so many times, what was one more? As he advanced toward the bed, he planned his moves out in his head. Five minutes—seven, tops.

With practiced skill, he got Gary/Garrett hard. It wasn't his best effort by any means, but it looked like five minutes would be enough after all. As he tightened his lips, bobbing his head faster, harder, Archer couldn't help wonder what Marguerite would think right now. He'd walked away from her funeral, from his responsibilities, for *this*. He felt her disappointment. But what did she expect? This is who he was. This is who he always would be.

Chapter 7

*R*yan lay propped up against the headboard of Emma's bed, with the little girl curled up on one side of him clutching a ragged stuffed animal of indeterminate species, and Dillon on the other, as he read to them. It was a moment of sweet perfection after an arduous day, but that perfection ended when he heard the front door open. His heart began to pound with a rare combination of anger and indignation.

Archer was back.

"Uncle Archie's home," Emma mumbled around the thumb in her mouth. The thumb-sucking was new, but Ryan had given up trying to make her stop. The books said she needed all the comfort she could get.

"So he is." Ryan continued reading, modulating his voice to snare the kids' interest again, ignoring the heavy tread of Archer's feet on the stairs. If Archer had been a child, Ryan would have known what to do: he would have let Archer know how much he had disappointed them all today. But Archer Noble was a grown man, and one with a strong personality to boot. Ryan couldn't very well send him to his room to think about what he had done. He supposed he should consider it a good sign that Archer hadn't stayed out all night.

A few minutes later, Ryan looked up from his book, surprised to find Archer standing there, watching them. He fidgeted in Emma's doorway like a guilty child. "Everyone okay?"

"Fine," Ryan replied, determined not to involve Dillon and Emma in his own private drama.

"Gonna hop in the shower."

"Go ahead. The kids have already had their baths." Ryan began to read aloud once more, proud of how calm and mature he sounded.

Moments later he heard the shower running in the bathroom across the hallway.

"Why doesn't Uncle Archie love us?" Emma piped up when Ryan paused to turn the page.

His eyes welled with tears. Ryan tried to think the best of people, but Archer clearly didn't deserve these kids. "He does, sweetie." Ryan stroked her soft hair. "Uncle Archie's just hurting right now too. And he's not used to children." He hoped that was true, but after today it was becoming more and more difficult to make excuses for Archer.

"I don't care if he doesn't love us," huffed Dillon. "I don't like him. I want him to go away so we can stay with you, Ryan."

The twist to Ryan's heart was surprisingly painful this time. If only things were that simple. He pressed a kiss to Dillon's temple. "Remember how at the start of the year you said you didn't like Matthew because he broke your lunch box? Now he's your best friend, isn't he? People can change. You have to give them time."

Ryan read a bit longer, until the thumb slipped out from between Emma's lips and her breathing told him she was asleep. Dillon, too, appeared on the verge of drifting off, his eyelids drooping as he struggled to stay awake. It had been a tough day for all of them. Ryan carefully extricated himself from the bed. "We'll finish it tomorrow," he whispered when Dillon protested sleepily. He debated telling Dillon to go to his own room but decided there wasn't any harm in leaving him where he was. "Go to sleep now."

"Don't forget the night-light," Dillon mumbled.

Ryan tucked the blankets around them, made sure the night-light was on, before he closed the door and left the kids sleeping.

He tiptoed past the bathroom door, went back downstairs, and made himself chamomile tea. Ryan had never fully understood the expression "weary to the bone" until now—it wasn't 10 p.m. yet, but he'd been up since dawn. The one good thing about being so busy was that he hadn't had time to let his grief take over, but now that he could actually stop and catch his breath, he sensed it waiting there, ready to pounce. He focused his thoughts on the kids instead. He'd planned to walk away after the funeral, but after Archer's selfish antics today, he wasn't so sure. As Ryan sat at the dining room table, sipping his tea, he heard Archer rummaging in the kitchen. Outrage choked Ryan, but he tried to rein in his contempt. The man was grieving. Surely he would come around soon.

Part of Ryan felt sorry for Archer. If even half of what Marguerite had confided to him was true, Archer had endured more than anyone should have to in one lifetime. He seemed so remote; as far as Ryan could tell there were no friends calling to see how he was doing, no one offering comfort. He'd stood apart at the service, aloof and cold, with only the tic in his jaw revealing any inner turmoil. It was that tiny vulnerability that had made Ryan finally go to him. No one deserved to be alone at a time like this—not even a man as unlikable as Archer Noble.

And then he'd blown it by running away.

"There's leftover pizza in the fridge," Ryan offered without turning around or otherwise acknowledging Archer's presence. After such a trying day, he had wanted to make it a special night for the kids, so they'd ordered pizza and eaten it right out of the box in front of the TV.

"We need to talk," Archer said, flinging himself into the chair across the table. Ryan's lips twitched at the abrupt tone. Over the last week of living together, he had learned that Archer Noble was not the type to beat around the bush. He was often blunt, sometimes to the point of rudeness—what else would he expect from a man who boasted about how many public places he'd had sex in? Now Archer was looking at Ryan with weary resignation.

"I agree. Today was . . . unacceptable. We need to start thinking about the kids' future."

"'We'?" Archer lifted a brow. He wrenched the cap off a water bottle as if it had personally offended him. "Seems to me like we've already got the perfect solution right here."

"Excuse me?"

"I want you to take the kids."

Ryan gasped, as if he'd been punched in the stomach. "What?"

"Why not? She obviously trusted you enough to put you in charge."

"Yeah, temporarily."

"You know that Margie made me their guardian. But what I didn't tell you is that she also appointed you as alternate in case . . ."

"In case what? In case you refused?" Ryan finished when it didn't appear Archer was going to continue.

"Regardless, whatever it says in the will isn't official."

"What?"

"According to the lawyer, in this province guardianship is not automatic. No matter if it's in the will or not. We have ninety days to file an application for permanent custody or else the courts will step in and appoint someone. I say you go ahead and file the application."

"But...you can't," Ryan stammered as Archer stood and began to pace. God help him, he knew it was wrong. But he couldn't stop the hope from bubbling in his chest.

"How am I supposed to take care of them? I travel all the time. I don't have a permanent address. I don't know the first thing about raising kids—never wanted any of my own. I mean, who in their right mind would want to bring a kid into this fucked-up world? The boy has an imaginary friend for Chrissakes. What the fuck am I supposed to do with that?"

"I don't think it's anything to worry about. It's his way of dealing with things."

"See?" Archer pointed a finger at him. "I don't really give a shit. But you do. What I learned about parenting is nothing I care to pass on. But you...you're amazing with them."

Ryan pounced on the unexpected concession. "So you *do* agree gay men can be good parents."

"I never said we *couldn't* do it," Archer returned.

"Oh yeah, I forgot. Your argument is that we shouldn't want to," Ryan sneered. "That those of us who want marriage and parenthood are 'conforming to heteronormative values.'"

Archer blinked. "I'm flattered. You memorized it. I didn't think you knew who I was."

"I didn't know you were Marguerite's brother. She said you were a writer—I never made the connection. But, oh yeah, I know all about Archer Noble."

"And you don't like him, judging by your tone of voice."

Ryan shrugged. "I don't like what he stands for. I don't like how he so easily dismisses others and puts them down for wanting different things."

Archer fisted his hands on his hips. "Why is it so wrong to like my life the way it is?"

"I wasn't talking about *your* life, but since we're on the topic, it's not only your life now. Shit happens. We don't always get what we want." Ryan's voice cracked. He knew that better than anyone. "Think about someone else for a change."

"I am thinking of them. This is what's best."

"Running away is never best."

"What the fuck would you know about it?" Archer snapped. "I bet you grew up in a nice house, with a nice family—"

"You don't know me."

"I know you're a naive kid who thinks life is all hearts and rainbows and that everyone deserves a happy ending."

Ryan considered himself an even-tempered person; he rarely got angry, almost never raised his voice and definitely never hit anyone. But Archer was testing the limits of his self-control.

"What's your problem?" Archer asked. "I thought you'd be thrilled. You're exactly the type."

"Oh? And what type would that be?"

"Mr. White-Picket-Fence," he answered with a smirk. "Go ahead. Tell me I'm wrong. I bet you've been dreaming of babies and Mr. Right since you played with your first Barbie doll."

In that moment, Ryan hated that smug, handsome face; hated that once again Archer had him pegged; and hated that he made Ryan's dreams seem like a fate worse than death.

Archer took a deep, steadying breath and shook his head. "Look, I can't do it."

"They should be with family," Ryan insisted. "Isn't there anyone—?"

"Jackson's dad died when he was a kid—the same cancer that took him. His mom's in some assisted-living facility with advanced dementia. There's no one else."

"Just you."

"Or you," Archer countered.

"Are you that selfish? Getting laid is more important than taking care of your niece and nephew? What would Marguerite think?" What the heck he was doing? He had a chance at a family and here he was still pushing them at Archer.

"I don't know," he shouted, jumping to his feet. "I don't know what the fuck Margie was thinking. She wasn't, obviously."

Ryan summoned his compassion and forced his voice to gentle. "I think she knew you better than anyone. And if she made you their guardian, then that's what *she* wanted. Are you really going to ignore that?"

Archer whirled on him. "Did she tell you about our mother?"

"Some," Ryan replied cautiously.

"And our grandfather? The abusive alcoholic?"

"I don't see what—"

"We have bad blood. With you they have a fresh chance."

"That's bullshit." Ryan gaped at Archer, who looked as though he actually believed that crap. "Marguerite has—had—the same blood as you and she was a great parent."

"Margie got the good parts." Archer ran a hand through his short dark hair. "Believe it or not, I'm not a complete asshole. They deserve better than me."

For a second Ryan almost agreed. Not because of any genetic nonsense, but because Archer seemed incapable of caring about anyone other than himself. Dillon and Emma deserved to be raised by someone who loved them, who *wanted* them. Then he thought of Marguerite, the promise he'd made in the school yard, and wavered. "What if I say no?"

"You won't," Archer replied confidently. "You already love them. It's written all over your face."

Ryan hesitated. Was he that transparent? This wasn't how he'd imagined becoming a parent. He'd always counted on having a partner at his side and starting with a baby first, not two school-aged children, but he could do this too—he had a steady job and a good salary. Wouldn't Marguerite want the kids to be loved?

But it was wrong. He felt that in his gut. Marguerite had known all these things about Ryan, and she had still chosen her brother. He had to trust that she knew best.

"They already love you," Archer continued, dangling the bait a little bit closer.

"And they'll love you too," Ryan returned, although he was only half-sure about that. Archer Noble was hardly the lovable sort. "They don't know you. Give it some time."

"I don't have time. I'm working on a proposal for my own show, and I need to get things squared away. If it's money you're worried about, don't. Thanks to the mortgage insurance, the house is now paid for. I'll even transfer the deed to your name and you can live here. There's not much in the estate, but after probate, there should be something to put in an education fund for the kids. It won't be a lot, but it's a start."

Ryan gaped at Archer. It was a generous offer. Instant home. Instant family. He may not have been Marguerite's first choice, but she had trusted him to step in if her brother wouldn't, right? So why did it still feel so wrong? If he said no too, the courts would appoint a guardian, the kids would go into the system, and who knew where they would end up. Would Archer actually let that happen? Ryan was afraid to call his bluff.

"I need to think about it," Ryan said finally, and it broke his heart a bit to say it out loud.

Archer sagged in relief, like a man who'd just heard he was being paroled.

Ryan was awakened by a bloodcurdling wail in the middle of the night. *Emma.* He bolted upright in the dark, windowless basement bedroom where he slept, listening. Another faint cry followed and then angry shouts from Dillon. Ryan shot out of bed, grabbed his robe, and raced up the two flights of stairs, nearly colliding with Archer in the narrow hallway outside the bedrooms.

"What is it?" Ryan demanded.

"I don't know," Archer replied, pausing to give Ryan's fuchsia silk robe a derisive glance.

Ryan brushed past him to shove open the door and flick on the overhead light. He found Emma sitting up in bed, and Dillon standing nearby with tears streaming down his face.

"What's going on?" As he moved closer, Ryan was assailed by the unmistakable smell of urine.

"I peed," Emma moaned in between deep, heart-wrenching sobs.

"She wet the bed like a baby," Dillon shouted angrily. "She peed all over me. Like a stupid baby."

"I'm not a baby," Emma shrieked.

"It was an accident," Ryan said gently. He turned to Archer who was still standing in the doorway wearing only a pair of tight-fitting boxers and a T-shirt, and a slightly dumbfounded expression. "Tissues, stat," he barked.

"What?"

"We need tissues. Lots of them."

Ryan didn't wait to see if Archer obeyed his order. He carefully lifted Emma's wet nightdress over her head and plucked her out of bed to stand on the floor. When a box of tissues appeared at his elbow, he gratefully grabbed a handful and wiped her face and runny nose. "It's okay, sweetie. It happens."

He was relieved to see Archer silently following his lead and doing the same for Dillon. His sodden pajamas were tossed on top of Emma's. Soon, the siblings' sobbing had dwindled to a few silent tears.

"See," Ryan explained. "No harm done. It can all go in the washing machine."

"Where's Mommy?" Emma whimpered.

"She's dead, stupid," Dillon snapped. "Don't you remember?"

To Ryan's surprise, Archer grasped him firmly by the arms. "I know you're angry Dillon, but don't take it out on your sister." His tone was gentle. "It's not her fault."

Dillon's eyes widened, and then without warning he launched himself into Archer's arms and sobbed against his chest. Pain, love, and fear flitted across Archer's face as he awkwardly cradled the crying boy, leaving Ryan speechless. In that brief moment Archer Noble seemed entirely human for the first time.

Archer blinked as though he had been caught in a nightmare and just woken up. He turned to Ryan in alarm. "What now?"

"Bed or bath?" Ryan asked.

"Huh?"

"You can either strip the bed or wash the kids." He didn't give Archer the choice of opting out.

Archer glanced at the wet sheets and wrinkled his nose. Ryan couldn't wait to see his reaction when he had to clean up puke. "Bath, I guess."

"Okay, put them in the tub but don't make the water too hot."

As Archer ran the bath, Ryan stripped the bed and carried the linens and sodden pajamas down to the laundry room to treat and soak in the sink. He would throw them into the washer in the morning. When he returned upstairs, he heard splashing from the bathroom, and when he ducked his head in was pleased to find Emma's sobs had diminished to watery sniffles. He handed Archer fresh pajamas for the kids.

Back in Emma's room, Ryan opened the window wider and tried his best to blot the mattress with paper towels. It would need a thorough disinfecting in the morning. By the time he was done, Emma and Dillon were washed, dried, and dressed again. He steered them toward Dillon's room.

"I wanna sleep in Mommy's bed," Emma declared.

"Me too," added Dillon.

They both turned pleading eyes to Ryan, who only shook his head. "Ask your Uncle Archer. It's his bed now." There. The challenge was issued. *Say no to their faces.* If the man didn't succumb to the two pairs of dark, wet eyes, there was absolutely no hope for him.

A muscle in Archer's jaw ticked madly. "Okay." He sighed, throwing a meaningful glance in Ryan's direction. "But everybody pees first."

Dillon and Emma stared at him, mouths open. Then Dillon giggled. And then Emma. Even Archer cracked a smile. Hope and sorrow mingled in Ryan's chest—an unsettling combination. Maybe things would turn out all right after all.

Ryan helped Archer get the kids settled in the big bed. "Don't forget Mr. Snuggles," Emma warned.

Archer's eyes widened in alarm. "Please don't tell me she has—"

"It's her stuffed animal," Ryan explained, suppressing a laugh.

"Oh, good." Archer returned a few seconds later with Mr. Snuggles and a quizzical look on his face. "What is this? A bear?"

"I thought it was a dog."

"It's Mr. Snuggles," Emma said simply, as though they were two dunces who didn't know the first thing about stuffed animals. She snatched up the toy and cuddled it against her chest. Ryan made to leave, but Emma grabbed the belt of his robe. "You too," she ordered.

A blush crept up his cheeks. It was wrong, on so many levels. It was one thing for Archer to share a bed with the two young children—he was a blood relative. But add another man—a gay man and a teacher—and they were asking for trouble. "Oh, no, sweetie. I can't."

Emma's lower lip began to tremble. Archer groaned as he slid beneath the covers. "Oh hell, will you get in? I can't take any more drama tonight."

With a sigh, Ryan turned out the light and lay down on top of the covers. He'd only stay until the kids fell asleep. The swirl of air from the ceiling fan ruffled the hem of his short robe and blew across his legs.

"Why is your robe pink, Ryan?" Emma asked in the darkness. "Girls wear pink."

"It's not pink. It's fuchsia."

"I like pink," she sleepily pronounced seconds later, and Ryan thought he heard Archer chuckle.

Ryan opened his eyes to the sight of dawn peeking through the blinds and the sound of birds chirping outside. It took him a minute to orient himself. He jolted fully awake when he realized he was still in Marguerite's bed with Archer on the other side of the king-sized mattress, the kids snuggled in between them. In his sleep, Archer had thrown a protective arm over both the children, and Ryan's hand rested on his wrist, anchoring them all together. His heart fluttered, the moment so perfect that he couldn't bear to move. It was everything he imagined for himself, except he didn't belong.

God, wouldn't Archer have a good laugh at his fanciful dreams?

Archer stirred before he could contemplate slipping away, so Ryan slammed his eyes shut, feigning sleep. If Archer got up first, he could make his own escape with some dignity. But when no further movement came from the other side of the bed, Ryan cracked open his eyelids a sliver and peered out from beneath his eyelashes.

Archer was awake, his gaze resting on the sleeping children, his forehead creased in reflection. What was he thinking to put so much pain, so much fear on his face? And something else. Something that looked suspiciously like longing.

Archer's gaze wandered to where Ryan's hand rested on his arm, and he tried not to tense in response. But instead of jerking away as Ryan expected, Archer remained still. Ryan's pulse skittered as he felt Archer's eyes on him. After a few more minutes, Archer slid his arm free. Only then did Ryan dare a soft sigh of relief.

Archer tenderly plucked a lock of hair off Emma's plump cheek. The barest hint of a smile teased his lips, transforming his usually stony face. He looked so much younger when he smiled—less guarded. Ryan's heart swelled until it felt two sizes too big for his chest. He forgot he was supposed to be pretending to sleep himself.

The quiet rumble of Archer's voice made him realize he hadn't been fooling anyone. "She reminds me so much of Marguerite."

"Yeah?"

"Even as a kid she liked to hog the bed. No matter if you started her off on one side, she would always end up sprawled in the middle all over you."

Ryan perked up. It was the first time Archer had volunteered any of his memories. "You shared a bed?"

"It was all we could afford. Sometimes we could only get a room with one bed and all three of us had to share." Archer's expression grew shuttered, as if he feared he had given too much away. "How do you always know what to do?" he asked suddenly.

"I don't," Ryan said. "Really. Half the time I fake it. The other half I put myself in their shoes."

"You must have a huge family to be such a natural."

Ryan rolled his head on the pillow. "Nope. Only child. I always wanted a brother or a sister though." In hindsight however, as lonely as he'd been growing up, he supposed it had been for the best. Arne and Karen weren't exactly the parental type.

"But you were so calm last night. It didn't even faze you."

"Not much you can do about it. It's bound to happen now and then." It seemed so intimate, to be having this conversation in bed with Archer, whispering so they wouldn't disturb the kids. Like something longtime lovers might do. "The first class I taught was kindergarten. Piss and puke are part of a grade-school teacher's life."

"Can't wait." Archer grimaced. His eyes widened as if he realized what he had just said. Whether he liked it or not, he appeared more resigned to his fate this morning. "About last night . . ."

"It was a crazy day; I know this isn't easy."

Archer sighed. "I really do want the best for them. And I'm pretty sure it's not me."

For a brief moment Ryan saw beneath Archer Noble's tough veneer. He was scared. He wanted to take the easy way out. But the look on his face as he'd watched Emma a few minutes ago showed that there might be more to the man; someone real buried underneath all that bluster and show. Was that what Marguerite had seen in her brother?

Ryan knew in his heart what he had to do. He would step in if he absolutely had to, but if there was the slimmest chance these three could make it as a family, he needed to make them see it. Even if it cost him his own happiness. That's what Marguerite would want. "Can I be honest with you?"

"Are you ever anything but?"

Ryan snorted. "The only wrong thing is not trying." He followed Archer's gaze as it landed on the two sleeping children again. He couldn't believe he was proposing this, but it felt right. "You said you had ninety days to file an application. Give it a bit more time. I can stay until school starts and help out if you want. If you still feel the same way come September, we can discuss it again."

Archer stared at him for a long time, his expression inscrutable. Then he nodded briefly, and the knot in Ryan's stomach loosened. He was setting himself up for a world of hurt, but he couldn't walk away now. He had seven weeks to convince Archer that the kids belonged with him—even if Ryan wasn't sure he believed it himself.

He rolled out of bed before Archer could see what it had cost him to make the offer.

"I'm going to start the coffee. Let them sleep," he whispered and left the new family cuddled together.

Chapter 8

"*H*ow is my favorite hedonist?"

Archer cringed as the familiar abrasive sound of his agent's voice blared through the phone's tiny speaker—she was a native New Yorker and had the accent and volume to prove it. He wished he'd let the call go through to voice mail, but he'd been so occupied in packing up Margie's things that he hadn't checked the call display before answering.

"Hey, Donna," he replied cautiously, bracing himself.

"How are those outlines for the next book?"

"About that . . . it's kind of a tough time right now." Archer cast a glance around Margie's bedroom, at the mounds of clothes piled on the bed waiting to be stuffed into trash bags. Now that the estate was somewhat settled, came the daunting task of packing up Margie's belongings. Ryan had volunteered to help, but Archer had turned him down. This was something he felt he had to do on his own.

He was struck with the memory of Gran doing this same chore after his *moosum* passed. Within days she had given away his possessions, telling Archer it was so his spirit would be free to depart the human realm. For Archer now, it was about getting rid of things they had no use for.

Emptying the closets had seemed like the easiest part of the job, so he had begun with that. The clothes were simply clothes—they held no sentimental value. He would let the kids pick through the other trinkets and knickknacks scattered across the dresser top for keepsakes before packing them up too.

Donna clucked her tongue in mock sympathy. "I know you've had a personal tragedy, but hon, we both know if you want to make it in this business, you've got to strike while the iron is hot. If we don't, in another month you'll be old news. No publisher will want you. Don't go getting all cocky because you've got a development deal. That's small potatoes."

"Didn't you see that editorial piece I did for the *Huff Post*?"

"I did. And I've been laughing my ass off at this Twitter war you've got going with that guy from the *Advocate*."

Archer grinned. He was pretty proud of that one.

"But Archer, honey, you're only going to be able to milk this cow so long before she runs out of milk."

His grin slipped. "I know—"

"You're not getting all domesticated on me, are you?"

"No, of course not," he replied quickly. The band around his chest tightened. He threw open the window and drew in a deep breath, but it didn't help much. Below, in the backyard, the kids and Ryan played in the swimming pool. Children were so resilient.

In the two weeks since the memorial service, he and Ryan had formed a wary partnership, with Ryan taking on primary care during the day as Archer met with the bankers, the lawyers, and spent hours on the phone with the insurance company. In return, Archer had made an effort to be more involved. It was halfhearted at best, but Ryan hadn't complained. They never spoke of it—how he had tried to unload Emma and Dillon like unwanted baggage. If he thought about it too hard, it made him uncomfortable.

True to his word, Ryan had moved into the basement bedroom. He probably believed the kids would grow on Archer if he held out long enough. What Ryan didn't know was that Archer's mind was already made up, and he had absolutely no intention of changing it. Even if it did make him feel a bit guilty now whenever he looked at their sweet, sun-kissed faces, as their smiles slowly returned and the giggles became more frequent. Sometimes he woke up in the morning to find one or both of them tucked in beside him, little bodies curled against him, trusting. In those moments, the most extraordinary sense of peace flowed through him. It dredged up long-forgotten memories of cold nights in strange beds, and he and Marguerite huddling together to keep warm, whispering stories to each other when they couldn't sleep. No matter how bad it had gotten, all he'd had to do was reach out a hand and know he wasn't alone.

"You sure?" Donna asked thoughtfully. "That might be a good angle."

Emma splashed happily in the pool, some sort of brightly colored flotation device strapped around her chest. Ryan stood nearby, waist-deep in the shallow end, a broad-brimmed hat obscuring his face as he instructed Dillon on proper diving stance. They seemed like such a happy family. Not for the first time, Archer felt like an outsider.

Ryan looked up then and must have noticed Archer standing at the window, because he waved for him to join them. Archer's stomach jolted with something he'd rather not analyze too deeply. He quickly turned away, and realized he hadn't taken in a word Donna had said.

"Sorry, what?"

"Think about it. Wild bad boy gets his just desserts when he's tamed by a pair of adorable orphans. It could work. You'd lose some readers of course, be accused of hypocrisy, but I think you'd pick up a lot more."

Oh fuck no. Archer winced at Donna's noticeable excitement. There were many things he'd do for his career, but starting a family was not one of them. "I'm only their legal guardian. I don't intend to let it change me. And it's only temporary anyway."

"Temporary?"

Archer explained the situation and his plans to his agent. She went quiet on the other end of the line. "You're going to give your niece and nephew over to a complete stranger? That's . . . cold, isn't it? Even for you."

"He's not a stranger," Archer replied defensively. "And you haven't seen him. He's perfect. Like Mary Poppins. Exactly the kind of man I wrote about in *I Don't*."

"The kind you derided?"

"Turns out they come in handy after all. Besides, this is about what's best for the kids." If he repeated that enough times, he might quell the glimmer of doubt that had been nagging him lately.

Margie and Jackson's wedding picture stared back at Archer from the dresser top, his sister's gaze suddenly accusing. Margie would have expected better. *But haven't I done enough*, he wanted to shout.

Things are finally coming together for me and still you want more? Archer ignored the twist in his gut and tossed the photo into the box with the rest of the items to be kept.

"Keep going," Donna encouraged, pulling him back to the conversation.

"What?"

"You've got something there. Write about your decision *not* to parent."

"Yeah, and get crucified in the process for abandoning my sister's children."

"Hey, you said it, not me. And there's no such thing as bad publicity. Since when do you care what people think of you anyway?"

Donna was right. His entire career so far had been based on stirring up trouble and being an arrogant asshole. Besides, he didn't have any other ideas right now. "I'll consider it. See what I can come up with."

"Well, think fast. I need an outline by the end of the month."

Archer pinched the bridge of his nose to keep his encroaching headache at bay. "Yeah, got it." Now that he had finished up most of the paperwork associated with settling the estate, he would have more time to get back to his writing.

"Do it again, Ryan," Emma cried from below. Archer clenched his teeth at the piercing squeal.

"Pull something together," Donna ordered. "Show me what you've got. But don't lose your edge. That's what the readers want." A few minutes later, with some choice words about getting his ass in gear, Donna hung up and Archer returned to his packing.

How had Marguerite accumulated so much? Archer's nomadic lifestyle meant he had little to his name except for what he carried in the suitcase and kept in a storage locker downtown. He didn't even have a fixed address these days—he got by on short-term rentals or bumming accommodation off contacts and people he met online. He liked it that way—with nothing to tie him down.

He lifted the lid on the small jewelry box sitting on the dresser and sifted through the jumbled contents. There wasn't much—a few plastic beaded necklaces, a couple of tarnished chains and mismatched earrings. He would put it aside for Emma to go through in the future. Little girls liked that sort of thing, didn't they?

His fingers stilled on a familiar child-size ring set with a single chipped pink rhinestone. As he pulled it free of the others, his heart seized.

Suddenly the walls were closing in on him—like they had at the funeral home—only now it was ten times worse. One minute he was thinking about Marguerite, and the next he was struggling for breath, black spots dancing in front of his eyes. His lungs burned. He sank to his knees on the floor, dizzy and nauseous. But just when he thought he was about to puke, the feeling abruptly passed, leaving him shivering, sweaty, and wondering what had happened. He curled his fingers around the tawdry childish token, the fake stone biting into his palm as he leaned his head on the corner of the bed and waited for his heart rate to return to normal. The sting grounded him.

What the hell was that? It had to be a stress thing. He'd heard of panic attacks before but never had one. It was probably normal given the sudden pressures in his life. But, fuck, there was no time to deal with this now, not with a book to write and an estate to finish settling. Slowly, he opened his clenched fist and stared at the ring in his palm. He had shoplifted it from the Eaton's department store on Donald Street for Margie's fifth birthday. Nearly got caught too. She had worn it faithfully until it became too tight for her growing fingers. He couldn't believe she had kept it all this time. It was junk. *Oh, Marguerite, why you?* If ever he needed proof there was no goodness in the world, this was it.

As Archer sat there, his phone chimed with an incoming text. He groaned and tucked the ring into his front pocket for safekeeping. It was probably Donna with a follow-up reminder. But when he checked, it turned out to be his hookup from the funeral seeing if he was free later. *God, yes.* A good, hard fuck was exactly what he needed. He typed a short response in the affirmative, which was returned soon after by a stimulating selfie that made the blood rush to his dick. He rubbed himself through his shorts. So he couldn't remember the guy's name, and the sex had only been so-so—he wasn't about to complain now that he could actually breathe again. So he pushed his strange episode to the side as they made arrangements for that night.

Afterward, Archer remained on the floor for some minutes, listening as the happy squeals of the kids playing in the pool drifted up from the backyard through the open windows. They were having fun. Without him. That was the way it should be. Still, something he didn't examine too closely made him get up and wander downstairs.

"Uncle Archie, watch me," Dillon cried excitedly when Archer slid open the patio door and stepped out into the backyard. The rectangular swimming pool had come with the house and the discolored liner was beginning to show its age. At first Margie hadn't been thrilled with the pool, but year after year it remained, taking up most of the shallow backyard although it only got used two months out of the year. Seeing how much enjoyment it brought to the kids, Archer was glad she'd kept it.

"Are you watching?" Dillon demanded, crouching forward on the edge, fingers pointing toward the water. He leaned forward and executed a spectacular belly flop. Even Archer had to wince. Dillon bobbed up to the surface sputtering and moaning. "Ow, I hurt my willy."

"Ouch." Archer struggled to contain his laugh. "Be careful. You're going to need that when you get older."

Ryan sent him a menacing glare. "Good job," he praised, but Archer was pretty sure he'd seen the younger man's lips curve ever so slightly.

He glanced around the yard, frowning at the colorful cluster of flowers under the dappled shade of the chestnut tree in the far corner. He didn't think they'd been there last week. "Where did these come from?"

"They're patients," Emma declared. "Aren't they pretty?"

"Impatiens," Ryan corrected.

"Red is for Mommy—"

"And purple is for Daddy," Dillon finished.

Jesus. Archer reeled as though he'd been slapped across the face. He turned his back on the garden, pushing down the emotion rising in his chest. "Was that your idea?" he demanded of Ryan when he could finally speak again.

Ryan nodded hesitantly.

Archer cleared his throat. "It's a good one," he said roughly. Grudgingly. "She'd have liked that. Margie always loved flowers."

Ryan's smile was cautious.

"Come and swim, Uncle Archie," Emma shouted gleefully, breaking the somber mood.

Archer grimaced, sticking to the safety of the patio. "I'll stay right here, thanks. Where it's nice and dry."

"But it's fun. Can't you swim?" she asked.

"Nope. Not even a little bit."

"Didn't your mommy take you to swimming lessons?"

Archer was taken aback by how much the innocent comment hurt, but he did his best to hide it. His childhood worry had been getting enough to eat, not learning to swim. Swimming lessons had been as unattainable as the white father he'd dreamed of. Thank God Emma would never have to know life like that.

"Not everyone is lucky enough to get swimming lessons, Em," Ryan counseled.

"Why not?"

Archer pulled himself together. Emma was only a kid. He didn't need Ryan to run interference for him. "For one thing, there was really no place to swim. For another, we didn't have the money." *Or a mother who gave a fuck.*

"You should learn," Ryan said. "With the pool and the kids, you'll need to. In case of emergency."

Nice try, Archer thought with a pointed scowl. *I'm not going to be around long enough to need to learn.*

His eyes fixed on Ryan, treading water in the middle of the pool. The man wore a wide, floppy sun hat, aviator sunglasses, and a long-sleeved T-shirt. Barely an inch of skin showed. "Do you usually swim fully dressed?" he jeered.

"Sun protection," Ryan replied. "I burn easily."

Yeah, Archer bet he did. All that fine, milk-white skin. He yanked his thoughts away from the direction they were headed and pulled his own T-shirt over his head.

"Sunscreen is on the table," Ryan told him.

"Don't need it. My people don't do cancer. Heart disease, suicide, and alcoholism, yes. But we don't make it to skin cancer." Archer tossed his shirt on a chaise lounge in the shade nearest the house. Oddly, Ryan had no response this time. When Archer glanced back toward the pool, he noticed that the man had stopped treading water and the parts of Ryan's pale face still exposed had turned unusually pink.

"Whoa. Cool tattoo, Uncle Archie," Dillon crowed.

He had lived with the large stylized Thunderbird on his back for so long that he tended to forget about it. It was from an earlier time. Intricate and colorful, the wings spanned the width of his shoulder blades. He turned, showing it off some more. "You like that?"

Dillon paddled over to the edge of the pool where Archer stood. "What is it?"

"It's Thunderbird."

"What's a thunderbird?"

Archer frowned. Had Margie not told them any of the old legends? No, of course she wouldn't have. He only knew a few himself. Archer sat down on the coping and dangled his legs in the water to cool off. This was as close as he got to water—unless he was sitting naked in some hot tub. "Well, Thunderbird is like an eagle, with a wingspan two canoes wide. He eats snakes and protects humankind from the Great Horned Serpent of the Underworld."

"Ew," said Emma.

"Cool," said Dillon.

"When he beats his wings, it sounds like thunder, and lightning flashes from his eyes. Sometimes he can take human form. Sometimes he disguises himself as black swirling clouds." His tiny audience was spellbound. Even Ryan stood in the shallow end staring at him.

"What else, Uncle Archie?"

"Well," Archer tried to recall some of the stories he had heard during the long winter nights. "His name is Pe-ya-siw. There's a Cree legend that somewhere out west there's a lake where a great struggle occurred between a huge serpent and Thunderbird. For hours they battled; the skies rolled with thunder and lightning, but finally Thunderbird tired and the snake pulled Pe-ya-siw beneath the water. Ever since then, the lake has rumbled because they still fight below the surface."

"Pe-ya-siw," Dillon repeated, sounding out the word. "Is that what we are? Cree?"

"Do you know more stories?" Emma asked eagerly, leaving Archer speechless.

"Maybe Uncle Archie could tell you another story at bedtime," Ryan suggested in that way of his that let Archer know he was supposed to comply. "It's time to dry off before you turn into popsicles."

Emma giggled, but her teeth were chattering as she climbed out. Dillon followed.

"How do you do that?" Archer demanded.

"What?"

"Make them listen to you."

"Habit. They're used to listening to me at school."

Dillon shook off like a dog, sending water spray everywhere. "Aren't you getting out too, Ryan?"

Ryan's cheeks flushed again, piquing Archer's curiosity. "Um, in a minute," he said.

Dillon and Emma wrapped themselves in towels and sat in the sun sipping juice boxes. Archer leaned back on his hands, savoring the sun's heat on his chest and face. The backyard was so peaceful and private with its tall evergreen hedge and screen of trees, that he almost forgot he was in the city.

Ryan tossed his hat and sunglasses onto the patio stones beside Archer and then slid beneath the water. He did two lengths of the pool, that long, lean body cutting through the crystal water before swimming over and folding his arms on the edge next to Archer. He smelled like coconut sunscreen instead of vanilla today.

"Why don't they know about any of that stuff?" he asked quietly

"You mean the legends? Shame is hard to let go of, I guess."

"Why would Marguerite be ashamed?"

Archer had to look twice at Ryan to make sure he wasn't being sarcastic. He wasn't. Genuine curiosity showed on his face. "How old are you again?" Archer asked.

"Twenty-five."

"That explains it, then—you're still young and idealistic. Where we come from shame is something you grow up with. It's inherited, like the shape of your eyes. The 'Peg is not Toronto. Things are different there. I have no doubt I'd be dead if I hadn't left. Maybe things are changing now, but twenty years ago you didn't advertise you were Native if you didn't have to. I was Dillon's age the first time I got beat up. There were four of them—older boys—they called me a dumb Indian." Archer shrugged. "Margie was lucky that way—she could pass for white. She didn't get it so bad."

"That's . . . that's awful," Ryan said, his eyes wide. "But you need to teach them about their heritage."

Archer snorted. "Like how their crack-whore grandmother left her kids alone in a motel room for three days? Like how our Grandpa Tom knocked his wife around and drank himself to death? That kind of heritage?" Ryan's lips tightened in disapproval, but that only grated on Archer's nerves. What did this privileged white boy know about where he came from? Archer wouldn't wish his heritage on anyone—it certainly wasn't something he wanted to share with the kids. "That noble-savage shit is long gone. These days you're lucky if you finish high school."

"They should probably hear about that too one day. But for now maybe you could start with the easier stuff."

"Are you crazy? No one wants to hear about how bad it is on the reserve. Why do you think Margie kept it from them?"

"Life isn't all Disney princesses and birthday parties. Dillon and Emma need to know that eventually. They're half Cree, they should know where they came from."

"They're only a quarter Cree," Archer spat. "Margie's father was white. That's about all anyone knows." He paused. "Doesn't that shock you?"

"I don't shock easily," Ryan said with a shake of his head. "Besides, Marguerite told me that. I may come from a small town originally, but my parents are . . . um, free-spirited. I've seen a lot."

"'Free-spirited'?"

"You might say they're hippies in the wrong decade." Ryan glanced over at the kids for a second. "Very spiritual, very open. About *everything*. They're both artists: Arne's a glassblower. He fancies himself a nudist—not of course while he's working. Karen paints, sculpts—she dabbles in a lot of things. She hates to limit her creativity to one art form." Ryan's eye roll told Archer what he needed to know about the two Erikssons. "Anyway, there were some pretty serious parties while I was growing up. Pot. Harder stuff on occasion."

Archer chuckled. Ryan's parents sounded like his kind of people. "Oh my God, and you're so straitlaced."

"That's about the only thing straight about me," Ryan teased with a flutter of golden eyelashes. They sparkled in the sunlight. "When I turned thirteen, I wanted a birthday party. I organized it all myself—Karen and Arne sure weren't to be trusted with it. I was determined they weren't going to embarrass me in front of my friends for once."

His lips twisted wryly. "It ended with Brendan Cavanaugh, whom I had a huge crush on at the time, finding Karen's panties behind the couch cushions. Black lace with a red bow. 'Oh, that's where they went,' was all she said. Can you imagine how that played out in a room full of teenaged boys? I can still see the looks on their faces. Needless to say, I never had friends over after that. And I got quite the reputation at school. So you see, everyone hides stuff about where they come from."

Archer scowled. "I'm not hiding."

"No, I guess not when you've got a huge reminder tattooed on your back. For a man who claims to hate his own culture you sure have a funny way of showing it." Archer ignored Ryan's sarcasm and stared out across the backyard as Ryan kept talking. "It must have been very difficult being gay on the reservation. I don't imagine you had anybody you could talk to."

"Fuck that. No one knew. Not even Marguerite at the time. I left at sixteen, dropped out of school, ran away to Winnipeg and then Vancouver. Did whatever I had to so I could save enough money for Margie to go to college." Oh, he would shock Ryan all right if he told him the things he had done in those hard years, most of it illegal. It was on the tip of Archer's tongue to lay out every sordid detail. At the last minute he couldn't bear to do it, because, heaven help him, he didn't want the other man's opinion of him to fall any further.

Christ, he was becoming like Emma and Dillon, angling for Ryan's approval. What was happening? He'd never cared what others thought about him before. His lip curled in self-disgust. "There, see what kind of example I'm going to set for these two."

"That's some big chip on your shoulder," Ryan remarked drily. "For your information, I think it's amazing how far you've come. When you're not being an ass and busting my dreams that is."

"You do?" Archer gaped.

"Of course. You could have easily given up, but you overcame your circumstances. Both you and Marguerite. That's something. You should be proud."

Archer started. Proud? It had never occurred to him to be proud. "I thought you hated my book."

"I didn't have a problem with the book. Only your viewpoints. The book is actually quite good—well written and engaging. You have a certain way with words."

Archer frowned. Had Ryan just complimented him? "What's so funny?" he asked when Ryan suddenly smirked.

"I don't know. I've been here for almost three weeks now and this feels like the first time we've really talked."

Archer found himself returning the smile. "You mean without yelling? Yeah, it does, doesn't it."

"Have you ever been back?" Ryan asked. "To the reservation?"

"No. I set up a bank account for Margie, made sure she had everything she needed but never went back. She was the only girl in her class to go on to college. When Gran died, Margie attended the funeral, but I stayed away. I guess things are improving now—there's a new school and a casino. But there are too many bad memories for me."

"I get that." Ryan planted his palms on the edge and levered himself out of the pool, sending droplets flying.

Archer ducked to avoid getting wet. "Hey," he started, but the words died in his mouth as his gaze drifted up, up, up Ryan's lanky frame. The wet T-shirt and swim shorts clung to his body, revealing every hard line and soft curve. All this time Archer had seen the younger man as some sort of sexless nanny, an overgrown boy really. His taste did not run to pretty twinks, and Ryan certainly fell into that category.

But his personal preferences seemed to have gone out the window, because he couldn't stop staring now as Ryan innocently wrung out the translucent T-shirt, flashing his pale, softly curving belly and indecently low-cut swim trunks. The bathing suit made Archer's eyes widen—it was shockingly small and tight, a bright turquoise, and not at all what Archer would have expected from a conservative teacher. The stretchy fabric hugged an ass this side of perfect, and showcased well-defined legs that went on forever—no doubt from the bike riding. The fine coating of flaxen hair on Ryan's calves shimmered with droplets of water.

Oh, shit, Archer thought frantically as his dick swelled in appreciation. This was a complication he didn't need.

Ryan Eriksson was not a sexless nanny; he was most definitely a man.

Chapter 9

"*P*ut that back, Em. It's full of sugar," Ryan told Emma as she held up the box of cereal with a hopeful grin. "We want *that* one." He pointed to a healthy alternative that she plucked off the shelf, fortunately without a fuss, and dropped into the loaded shopping cart.

He turned to Dillon who shuffled along beside them, subdued. "What do you say we invite Matthew over sometime to play in the pool? You guys haven't seen each other since school let out."

"Can Cami come too?" Emma cried eagerly. Cami was Matthew's little sister, three years old and adorable.

"Sure. Maybe we can have a pool party. Would you like that, Dillon?"

"I guess." Dillon gave a less-than-enthusiastic shrug. "But Sam doesn't like other people."

Ryan sighed. Dillon's lack of interest in his friends, in leaving the house, was beginning to worry him. Dillon had always been quiet and reserved, but this listlessness was new. It had been almost a month now since Marguerite's death, and while Emma was bouncing back to her usual outgoing self, Dillon showed no sign of similar progress. He seemed more than content to spend time by himself or with the invisible, but ever present, Sam. In fact, Sam came up in conversation so often, Ryan was beginning to think of him as a real person too. He would have to ask Jill about imaginary friends later. For now he would take things slowly. He didn't want to push Dillon into something he wasn't ready for.

Ryan checked his shopping list again. Tonight he thought they could grill if he could figure out how to work the barbeque—it was too hot to turn on the oven—and he would do a light cucumber and tomato salad. But he'd forgotten the main ingredient. "Hey, Dillon, will you go get me a cucumber? I forgot to grab one."

Dillon sprinted toward the produce section as Ryan continued down the aisle. Grocery shopping with two children in tow was a new experience. It was more work than he expected, but he was trying to get them out of the house and out of Archer's hair so the man could get back to his writing career. He'd been chafing at something the past week, quick-tempered and restless, spending his nights out—and Ryan had a pretty good idea what he was doing on those nights. But he'd done his best not to take his frustrations out on the kids, and for that Ryan had given him some leniency. The adjustment had to be difficult, but he was making an effort. Ryan was used to spending his days with kids. Archer wasn't.

And maybe, if Ryan was being honest, he needed a break as well. It wasn't enough that he found Archer attractive, but the man had to have a tattoo too: a big, beautiful, hot-as-hell one that got Ryan hard simply picturing it. So far Archer hadn't noticed his reaction—Ryan had been lucky. He could only imagine the ribbing he was in for if Archer ever did.

Ryan had lied to Jill. From the moment he'd first seen a picture of Archer Noble, he'd been intrigued. Physically, he found Archer gorgeous, with his deep-brown eyes and tanned skin. Plus Ryan had to admit the idea of a bad boy had always excited him, but only in theory—the reality, not so much. Bad boys didn't tend to be interested in things like love and commitment. Knowing that, however, didn't seem to stop his unwanted attraction from popping up at the worst possible moments now that they lived together. Like when Archer brushed his arm as he reached for a glass in the cupboard, or when he overheard Archer trying to avoid answering the kids' endless questions about their heritage, and most definitely when he joined them during afternoons at the pool. The subtle shift in their relationship—from adversaries to, at the very least, wary colleagues—didn't help matters either. It was easy to dismiss Archer when he was being a dick, but the damaged man beneath the hardened exterior was much more difficult to ignore.

"Ryan? Ryan?" He heard Dillon cry from somewhere nearby, his voice edged with panic. "Ryan where are you?"

"Next aisle, silly Dilly," he called, wheeling the cart in Dillon's direction and nearly colliding with the tear-stricken boy at the end of the aisle.

"I couldn't find you," Dillon sobbed, gasping and shaking like a leaf. "I thought you were gone. Don't leave me like that."

Oh shit. Ryan crouched in front of Dillon and took hold of his arms, hanging on until he began to quiet. He ignored the curious looks of the other shoppers around them. "I'm right here, okay? I'm sorry. I should have stayed put."

"You shouldn't do that," Dillon accused.

"I know. I didn't mean to make you worry. Okay, now?" Ryan wiped the tears from his cheeks.

Dillon nodded and looked down at his feet. "I lost the cucumber."

Ryan stroked his soft hair, his throat tight with an emotion he didn't dare let loose. "Well, let's go find it, then. It can't be far. Unless it ran away."

Emma giggled. "Cucumbers don't have legs, silly."

"They don't?" Ryan made his eyes wide in mock surprise. "How do you know?"

"It's a vegetable," Dillon answered, all serious.

"Well, if potatoes can have eyes, why can't a cucumber have legs?" His bad joke earned him a weak smile from Dillon, so Ryan kept up the teasing as they located the missing cucumber on the floor of the next aisle. His puns became more and more ridiculous as they continued toward the checkout and past a display of brightly colored cut summer flowers. "What do you say we pick up some flowers? That would be nice, right?"

The kids heartily agreed, and Ryan let them each pick a bouquet and then, at their insistence, chose one himself, which prompted Emma to say they should get one for Uncle Archie. Ryan let them argue over which one it should be. It was an encouraging sign they had remembered Archer.

"What about Sam?"

Ryan winced. "Can't Sam share yours?"

Dillon shook his head. "He wants his own."

Five bouquets was definitely overkill, Ryan thought as he loaded the cart, but they were only a few stems each, and he didn't feel ready for a battle. Besides, you could never go wrong with flowers, and the house sure needed cheering up.

He wondered if it would be a good idea to change things around a bit—redecorate—or if it would seem like he was trying to eliminate all traces of Marguerite and Jackson. The kids had few enough memories of their father as it was. But maybe they could make some simple changes, like hanging new draperies, or adding some throw pillows. He could get the kids involved. Ryan stowed the thought away; another thing to ask Jill about later.

As Emma and Dillon laid out their groceries on the conveyor belt, Ryan's eyes were drawn to the two men ahead of him in line, bagging their own. They were both older, silver-haired, but still attractive. They didn't speak much to each other but moved with a familiar rhythm as they packed, as if they had done this hundreds of times before. Couple or not? It was a game he played all the time—in the supermarket, in the department store, on the street. Who belonged to whom?

A minute later, the shorter man patted his back pockets looking for his wallet; the taller one produced it without a word, like he had read his companion's thoughts. Definitely a couple, Ryan thought fondly.

His eyes misted over, a stab of jealousy slicing through his chest. He wanted to grow old with someone too. He wanted to do mundane things like grocery shop and argue over paint chips in the home-improvement store. And he wanted it *now*. He'd been so close to having all of that. Memories of Kenny set up that old ache in his heart and brought a lump to his throat. Did Kenny ever think of him? Had he moved on? Or was he as miserable as Ryan?

Marguerite had understood him, his need for a family. It was something they'd both had in common. But Marguerite was gone. Really gone. He felt the tears building behind his eyes.

"Are you crying, Ryan?" Dillon asked.

Ryan blinked rapidly to clear his vision. It wouldn't do for the kids to see him so low. "Just some sad thoughts, kiddo," he replied, draping his arm around Dillon's shoulder and pulling him in for a hug. In another year or so Dillon would be at that age where he hated to be cuddled, but for now, *especially* now, he seemed to crave it. Ryan couldn't blame him. And he was happy to oblige.

"Then we need to make happy thoughts, right?" Emma asked. "That's what you said."

Oh crap, he was going to lose it in the middle of the supermarket. These kids made him so damned proud. "Right," he agreed with a watery smile. "Happy thoughts. Like . . . ice cream?"

Their whoops of joy were loud and enthusiastic enough to make the check-out lady laugh. A short time later, Ryan and his two sticky-fingered-but-happy charges made it home. He had to park on the street because there was an unfamiliar car sitting in the driveway. They had company.

"Who's here?" Emma asked, her mouth ringed with chocolate as Ryan unbuckled her from the car seat. He had borrowed Archer's rental for the grocery trip. It had to be costing Archer a fortune, but he was too stubborn to give in and buy a permanent vehicle.

"I don't know."

The inside door stood open and the storm door unlocked as Ryan, loaded down with bags of groceries, and the kids trooped inside. Emma and Dillon carried the flowers. All three of them stopped as Archer and another man stumbled down the stairs. Archer was shirtless. Both looked rumpled. Ryan's face burned with a mixture of embarrassment and fury as the situation became clear.

The two groups stood there, like warring factions, staring at each other until Emma finally spoke. "Who are you?" she demanded.

The man turned to Archer and then back. "Uh, I'm Max."

"He's a friend of mine," Archer added.

"Is he your boyfriend?" Dillon asked. Emma giggled.

Ryan watched Archer's eyes widen. Panic crossed his face. He cast a pleading glance at Ryan, but Ryan remained silent. Oh, hell no. He was not helping Archer get out of this one. The asshole could squirm. He deserved it.

"Um, no," Archer answered. "Just a friend."

Ryan suppressed a snort. Archer's "friend" was big and stocky, with short black hair and a thick beard speckled with silver. The tail end of a snake tattoo peeked out below his shirt sleeve. The body emerged from his collar, winding around his neck so the head sat directly below his ear. *Holy crap, that had to hurt. This* was Archer's type?

"Do you have tattoos everywhere?" Dillon asked, his expression a mirror image of Ryan's own.

Ryan prided himself on being even tempered, but this was too much. He gave Dillon a gentle nudge in the back. "Let's take the flowers into the kitchen and get them in some water, huh?"

"But—"

"Now," Ryan said using his classroom voice. He ushered them to the kitchen, set down his load, and began washing off sticky faces and fingers before he unpacked. Dillon's pout concerned him.

"What's wrong?" Ryan asked.

"I thought you could be Uncle Archie's boyfriend."

"Me?"

Dillon nodded. "Because you like boys too. Like Uncle Archie."

Ryan was speechless. As much as he hated to reinforce stereotypes, he knew his orientation was fairly obvious, but he hadn't realized that his students were aware of it. They were so young, and he tried to be careful at school. "How . . . Where did you hear that Dillon?"

He shrugged. "I heard Mommy talking about it. She said she wished Uncle Archie had someone like you." Dillon bit his lip and stared down at his feet. "If you liked him, then you could get married and stay here."

Ryan was doubly shocked. "What?"

"Allison has two moms."

"It doesn't work like that, kid," Archer said, startling them all with his appearance in the kitchen. He had put on a shirt, and Ryan guessed Max was gone. "Think of it this way: just because Daddy liked girls didn't mean he married the first one he met, did it? He needed someone special, like your mommy."

"Ryan's special," Dillon said defensively.

The heat rushed to Ryan's face. "Dillon!"

Archer scrubbed a hand over his jaw. "Wow, I really wasn't planning on having this discussion so soon."

"Maybe you should have thought of that before you brought . . . friends home," Ryan snapped.

"It wasn't planned."

"And that makes it better?" Ryan was aware of both Emma and Dillon staring at them in fascination. "Dillon, take your sister downstairs and watch TV."

Dillon's eyes widened. "You *want* us to watch TV?"

Ryan couldn't blame him for being shocked. Television was considered a treat in Marguerite's house. "Right now I do, yes."

"So you and Uncle Archie can fight?" Dillon asked curiously. "Mom always made us leave the room when she and Dad were fighting."

He blinked in surprise. "We're not going to fight. We are going to have a discussion." Archer's snort made him furious.

"Go on, guys," Archer urged with a wave of his hand. Ryan was stunned and a little bit disappointed when the kids obeyed so quickly. Helping the kids adjust to Archer had been the whole point of him staying, hadn't it? So why did it leave him so sad?

"Okay, let me have it," Archer began, but Ryan held up a cautionary hand and stood at the top of the basement stairs until the sound of the television drifted up from below. Then he rounded on Archer.

"Look, what you do in your own life is up to you. It's bad enough you're out every other night, but don't you ever bring your fuck buddies into this house."

"I told you—"

"I don't care. *They* come first. Those kids downstairs. They need stability, not shifty strangers passing in and out." Ryan began throwing random dry goods into any available space. Damned soft-closing cupboards. You couldn't slam them when you were angry, and right now Ryan needed something to slam.

"Max was not shifty."

"Are you listening? Kids don't understand biology. They shouldn't have to at this age. They see you with a different guy every week and they get confused. They get scared because they don't know what's going on. Never mind what it teaches them about healthy relationships."

Archer cocked his head. "This is personal, isn't it? This isn't all about the kids. It's about you. You disapprove of my lifestyle because I don't fit with your fairy-tale, true-love happy ending."

"That's not true. Unlike *some* people, I don't push my views on others."

"Haven't you ever needed to . . . I don't know . . . let go?"

"Not really, no."

"Well pardon me, Saint Ryan. Just because you're living like a monk doesn't mean I want to."

Ryan flinched. "Nice. So I'm supposed to spend all my time with the kids, do everything around this house, and you get to go out and play whenever you want?" He froze. Holy crap. He sounded like an aggrieved spouse. He stumbled into the dining room and sat down, shaken. He was too close to this. When had he begun thinking of this as *his* family, *his* home? Jill had warned him, but he hadn't listened.

"What does it matter?" Archer continued, close on Ryan's heels and apparently heedless of his inner turmoil. "I warned you I wasn't parent material. Let's file the application and get it over with."

Ryan swung around in his seat. "You haven't even given it a chance."

"I don't *want* to give it a chance."

"You said you'd wait until the end of summer."

"It's only going to be more difficult then."

"For you or for them?"

Archer's lips thinned. His eyes slid away from Ryan's like a guilty child's. Ryan hated to admit it, but the man was right—the longer they waited, the harder it would be for *all* of them. He'd seen the way the kids watched Archer—warily but with great interest—as though he were a new toy they weren't sure if they could play with. Dillon especially seemed fascinated by his uncle, and Ryan wondered if Archer had noticed how he silently shadowed him. There was, he realized, still a small part of him holding out hope that Archer would come through in the end, that Marguerite's faith in her brother wasn't misplaced. But it had definitely been a mistake to move in and play house as though they were one big happy family.

Ryan could no longer fool himself. He wasn't doing this simply for Marguerite or the kids. Or even Archer. He was doing this because he wanted a family of his own so badly he was willing to borrow someone else's.

"I think I have to go," Ryan blurted.

"Go where?"

"Home."

"What? No!" Archer began pacing. "What happened to staying until the end of summer?"

Ryan shook his head tiredly. His stomach rolled. "I don't know anymore. It might not be good for me to stay. They're getting too attached. And I . . ." *I can't tell reality from fantasy*, he wanted to say. *I'm going to get hurt.*

"If you walk away now they're going to be crushed. It will be like Marguerite and Jackson all over again." Leave it to Archer to hit below the belt like that. Ryan recalled Dillon's reaction in the grocery store and knew he was right. His sudden departure could make things worse. But so could Archer's.

"You just don't want to lose your nanny," Ryan retorted, his suspicions confirmed when the muscle in Archer's jaw twitched. He'd been used. Archer had never had any intention of following through. Archer the good guy didn't exist. Ryan had been dumb enough to play right into the man's hands. It made him furious—with himself most of all. "If you're not going to make an effort, why should I?"

"Why are you being so stubborn about this? There's no way I can take care of them on my own."

Ryan wasn't a gambling man. He didn't enjoy taking risks, he liked knowing what was coming—something Kenny always chided him for—but he decided to take a chance now.

"I guess you could always put them in foster care," he bluffed. He would never let it get that far—he'd promised—and besides he recalled that first tragic phone call when Archer had been as eager as Ryan to avoid Children's Aid. Had it really only been a month ago? "I'm sure you know what happens after that. Marguerite did. They go into the system. They're shuttled from home to home, thinking nobody loves them. They—"

"Shut up," Archer snapped.

"They might be split up." Ryan continued to push, confidence growing when fire flashed in Archer's eyes. His anger was a good sign. If the man truly had no heart, he wouldn't care who reared his niece and nephew. He might not want them, but he didn't want a stranger to have them either. "They're your blood. They're Marguerite's blood.

Are you going to let somebody you don't know raise them? How do you know that wouldn't be even worse? I've heard so many horror stories . . ."

"Fuck you. That's a low blow." Archer's phone buzzed. He checked the display, swiped his thumb across the screen, and tucked it back in his pocket.

"Don't you want to take that?" Ryan asked.

"My agent." He grimaced. "I'm late on a deadline."

"Oh, writing not going well?" Ryan gibed with a distinct lack of sympathy.

Archer yanked the chair opposite him so hard it scraped the floor. He sat down angrily. "I think you're bluffing."

"Maybe I am. Maybe I'm not. I have a life too, you know. I could walk out of here tonight and then where would you be?" Ryan called on every ounce of experience dealing with stubborn seven-year-olds he possessed. The key was to never, ever let them think you didn't mean what you said. "I think you need *me* more than I need you."

A minute later, Archer folded. "What's it going to take to keep you here?"

"We abide by the original agreement. But you take it seriously this time." A small rumble of disquiet filled Ryan's belly. God, he hoped Marguerite had known what she was doing. He had a little more than a month to wean the kids off him and push them toward Archer. A month to make Archer fall in love with them. "And we would need to set some ground rules."

"Ground rules?"

"Like splitting up the work. No more being out every night. You need to spend more time with them. You're still their uncle."

Ryan practically heard Archer's molars grinding together. "Are you trying to kill me? What if we took turns having nights off? So you can get back to this life of yours."

His life. Ryan grimaced. The thought held absolutely no appeal. He would much rather have movie night with the kids than go out clubbing, but if it would get Archer to stay home more, then he would make the sacrifice. Besides, it was for the best. The kids needed to get used to being alone with their uncle.

Archer plucked the calendar off the bulletin board and spread it out on the table. "We could each have one night a week—I'll take Saturdays. What do you say?"

"*Alternate* Saturdays," Ryan countered which earned him a scowl from Archer.

"Fine," he grated.

"And what about . . . friends?"

Archer leaned against the back of his chair and sighed. "For the last time, I didn't invite Max over here."

"Couldn't help noticing you didn't exactly kick him out though."

"Look, I get that things can't be the same. I don't like it, but I do get it. My mother was a prostitute remember? Sometimes there was only enough money for one room, so Margie and I would have to wait outside until she was done. Once or twice we hid in the bathroom when it was too cold out. I know exactly how it feels."

Ryan gaped. How could the man say things like that so dispassionately? As if it were an ordinary occurrence, something every kid went through. No wonder he was so uncertain around children—he'd never had the chance to be one himself. His heart turned over for that little boy. Damn it, how did Archer do that so easily? Turn Ryan's anger to pity in a flash. He didn't want to feel sorry for him.

"No more hookups under this roof," Archer conceded, with a wry curl to his lips. He raised his right hand as if taking an oath. "I promise."

"Are you done?" Dillon called from the basement stairs. Ryan looked at Archer, who stared back, one brow slightly raised. It was an expression he had seen Dillon use on occasion, and for the first time he noted the resemblance between uncle and nephew. He wished Archer could see it.

"Yes, we're done. You can come up." Ryan sighed. He couldn't escape the feeling he'd made the wrong decision.

It was going to kill him to leave come September.

Chapter 10

"He's using you."

Archer froze outside the basement guest bedroom at the sound of the female voice. The door was ajar, and Ryan's curvaceous roommate, whom he'd met at the funeral, was a loud talker. She obviously wasn't his biggest fan either. He wasn't eavesdropping he told himself; Emma had left Mr. Snuggles down here, and she needed the stuffed toy to sleep. Still, he waited to hear Ryan's response.

"I know," Ryan finally said in that soft, melodic voice of his. It was Saturday night, Ryan's first night off under their new arrangement, but he didn't seem too excited about it. Neither was Archer if he was being totally honest. All day long he'd had this squirmy, unsettled feeling in his stomach, which he now attributed to his apprehension over spending an entire night on his own with the kids.

"And that doesn't bother you?" Jill asked.

"I'm happy, Jill. The kids are happy."

"And you're the freaking nanny."

"Only until September. Where's the harm?"

"The harm is you're going to end up with a broken heart when summer is over."

Another pause from Ryan. "I know."

"You're in deep, aren't you?"

"Yeah." Ryan sighed. "And please don't say 'I told you so.'"

Jill grumbled. "Why do I even bother? I swear you're addicted to being needed."

Archer moved away from the door, confused and more than a little guilty. Jill was right. He *had* taken advantage of a generous young man, used Ryan's obvious affections for the kids to his own end.

And now to top it off, here he was invading the man's privacy. When had he become such a dick? If Margie were here, she would rip him a new one.

That didn't stop him from straining to hear the rest of the conversation while he silently scoured the rec room for the missing Mr. Snuggles. "I'm doing this for Marguerite," he heard Ryan say.

"Really?" Jill asked drily.

"Yes. She adored those kids, and she adored her brother. You should've heard the way she talked about him, like he was her hero. If she saw the good in him, then I have to believe it's there too."

"Yeah, way, way down."

"Jill!"

"Oh, you're defending the manwhore now. It's worse than I thought. You must really like him."

"Shh, he'll hear you."

"So what? He should know you have feelings too."

Archer found Mr. Snuggles tucked between the couch cushions and seized the mangled toy with a sense of relief. Listening to Ryan defend him was stirring up confusing, unfamiliar emotions: shame, guilt, and most worrying of all, pleasure. Especially when Jill cried, "Oh my God, you *do* like him."

"Jill," Ryan warned. "Shut up and tell me how this looks."

"Cute."

"Cute?"

"Sorry. Hot. Very hot. You'll definitely get laid tonight." She laughed again, and Archer wondered why. "You're the only man I know who would turn his nose up at that."

"I'm after more than sex, remember?" Ryan grumbled.

"I know, honey. And you'll find someone who wants the same things, I promise. Just because Kenny wasn't interested doesn't mean there's not someone else for you. You don't need to hide behind this fake family. Tonight is about having fun."

"I'm not hiding."

"Aren't you?"

"Bitch," Ryan spat without rancor. It was the first time Archer had ever heard him swear. "I hate it when you go all psychoanalyst on me. Did I ever tell you Marguerite tried to fix me up at her Christmas party?"

"No, what happened?"

"He didn't show. I don't know who she had in mind, but he obviously wasn't interested either."

Archer clutched Mr. Snuggles to his chest at a sudden, crazy thought. Had his sister been playing matchmaker? *He* was supposed to have attended Marguerite's party; she had pressed him like crazy about it, but he'd canceled at the last minute. His heart stuttered. *Oh, Margie, you didn't. You didn't try to fix me up with this pretty twink. What could you have been thinking?*

"His loss," Jill sang. "Are you almost done? And Alex says I take forever to get ready."

"Maybe I shouldn't go out tonight," Ryan said abruptly.

"You said it was your turn."

"It is. But what if the kids need me?"

"They're already getting ready for bed."

"What if there's an emergency? Crap. We haven't talked about that—"

"Oh no, you are not backing out. I am forcing you to have fun no matter what."

"No matter what?"

"Think of me as the fun police. We're going to dance until our feet hurt. Now are you nearly ready?"

Archer scrambled up the stairs. He had only made it back to the first floor when he heard Jill and Ryan emerge from his room and start up the stairs, so he quickly swung around to make it appear as though he was coming from the kitchen.

"You guys heading . . . out," he finished, voice wobbling at the end when he saw Ryan.

Those long, lean legs that had mesmerized him before were encased in a pair of bright-yellow jeans, snug enough for Archer to clearly see that Ryan tucked to the left. A blousy silk tank clung to his shoulders and chest. The fair skin of his collarbone sparkled beneath it. The outfit was ridiculous—something no man should ever wear if he wasn't walking in a runway fashion show, and yet Archer's dick thickened alarmingly. His chest tightened.

Ryan had slicked his hair back, which highlighted his cheekbones and slimmed his face. Those large hazel eyes stood out even more.

The lashes seemed extraordinarily long. "Are you wearing makeup? And glitter?" Archer spat, confused by his reaction. He didn't go for feminine men. Just the opposite. The bigger, more masculine they were, the more he got off on taming them. But for some reason he couldn't take his eyes off Ryan. And if he couldn't, then other men wouldn't be able to either. Like him, they would want to touch that pale, smooth skin and see if it was as soft as it looked, and would want to know how far that trail of glitter went. Archer's stomach twisted. God, no, it wasn't jealousy, couldn't be . . .

Christ, he'd written off that earlier moment of poolside attraction as a horny aberration. But here it was happening again.

"It's only mascara," Jill sneered. "Or do you have a problem with that too?"

"You can't go out like that," he snapped, taken by surprise at the sudden surge of protectiveness. Yes, that was it—*protectiveness*, not jealousy. Ryan was young and naive, a walking target for every hatemonger and homophobe in the city. "It's not safe."

"Relax," he said. "I've been out like this plenty of times. We're going to the Village."

"Yeah," Jill interjected. "Good thing he didn't see you at Pride," she added with a wink that made Ryan blush, and only fueled Archer's imagination.

"I think you look pretty," Emma crowed, startling them all. She stood behind them in her nightgown, on the top step with Dillon at her side.

Ryan's shiny lips parted on a smile. "Thank you, sweetheart. *Some* people know how to give compliments." The dig was clearly meant for Archer.

"You're coming back, aren't you?" Dillon asked fearfully.

Ryan's expressive eyes glistened. He moved to hug the boy. "Of course, Dilly."

"Did you find Mr. Snuggles, Uncle Archie?" Emma demanded.

Archer glanced down to find his hands wrapped around the stuffed animal's neck, mangling the poor harmless creature. "Got him."

"Do you need me to get her to sleep?" Ryan asked eagerly with one arm still holding Dillon as if afraid to let him go. "I don't mind. She likes you to—"

"Rub her back, I know," Archer finished.

"Ryan," Jill warned. "He can manage on his own for a few hours."

Ryan ignored her. "If you're reading to her, she likes you to do the voices. You know what, I can do it. It won't matter if we leave later."

Archer was tempted to feign incompetence so that Ryan would stay. But in his head he saw Margie's disapproving face and knew it wasn't fair. Ryan deserved a night off more than anyone, and Archer needed to get his strange response to the man under control.

"Ryan," Archer and Jill said at the same time, in the exact same tone of exasperation. They looked at each other in amazement. Jill gave him a tentative smile.

"Go have fun," Archer told them, injecting a parental note in his voice. Yeah, that was it. He should think of Ryan as the younger brother he never had.

"Oh, he will," Jill said, flashing a long string of condoms from her purse.

Color bloomed in Ryan's cheeks. "Oh my God," he gasped and tried to stuff them back into her handbag. "Seriously? Put those away. There are children present."

Archer wanted to snatch the damned rubbers out of her hand. She was supposed to be Ryan's best friend. Did she honestly think he was going to hook up in a grubby dance club restroom? Mr. White-Picket-Fence? Ryan was the romantic type—Archer had known that as soon as he met the man. He would want a soft bed, lots of kissing and foreplay, maybe some candles. Archer meant it to sound mocking and derisive in his head but somehow it didn't.

"Come on, the cab's here." Jill tugged on Ryan's arm, practically pulling him out the door.

"You still have my number right?" Ryan asked, glancing over his shoulder at Archer. He looked as though he were being dragged to his death. "In case there's an emergency."

"Yes, I have your number. Don't worry about us. And don't do anything I wouldn't do."

Ryan's grin didn't quite hide his trepidation. "That doesn't leave a lot does it?"

With surprisingly little fuss, Archer got Dillon into the bath and settled Emma into bed. He curled up beside her to begin reading from the picture book she asked for almost every night. She pillowed her head against his arm, and he fought back a sudden smile, thinking how they were already pint-sized people with their own personalities. Emma was loving and open, a happy child. She cried and got over it. Yelled and moved on. Although she resembled Margie, she had Jackson's easygoing temperament. Dillon, on the other hand, was more like him—cautious, reserved, always hanging back, wanting to be a part of things but afraid to make the first move. He kept things inside. Archer could see him trying so hard to be grown-up, independent, but he hadn't learned yet how to hide the longing in his eyes or completely mask his feelings. Occasionally Archer wondered if the same applied to him.

After a few minutes of reading, he became aware of Dillon standing hesitantly in the doorway, a teal-blue blanket clutched in his hand and dragging on the ground beside him. "What have you got there, kiddo? You're a little old for a blankie, aren't you?"

"It's Mommy's scarf. I gave it to her for Christmas."

"Where did you find that?"

"In the bags in the garage. Ryan said I could have it."

His giveaway bags—which he hadn't found a home for yet. "Oh he did, did he?"

Dillon took a step backward, like he was two seconds away from bolting. Ryan, in one of his many lectures, had advised him that the key to dealing with Dillon was to treat him like a skittish animal and let him come to you on his own terms. The more you pushed, the harder he would resist. It shouldn't have been so surprising to Archer; he was the same.

He listened to that advice now, tucking Emma closer to make room and motioning for Dillon to hop up on the bed. He did, in a flash of superhero pajamas, squeezing in on the other side of his sister. Archer's chest swelled with an emotion so unexpected it took him a minute to identify it: contentment. It felt so right that for the first time he could see them doing this every night, like a real family. He faltered. When had that happened? When had he stopped seeing them as burdens and started caring about them?

The old fear resurfaced—the feeling of being trapped suddenly overwhelming. There was no way he could do this on his own. He wasn't ready for that sort of responsibility. He had a career to think of. The network people had already been trying to pin him down for a "meet and greet." He doubted they'd be enthused if he showed up with two kids in tow.

"Ryan always sits in the middle," Emma protested, drawing him from his thoughts. "Between us."

"I'm not Ryan," Archer pointed out, bridling at the comparison. There was no way in hell he could ever live up to Ryan's lead. Why bother? Even the kids knew he was a second-rate guardian. "Aren't you old enough to read this by yourself, anyway?"

"Yes, but sometimes I like to listen," Dillon replied. "But I can't see the book like this." With a deep sigh, Archer changed position, not crawling between them as Ryan would do, but stretching out his arm so that Dillon had a clearer view.

"There. Better?" Dillon nodded, giving Archer a whiff of fragrance that smelled oddly familiar. He leaned in further and sniffed him. "Are you wearing perfume?"

Dillon's eyelashes lowered. "Yes," he said quietly. "It's Mom's."

That was why it smelled familiar. Marguerite's favorite lily of the valley scent. How had he missed that in his cleanup? "Did you take that from my room?" It must have been in her nightstand, which he hadn't gotten to yet.

The fear in Dillon's eyes made Archer feel like a monster, but Dillon bravely held his head up. "I missed her smell," he asserted in a wavering voice. "Are you mad?"

Archer forced his lips into a smile. "No, no, I'm not mad. But next time, ask first, okay?"

"Okay."

Sometimes Archer listened in when Ryan read to the kids. He tried to imitate him now, using a different voice for each of the barnyard animals, but he didn't have Ryan's talent for being silly. It had been decades since he'd read aloud to anyone, and he felt stiff and self-conscious. Emma kept correcting him. "No, do it like this, Uncle Archie. *Mooooooooo.*" Her cow imitation was dead-on. When Archer tried again, he sounded like a dying bullfrog, which only set Emma to giggling. Then Dillon chimed in and soon all three of them were lowing like a herd of demented cattle and laughing. It was the sweetest sound he'd ever heard, and it sent up an ache somewhere deep in his chest. He watched the kids in astonishment. *He* had done that. Made them laugh. Brought them a moment of happiness. He couldn't wait to tell Ryan.

What would Donna say if she could see him now? The thought immediately sobered him. He finished the story with a sense of relief.

"Why do you keep looking at your watch, Uncle Archie?" Dillon asked.

Archer started, surprised to find he'd been doing just that. "Am I?"

"Yeah. Ryan's coming back, isn't he?" Dillon's eyes were anxious.

"Of course he is." Archer tucked his arm behind Dillon's shoulders and ruffled his hair. He was worried about Ryan, that was all, he told himself. A kid like that, looking all pretty and effeminate wouldn't be able to handle himself. Ryan was way too sweet and gentle and easily taken advantage of.

"Will you tell us a story, Uncle Archie?"

"I thought I just did."

"About Mommy, when she was little," Emma chimed in. Archer thought about refusing—what could he possibly tell them that wouldn't frighten them or set off a whole series of questions he wasn't yet ready to answer?

Still, he sifted his memories for something suitable. He grinned when one particular recollection leaped to mind. "Well, your mom, she had a sweet tooth. Didn't matter if it was chocolate or candy or cookies."

"Like me," Emma mumbled around her thumb, which was now firmly entrenched between her lips.

"Yes, like you. She was a greedy little thing. You couldn't look away for a second because she'd steal your candy too. Not that we had a lot. Anyway, one day when she was not much older than you Emma, she got hold of some bubble gum." He neglected to add that the haul was part of his five-fingered discount at the local corner store. He'd been aiming for a candy bar but the gum was closer and easier to grab. "She had recently learned to blow bubbles and loved to show off. I think she managed to stuff the whole pack in her mouth because when I finally noticed, she had blown a bubble the size of her head." Archer glanced at the kids. Dillon was regarding him avidly; Emma's eyelids kept fluttering closed before she forced them open again.

"You can guess what happened next. The bubble burst, and your mom's face was covered. It was in her hair, stuck to her skin." Archer laughed at the memory, just as he had laughed at the sight so many years ago. "Margie liked her hair long, but there was so much gum in it and we couldn't get it out, so I had to cut it. Oh, she cried the whole time, and then she wore a hat until it grew again. But she never chewed gum after that." God, he'd forgotten this story until now. There had been *some* good times.

Still smiling, Archer saw that Emma had finally fallen asleep. Dillon too, appeared on the verge of drifting off, his lips curved in a sleepy smile. Was that all it took to make them happy? A simple story? The idea was so uncomfortable that he pushed it away and slipped from the bed.

"Night, Daddy," Emma mumbled, curling into the space he'd vacated. His breath caught at the stabbing pain in his chest. He couldn't move.

"He's not our daddy," Dillon admonished, but she was already fast asleep. Archer recovered. Best not to think about it too much. It was an innocent slip. As he reached to turn out the light, Dillon called his name.

"Will you tell us another one tomorrow?" he asked.

Emotion clogged Archer's throat, and it took him a minute to answer. "We'll see, kiddo. We'll see."

It was after two in the morning when Archer heard a car slow down in front of the house. He lowered the book he'd been pretending to read and listened, as he had done repeatedly over the past three hours every time a car passed beneath the open window. This time the vehicle stopped. Next came the sound of a car door opening, followed by lots of giggling, and so Archer threw back the covers and padded to the window on bare feet. Sure enough there was a cab idling in the driveway but no sign of its passengers.

Archer pulled his discarded jeans over the boxers he'd been wearing to sleep in and went to stand in the hallway. Someone fumbled with the key in the lock below. More giggles. More than one voice. What if Ryan had brought someone home to fuck? The thought made Archer sick and angry at the same time. They'd made a deal.

He quietly descended the stairs until he could see the foyer but they wouldn't be able to see him. Great. Now Archer felt like an overprotective parent, lurking in the darkness, and he scowled. He had left a light on for Ryan, so he saw clearly when the front door finally opened and a pair of hunched figures barreled in with all the subtlety of a herd of elephants. One of them stumbled and went down in a tangle of long, bright-yellow legs.

"Shh, shh," Ryan hissed in between giggles as he lay on the tile floor. "Don't wake the kids."

"I'm not the one flailing around, you idiot," Jill snapped, trying to get Ryan to his feet. She staggered beneath his weight.

Archer decided to take pity on them both and moved out of the shadows. "Looks like someone managed to have some fun after all."

Jill started so violently at his appearance that Ryan almost tumbled again.

"Let me help," Archer offered, grabbing a pliant Ryan around the waist. He regretted his offer almost immediately when Ryan looped both arms about his neck and sagged against him, warm and soft and smelling like sweat, vanilla, and something fruity. The combination went straight to Archer's head, as if he were the one who'd been drinking. Lust pooled in his groin. Thank God Ryan appeared too drunk to notice the reaction.

"Thanks." Jill relinquished her load with a sigh of relief. "He's heavy."

"Have you ever had Sex on the Beach, Archer?" Ryan grinned. "It's delicious."

Archer's heart stopped.

"He's talking about the drink," Jill qualified and his heart resumed its odd, off-kilter beat again.

"Yeah? From the looks of it, I'd say you had a bit too much. And I didn't think anyone over the age of nineteen drank that shit. Seriously, where did you take him?" he asked Jill. "A sorority party?"

Ryan giggled in Archer's ear. His hands roamed freely over Archer's bare back. "Definitely not a shororirty. Lots of men."

Archer didn't know whether to laugh or cry. This was an entirely unexpected side of Ryan he was seeing.

Jill saved him by letting out her own full-bellied laugh. "He's going to be mwort . . . mortified tomorrow."

"Shhh . . ." Ryan warned, one finger pressed to those full, shining lips. How did they stay so shiny? Was it the lip balm he always saw Ryan applying? Did it taste fruity? Did it make Ryan's lips smooth and slippery, or sticky? Archer caught himself longing for a taste and gave himself a mental shake. "I also had a couple of Blow Jobs," Ryan added. "But those weren't as good."

Oh. My. God. "Please tell me that's a drink too," Archer begged Jill. "Or else there's something seriously wrong with this kid."

"It's a shot," Ryan explained, slurring only slightly. "It's creamy and you can't use your hands. But the whipped cream goes up my nose."

Archer couldn't help himself. He laughed. "I'll take care of the lush, here," he told Jill. "Are you okay to get home on your own?"

"Me? I'm fine. I told the cab to wait." Jill suddenly seemed to notice Archer's shirtless state and the way Ryan clung to him, his fingers still exploring Archer's skin. Her eyes narrowed in warning. "Don't take advantage of him."

Archer had the feeling she wasn't talking just about sex. "I won't," he surprised himself by saying.

"He's not as strong as you think he is."

Archer simply nodded, unable to find the right words. He understood Jill's protectiveness because he suddenly felt it too. His hold on Ryan tightened.

Jill seemed to come to a decision, because she leaned in and kissed Ryan's cheek. "I'll call you tomorrow, okay, hun? See how bad you're hurting."

"I'm guessing pretty bad," Archer quipped, which made Jill laugh again. He watched from the door to make sure she got safely in the cab and then jumped when Ryan's fingers slid under the loose waistband of his jeans and boxers and skimmed across his ass.

"Your skin's so beautiful," Ryan murmured. "And the color. Like cinnamon. Makes me want to see if you taste like cinnamon too."

He bent his head and, before Archer could stop him, flicked his tongue over Archer's bare shoulder.

"Oh no you don't," Archer said, calling upon a reserve of honor he didn't know he had. He grabbed Ryan's wandering hand and put it back safely around his neck, steering the younger man toward the basement stairs. "Never would have pegged you for a handsy drunk."

Ryan pulled back, swaying unsteadily without assistance. "Why not?" he demanded, clearly offended. "I *like* sex."

"Oh-kay." Archer got the feeling there was a story there, and was suddenly very interested to hear it.

"Jill says I'm a prude. I've only ever been with four people. Is that really weird?"

"I'm the last person to ask that question."

"It's not like I did it on purpose. I've just always had a boyfriend."

Archer reached for Ryan as he stumbled, but Ryan waved him away. "I can do it." He made it down four steps before his feet slipped out from beneath him, and he slid all the way to the bottom where he landed in a motionless heap.

"Ryan!" Archer rushed to his side. "Are you hurt?"

"Only my ass," Ryan moaned and rubbed his butt as he struggled, like a turtle on its back, to sit up.

"Oh well, that's okay, then. Your ass doesn't seem to be getting much action lately anyway."

Ryan blinked, as if seeing him for the first time. "Oh God, why did it have to be you?" He covered his face.

"You know I can still see you, right?" Archer grasped Ryan by the biceps and hauled him to his feet. "Actually, I'm really enjoying this. You're so damned perfect all the time, it's a refreshing change."

Ryan frowned. He stood close enough that Archer had to look up at him now. "I'm not perfect," he mumbled, his sparkling brow creasing.

"Close enough."

"If I was perfect, Kenny wouldn't have left."

Ah. "Is Kenny your boyfriend?"

"Was. He said we needed a break. That means he wants to fuck around, doesn't it?"

"How long ago was this?"

"Before Christmas."

"Ouch. I hate to be the one to say it, but I think that's more than a break."

"I know." Ryan broke free from his hold and weaved toward the bedroom.

Archer trailed behind to make sure he didn't hurt himself again. "What else did Kenny say?"

"Where's the switch?" Ryan fumbled for the light switch in the pitch-black room. Archer found it first, and the sudden glare made them both blink.

"Chemistry," Ryan exclaimed, standing motionless in the center of the room.

"What?"

"He said we didn't have chemistry anymore."

"Oh, well, that can be important."

"Seems like there should be more than that in a relationship."

Archer fought back a smile at the way Ryan chewed his lower lip in concentration. "Probably. But if there's no chemistry, then you're just . . . friends."

"I guess." Ryan whisked the blousy tank top over his head and let it flutter to the floor as he began to work on the top button of his jeans. *Do not help*, Archer thought, still frozen in the doorway. *The man is perfectly capable of undressing himself.*

"And he didn't want to be tied down." The top button freed, Ryan frowned at his crotch, as if he couldn't quite figure out what to do with the rest of them.

"I assume you're speaking metaphorically, right?"

"Huh?" Ryan wobbled unsteadily and nearly fell over.

"Never mind." Archer stepped forward with a grunt and brushed Ryan's fingers aside. "Let me do it before you hurt yourself again."

As he wrestled with the buttons, Archer tried to summon that sense of almost brotherly affection he'd felt earlier. He was helping out a friend—there was nothing sexual about it. But his good intentions evaporated the second his knuckles encountered lace hidden beneath the colored denim. A bolt of heat shot to Archer's groin. Well, well, Ryan was full of surprises.

Ryan hooked his thumbs under the waistband and worked them over his narrow hips inch by inch. It was a decidedly nonsexy shimmy, but Archer was rooted to the spot, watching as the skimpy white lace briefs were revealed. He tried in vain to ignore how nicely Ryan filled out the basket of those briefs or how that lace-clad bulge seemed to be growing right in front of him.

At last the damned jeans were around Ryan's knees. He raised one leg to step out of them and swayed. Unbalanced, he clutched at Archer to steady himself, but it was too late. Ryan fell back onto the mattress, pulling Archer with him.

The breath whooshed from Archer's lungs as he tumbled on top of Ryan's long, lean body.

"Oh," Ryan gasped, gazing up at him. His arms went around Archer's back, palms sliding over the bare skin and preventing Archer from rising.

Something turned over in Archer's chest as he stared down at Ryan's fragile features. Smudged mascara lined his dazed eyes, making them seem impossibly huge and deep, and trusting. His tongue snaked out to wet his already slick lips, and Archer groaned. Margie would get such a kick out of his bewildering attraction to a man far too young and too innocent for his taste.

But Ryan was so soft and warm beneath him. They fit together perfectly. Archer was unable to stop himself from plucking a strand of golden hair off Ryan's cheek, and letting his thumb caress the smooth fair skin. The barest hint of stubble lined Ryan's jaw. Remnants of glitter stuck to Archer's fingers. Ryan's eyes slid closed. He turned his head into the touch.

"So, you're not a fan of Blow Jobs, then," Archer teased.

"It's a shooter," Ryan insisted. The heat of his blush seared Archer's fingers. "The other kind I'm more partial to."

"Show me a man who's not."

Ryan's fingers stilled on Archer's shoulder blade where his tattoo ended. His eyes opened. "Did it hurt?"

"What?"

"The tattoo."

Archer swallowed, his throat tight and dry. "Yeah, it hurt."

"Was that the point?"

A shiver ran down Archer's spine. How could Ryan possibly know that? Not even Marguerite had known about the dark place he'd been in when he'd had the tattoo inked on his back like a brand.

"Partly," he responded once he found his voice. "It's supposed to remind me where I came from."

"But not in a good way."

"No."

"That's too bad. It's beautiful."

"You like it?"

Ryan nodded shyly, a slow smile tugging at his shiny lips as he continued to trace the lines on Archer's back. Archer was mesmerized, the slow throb of arousal stirring in his groin, but something else entirely stirring in his chest.

"What's happening?" he asked with no idea why he was whispering.

"I can't help it." Ryan's breath was hot on Archer's face. He wriggled and that's when Archer became aware of Ryan's erection prodding his hip. "You're on top of me. And this is my favorite position."

Oh. My. God. Blood roared through his veins, a surge of lust so strong that Archer shook with it, his cock hard in an instant. He closed his eyes and rested his forehead against Ryan's until he could regain control. "And here I thought you couldn't stand me," he quipped, trying to turn it into a joke.

"Only sometimes," Ryan said seriously. The rhythmic sweep of Ryan's hands on his back, on his neck, and the way Ryan squirmed beneath him as he kicked off his jeans, was making Archer melt, stirring up longings he hadn't realized he possessed. Longings to be touched, to be loved.

The air around him vibrated with electricity. Wherever Ryan touched him, a tantalizing warmth bloomed, heady and seductive, and Archer's head swam with the need to chase after it, to grasp hold of it and never let go. Did he dare? The dangerous fluttering of his heart warned him, but he was past listening. He *needed*. With a sigh of surrender, he skimmed his lips across Ryan's.

It was a soft kiss. Gentle. Far more tender than Archer thought himself capable of, but the unexpected power of it made his chest seize. He raised his head in surprise. *I shouldn't. We shouldn't.*

Then Ryan's fingers were in his hair, drawing him back down, and Ryan's tongue was tentatively probing at the seam of his lips, making Archer tremble.

Cherries. Ryan tasted like cherries. The flavor exploded in Archer's mouth and just like that he wanted more. He *needed* more. What was happening to him?

Suddenly Ryan turned his head. "Mmmpf," he mumbled. The hands that had been clutching Archer close were now pressed up against his shoulders, pushing him away.

"What's wrong?" Archer asked.

"Get off me."

"What?"

"Get. Off!"

Stunned, Archer rolled to one side. Ryan darted out from under him and streaked from the room, a pale blur. Archer sat up, confused until he heard the clink of the toilet lid being raised in the bathroom next door and the unmistakable sounds of Ryan's guts emptying into the bowl. *That's the end of Sex on the Beach*, he thought with a little laugh. The poor guy was going to have a massive hangover tomorrow.

Oh God, tomorrow. What had he done?

Nothing, he assured himself as he slid off the bed. He adjusted his confused cock and noticed with dismay that his hands were shaking.

Shit. He'd almost made the stupidest mistake of his life. If all it took to tie him up in knots was one kiss, who knew what would have happened if he'd actually slept with the man. Thank God he'd never find out.

Chapter 11

"*R*yan? Are you ... hungover?"

With the mother of all headaches thundering between his temples, and his foggy brain struggling to accept the unexpected sight of his ex-boyfriend on the front porch, Ryan was slow to respond.

"Sure feels that way," he croaked, slightly amused when Kenny's eyes widened further. It was a first for him too. In college, he had never been one to party very hard—always focused on his studies instead. Once he met Kenny—equally driven—in his sophomore year, his social life had dwindled further.

"Jill and I went out last night," he boasted now. And he was going to kill her the next time he saw her. It was bad enough that she had practically kidnapped him, and then plied him with sweet, fruity cocktails he couldn't resist, but she had obviously told his ex where to find him too.

"Oh? Where?"

When Ryan named the club, Kenny's jaw practically dropped. He stared at Ryan as though he were a stranger. "I thought you didn't like dance clubs."

"I'm discovering a lot of things I didn't know I liked." When Kenny flinched at the accusation in his voice, Ryan felt a glimmer of regret. He sighed, tugged the silk robe tighter around his nearly naked frame—and winced because even his skin hurt. He was never ever drinking again. "Look, I'm sorry. Apparently being hungover doesn't agree with me. What are you doing here?"

"You texted me last night. I guess now I understand why."

No, no, no. Not that. Anything but that. Ryan gaped in horror, his face burning. "I—I—"

Kenny touched his arm. "No, I'm glad you did . . . Really. I've wanted to call you so many times, but I was afraid you wouldn't answer. Can I—can I come in? I mean if it's okay."

Ryan hesitated. He wasn't ready for this: emotionally or physically. His hand shook as he brushed his hair off his sweaty forehead. This wasn't how he'd imagined their first postbreakup encounter would go. It had been seven—no eight—lonely months since Kenny had officially moved out, and Jill had taken over the second bedroom they had once planned to make into the nursery. Ryan's stomach lurched, although he knew firsthand there was nothing in it right now.

Whenever he'd thought about this moment, let it spin out in his head, he had always been cool and confident—he would show Kenny that he'd moved on, that he hadn't been broken. He certainly hadn't envisaged this: the overwhelming need to throw himself into those familiar arms and cry out all his heartbreak as if the last few months had never happened.

He realized Kenny was still waiting for an answer. Not wanting a messy confrontation, he stepped back and allowed him to enter. Ryan swallowed as all the memories he'd tried so hard to forget surged to the surface and sucker punched him in the heart.

With his hands stuffed in his chinos, Kenny hesitated in the foyer and offered up a weak smile. His gaze flitted over the myriad of family photographs lining the walls, and his mouth pulled down at the corners. "Looks like you got your family after all."

"I'm helping out a friend," Ryan replied a touch defensively. Friend? Was Archer a friend now? A vague memory of coming home last night, of lying in bed with Archer on top of him, seeped into his consciousness. That had to be a dream, right? When he'd finally crawled out of bed not long ago, shocked to find it was almost noon, a note on the kitchen counter had said Archer had taken the kids to the park. He had no idea when they'd return.

The skull-splitting shriek of the kettle pulled him back to reality, and he clutched his head. "Oh God, make it stop."

Kenny beat him to the kitchen and took the kettle off the stove. "Thanks," Ryan gushed gratefully as he shuffled behind. He felt like he was moving in slow motion. "Want some tea?"

"Oolong?"

"No, green." Ryan curled his lip. Kenny had always been picky about his tea. But to Ryan's surprise, he readily accepted the substitute. Too impatient to wait for a pot to steep, Ryan dropped a tea bag in each mug and added the boiling water directly. Kenny would have to suck it up. Despite his aching body, Ryan managed not to spill as he carried both mugs to the table and cautiously sat down opposite the man he'd once planned to marry and start a family with.

He was actually surprised at himself for remaining so calm in front of his ex. Maybe the hangover was a good distraction; the effort needed to keep his stomach under control stopped him from being nervous. He didn't have the energy to make a long, drawn-out scene.

"You kept it," Kenny commented with a nod to Ryan's robe. It had been a Christmas gift, brought back from one of Kenny's trips home to the Philippines. The trips Ryan had never accompanied him on because his family was ultratraditional. That should have been the first tip-off. Ryan had hung on to the robe, partly out of sentimental attachment, but mostly because it was beautiful, and he loved the way the silk slid over his skin. He didn't tell Kenny that. Simply nodded and sipped his tea.

"How have you been?"

"Are you really going to do this? Sit here and make chitchat?" Ryan asked. *Yeah, hungover Ryan was definitely cooler.* "Why are you here?"

Kenny mirrored Ryan and cradled his mug between his hands. "I've been thinking a lot. About us. About what went wrong."

"Um, it went wrong when you walked out," Ryan muttered.

Kenny's tanned face flushed. "I know." He removed his glasses and pinched the bridge of his nose. It was something he always did when he became stressed. "Look, I'm not trying to make excuses here. I got freaked out by the whole settling-down thing. I mean, we're still young, Ryan. And you were getting a little obsessive when it came to marriage and kids." He held up his index finger and thumb. "You were this close to turning into Bridezilla."

Ryan grimaced. "Then why did you let it get so far? Not once in the whole process did you say 'stop.'" That was what tortured Ryan, even now. Kenny had indulged all his fantasies. He'd picked out baby names, went window-shopping for cribs, scouted wedding venues without a word of protest. So it had blindsided him when Kenny said he didn't want any of it.

Sometimes he wondered if Kenny *had* simply used him. Jill certainly thought so, but best friends were known to be biased. For the most part he'd refused to believe it and defended Kenny assiduously. The man he loved, the man he'd shared his life with, wasn't capable of that. Now he was here. Surely that mean something. Ryan was afraid to get too excited. He certainly wasn't the best judge of character— look at how Archer had manipulated him. But at least Archer was open about what he wanted.

"I didn't know how to." Kenny's voice cracked. "Getting married, the adoption . . . it was all you talked about. It made you so happy, and I didn't want to let you down. But then everything seemed to be happening so fast. One day I woke up and realized I wasn't ready for that. My entire life up to that point had been about school and you. I needed some time for myself."

"Good thing you figured out I was holding you back," Ryan muttered as he stared into his mug. The old, familiar hurt rose like bile in his throat.

"That's not what I meant. We were so young when we met, Ryan. Neither of us ever had a chance to see what else was out there. Didn't you ever wonder about that?"

"No," he replied. "I didn't."

"Well, I did. I tried to tell you so many times . . ."

Ryan frowned. He'd repeatedly combed through the ashes of their relationship in the months after the breakup, analyzing every little detail. Yes, Kenny had been absent from most of the wedding planning and left all the big decisions to Ryan, but he'd always assumed it was because of the stress of his new job. Clearly it had been more. And Ryan hadn't noticed. Tears stung his eyes. "Why couldn't you have told me you were having cold feet, Kenny?"

"I didn't want to hurt you."

"Well, you did." Ryan sniffled.

"Look," Kenny said gently. "I didn't come here to dredge up old history."

"Then why did you come? And now? You know what next weekend is."

"Of course I know. It was supposed to be our wedding day."

Ryan refused to look up from his mug. He couldn't. Not until he got his emotions under control. He could still see the invitations sitting on the coffee table, ready to address and mail. He'd kept them for three weeks after Kenny left, just in case he changed his mind. Finally Jill had tossed them in the recycling bin.

"That's why I'm here," Kenny said. "To talk about the future."

"I don't understand." Ryan squinted at him. "Are you saying you want to get back together?"

"I'd like to give it a try. You're not seeing anyone, are you?" Wasn't it like Kenny to assume he was still single? Ryan wished he could say differently.

Yet despite every warning Jill had uttered, and every misgiving he held deep down inside, Ryan's heart gave a little leap. "Why? What changed your mind?"

"I miss you. I still love you, Ryan. That hasn't changed. That never changed."

Ryan searched Kenny's earnest face. Tendrils of old, familiar feelings wound around his heart. He wanted to believe him so badly, but why had it taken Kenny eight whole months to come to that conclusion? A harsh laugh burbled up in his chest. "What happened? Did you flunk out on the dating scene? What about our 'lack of chemistry'? Or me 'smothering' you? Did you forget about that?"

"I said a lot of things I'm not proud of. Mostly because I was scared as hell." Kenny licked his lips. "I think I finally realized what you'd been saying about other things being more important. We were good together. We could be good together again."

Ryan's throat tightened. God, he was tempted. The old feelings were still there, maybe not as strong as before, but they could be if he let them. He and Kenny were compatible in almost every way except for maybe the bedroom. When it came down to it, surely things like friendship and trust outlasted passion. "What about marriage? Kids? I still want those things."

Kenny reached across the table and took his hand. "I do too. I've given this a lot of thought. I'm ready to commit to you." He smiled, and Ryan's bruised heart swelled with new hope. "Whenever you want. We can do it like we planned. But . . . I'm being honest here—I'm not ready for kids yet. In a couple of years, definitely. But right now things are so new and unpredictable at the firm. And maybe we need to spend some time on *us* first."

Ryan would be lying if he said he wasn't a bit disappointed, but beneath that the glimmer of a future together teased his heartstrings. But his hangover was making it difficult to focus.

"I don't know," Ryan said softly. "I need to think about it."

Kenny nodded. "Sure. I understand." His smile was tentative but seemed genuine, and Ryan found himself remembering the way things had been before: the long walks on the beach in summer; the surprise party Kenny had organized for his graduation; even the vacation to Mexico one spring break when he'd gotten horribly sunburned and ruined the whole trip, and Kenny had patiently rubbed aloe over his peeling skin.

He could have that again.

Ryan smiled back. He threaded their fingers together, his throat tight with memories.

The peaceful moment was broken by the thunder of running feet in the foyer and a chorus of happy voices shouting his name. "Ryan, where are you?"

Ryan's headache threatened to split his skull in two. He released Kenny's hand, let his pounding head sink to the table, covered it with his arms, and wished he could sink into the ground as easily. The wooden surface felt cool against his forehead. "Please don't shout," he moaned.

With enough noise to wake the dead, Emma and Dillon trooped into the kitchen, followed by Archer. "Uncle Archie said you were sick, so we picked you some flowers." When Ryan raised his head, Emma proudly thrust a tortured bouquet of dandelions in his face. She wrinkled her nose up. "You smell funny."

"What's wrong with Ryan?" Dillon demanded.

Archer had the nerve to chuckle. "He had a little too much fun last night."

"He doesn't look like he had fun."

Archer laughed out loud. Ryan winced. "Stop," he gasped. "Please stop. Can't you see I'm dying here?"

"Oh, we see it all right," Archer responded. He held out his hand. "Hi. I'm Archer Noble." That's when Ryan realized he'd forgotten all about Kenny.

Kenny shot to his feet and shook the proffered hand. "Ken Lee."

Archer paused, his eyes narrowed. "Kenny, the ex?" His tone was decidedly less welcoming than it had been only a moment before. He moved to stand behind Ryan's chair.

Hang on. How did Archer know Kenny was his ex? And why did he suddenly feel caught in a pissing contest. Ryan saw similar questions in Kenny's eyes.

He cringed. What would Kenny think of the agreement he'd made with Archer? If the worst came to pass and Archer walked away, would he have to choose between Kenny and the kids?

Kenny gave him an encouraging smile and rose. "I should let you go. I'll call you later, okay? We can talk some more."

"Sure," Ryan murmured. He didn't get up to see Kenny out, but his head hurt too much to feel guilty about it. It felt so heavy, he had to prop it up with an elbow on the table.

Archer ushered the kids upstairs to change into bathing suits and then poured himself a cup of coffee. Ryan waited for him to say something, to gloat, but the silence stretched out interminably.

"So," Archer said after a few minutes had passed. "You and Kenny? Back together?"

"I don't know yet. I was as surprised to see him as you were." Ryan's hand shook as he sipped his tea. "How did you know he's my ex anyway?"

"You mentioned him last night. From the stuff you said, I got the impression he didn't really appreciate you."

Ryan stilled. He swung around, his gaze flying to Archer's face in alarm. "What else did I say last night?"

Archer's expression was carefully neutral. "You don't remember? Anything?"

Ryan searched his memory. He recalled a fast, heavy beat and lots of hard, sweaty bodies pressed in around him. He thought he'd danced with a couple of guys. One had wanted to take him home, and he'd actually been tempted for a change, but Jill had pulled him away, bought him another drink and . . . that was it. Except that Archer was watching him rather closely now, confusion written clearly on his face, and Ryan had the feeling he might have missed something important.

"Oh no," he moaned. "What did I do?" If he'd been stupid enough to drunk-text Kenny, who knew what else he'd done?

"You mean other than fall down the stairs?"

"I guess that explains why everything hurts," Ryan murmured.

"All in all, it was a very entertaining evening."

Ryan groaned and buried his face in his hands. Archer already dismissed him for being young and naive. What would he think now? For some inconceivable reason, he wanted to impress Archer, and at the moment Ryan felt a bit like a teenager facing his parents the morning after. Except in Ryan's case, both Karen and Arne would have been overjoyed to see him like this. Hell, they would have been right there with him.

Ryan's eyes snapped open with a sudden thought. He could use this to his advantage, couldn't he? Given Marguerite and Archer's family history, maybe Archer would think twice about leaving his niece and nephew in the care of a man who got tanked on a regular basis. Ryan sat up straighter.

"You'd think I'd be used to this," he said casually.

"Oh, this happens a lot does it?"

"All the time," Ryan bluffed. "I love a good party."

Archer smiled. "Anyone ever tell you you're a terrible liar? Do you want some toast?"

"Ugh, no." Ryan's stomach gurgled at the mention of food. "And in future I think I'm sticking to wine."

Archer's laugh had a hard edge. "The first, and only, time I got shitfaced scared the crap out of me." Something in his tone made Ryan look at him, and when he did, there was a haunted, far-off gaze in Archer's eyes. "I think I was twelve or so. Uncle Russ took me out in his truck with a case of Labatt's and a forty-ouncer of whiskey, and we parked in someone's field. I don't remember much about that night—don't *want* to remember—except for how damned good I felt. Like I was nothing and everything at the same time. And if I was nothing, then nothing could ever hurt me. I was free. It would have been so easy to keep going like that. Easier than you could possibly know." Archer blinked, clearly emerging out of the memory that had gripped him. "But then I realized there would be no one to protect Margie. I haven't touched a drop since."

"Jesus, Archer. Twelve?" The words burst from Ryan's lips before he could stop them. He was horrified.

Archer shrugged like it was nothing. "Don't worry about it. All I'm saying is that everyone needs to blow off a little steam now and then. You wouldn't be human if you didn't."

Ryan sighed and slumped back in the chair. "Well, I've obviously discovered my outlet is overpriced cocktails. What's yours?"

"Sex."

Heat surged into Ryan's face as Archer's blunt gaze raked over his body. He felt absolutely naked under the weight of that stare. When he glanced down, he saw that his robe had parted again, revealing a swath of pale chest and thigh. Some perverse instinct made him want to keep it like that, see what happened next, but he knew Archer wasn't truly interested—he played in an entirely different league—so Ryan tugged the silk so it covered his exposed thighs.

"Jeez, rein it in will you," he grumbled. "I'm only human."

Archer's brow wrinkled, like he was trying to figure something out. He even gave his head a shake, but then his lips twitched and split into a wolfish grin. "You're the one giving me a show, walking around in nothing but glitter and 'fuck me' panties."

Ryan squawked and stood, gathering his robe around him. When Archer was being all flirty, he was irresistible. Teasing or not, a few minutes more of that intense scrutiny and he would start getting hard. And that would be mortifying. Way more mortifying than being caught wearing lace or texting his ex. "They're *not* panties. They're men's briefs."

"Look like panties to me. They're lace for Chrissakes."

Ryan's face burned, but he was done feeling ashamed about his tastes. He would not make excuses for them anymore. His attention caught on a shimmer below Archer's left ear. "Speaking of shows . . . Is that glitter on your neck?"

Archer slapped a hand to his neck and then scowled when he pulled it back and saw glitter on his fingers. "Must have been when I was hauling your butt off the floor," he muttered, twisting away.

That image of Archer pressing him down into the mattress flitted through Ryan's brain again, so vivid he could almost feel the man's weight hitting in all the right places. Even with the pounding head, his body began to warm. But the idea was ridiculous; he'd had too many lonely nights lately was all.

It was a good thing Archer had zero interest in him. If he ever changed his mind, Ryan wouldn't stand a chance against a man like that—a man he was already attracted to—and the last thing he needed to worry about was awkward sexual tension making things more complicated than they already were.

Whatever subtle flirtation Ryan might have imagined between him and Archer vanished a few days later when he and the kids returned from an afternoon at the park to find a familiar suitcase in the foyer.

"Is Uncle Archie leaving?" Dillon asked, his eyes dark with worry.

Ryan's stomach tightened as Archer strolled down the stairs with his laptop bag slung over one shoulder. "Oh, good, you're back," he said. "I'm heading out in a couple of minutes."

"Out? What's this?" Ryan demanded, forcing the words past his dry throat. Sure things had been a little strained between them since he'd made a fool of himself last weekend, but that didn't mean Archer was ready to walk, did it?

"I've got to fly to Vancouver for a few days."

"Vancouver?" Surely he'd heard wrong.

"To meet with the PROUDtv execs. I've got an interview. For the pilot."

"Seriously? The network whose claim to fame is *The Real Escorts of Beverly Hills*? Nice, Archer." Anger flooded his body. "And you weren't going to say anything?"

"I told you about the deal I was working on."

"You mentioned a television show. A month ago. You never said anything about an imminent trip. A heads-up would have been nice." Archer wouldn't meet his stare, which told Ryan all he needed to know: Archer had deliberately kept this to himself. "Jesus, Archer, you can't just up and leave whenever you feel like it. What about the kids?"

"I don't see the problem. You're here."

"You can't go," Dillon cried. He swung to Ryan, clutching his arm and trembling as he had that day in the grocery store. "What if he doesn't come back?"

Archer's forehead creased. "It's only for a few days, kiddo. I'll be back."

"That's what Mommy said too." With a strangled sob, Dillon ran up the stairs, Emma, as always, close on his heels.

Archer stabbed his fingers through his hair and for a second he looked lost. The honk of a horn outside made him start. "That's my cab."

But Ryan wasn't done. He trailed Archer out the door and down the steps. "Archer! What the hell is wrong with you? Can't you see they need you here?" The cab driver gave them a wary look as he threw Archer's suitcase in the trunk and hopped back in the car. "Oh right. I forgot. Nobody but Archer Noble matters."

Archer stopped, his shoulders stiff. When he spun around, his face was drawn tight. His brown eyes blazed with anger. "I don't *want* them to need me. Don't you get that? This is my career. It's what I *do*. I don't have a nice little nine-to-five job and get summers off. I don't have a fancy degree to fall back on. I have to go where the work is. I can't put it on hold because it's inconvenient. I already told you all this."

Ryan flinched. "What about them? Or are they inconvenient too?"

"You're making too much of this," Archer huffed. "It's two fucking days, Ryan."

"Fine. Go." Ryan crossed his arms over his chest. "I hope it works out for you," he said, choking on his bitterness. "Your career is obviously far more important than the people in your life."

Chapter 12

*T*he fucking cursor mocked him with each flash on the blank screen as he held his phone tucked to his ear and listened to Darren drone on. *I'm waiting*, it seemed to say. *Come on, you slacker.* Archer was sorely tempted to put his fist through the laptop to silence it.

"They loved you," Darren Burns, development producer for PROUDtv gushed as Archer perused some of the racier emails in his inbox before deleting them. "You were a big hit. Expect a contract offer soon."

Archer paused on a hot dick-pic and typed a quick one-handed reply. "That's great, Darren," he offered, wishing he sounded more enthusiastic. Normally Donna would handle this sort of thing, but Darren had been awfully chummy during his visit, and Archer . . . well, Archer never ignored an opportunity.

It'd been more than a week since his return from Vancouver and he was still enduring the silent treatment from Ryan. The kids had been more forgiving: their excited welcome, the way Emma had hurled herself into his arms and clung to his neck as though she'd actually missed him, had caught him by surprise. His chest warmed at the memory. He'd been so eager to escape, but the scary thing was, he'd missed them a bit too.

The sense of relief generated by his trip had quickly vanished. Now into August, Donna's deadline for an outline had come and gone, and he had nothing to show—not even the glimmer of an idea. It was as if all his creative energy had been drained. He knew he wouldn't be able to dodge Donna much longer. She had already given him one extension; she wouldn't be so generous the next time.

Thank God the television deal was still on the table. If his writing career ever ended, he'd need that to fall back on. And he'd put on quite a show in Vancouver.

Darren was still talking. Archer switched his phone to the other ear and waited for a break in the monologue. "Well, I can't wait to work with you guys. I'm looking forward to doing the travel series."

"Oh, change of plans," Darren announced.

"But I thought we agreed—"

"After you left, my intern came up with this great idea. Right up your alley, so to speak. Ever hear of a show called *Temptation*? It's where one spouse sets up the other to see if they'll be faithful."

Archer jerked to attention. "You want me to be bait?" he asked tightly.

"No, of course not. You'll be the host."

"Of a show that breaks up happy queer couples I'm guessing." Jesus. *What would Ryan say?* Archer immediately berated himself for worrying. What did it matter what Ryan thought?

"Hey," Darren admonished, "your whole thing is that monogamy doesn't exist. Here's your chance to prove it."

Archer made a face at the phone. He'd been hoping for something with a little more substance, like his own talk show, but he couldn't afford to be too picky right now. Once he was under contract and got out to Vancouver permanently, he could pitch his own ideas.

"Fine. I'm on board with that," he lied.

"Good. You've got that edge we need. And with your name on the project, this could actually find an audience. The execs agree."

And with the tie-in to my book, it might help my sales. So why did he have this bad taste in his mouth?

"I'm planning to film the pilot in November. We'll see where it goes from there."

November. Perfect. He'd have the estate settled by fall, and the kids safely ensconced with Ryan. He would have to keep his distance between now and then so he didn't slip up again. He didn't really understand the effect Ryan had on him, but he knew enough to be cautious. If he wasn't careful, he'd find himself fully domesticated as Donna had predicted weeks ago. "Sounds good, Darren. I'll look forward to hearing from you."

"And . . . you know, if you were to stir up a little controversy in the meantime . . ."

Archer sighed. "Got it."

"I knew you would. Let's keep that momentum going, shall we? Talk to you soon."

Keep the momentum going, he thought with a groan as he hung up. What momentum? He was going nowhere. Fast.

Archer leaned back in the chair and threaded his hands behind his neck. He should be out *there* launching his career, not playing house. All too familiar pressure built behind his eyes. His skin felt too tight. Even though he'd only been back a week, he needed to get out of here again before he went crazy. He needed . . .

Well, he knew what he needed. But Saturday was still half a week away, and goddamn Ryan had him under house arrest.

Unbidden, the memory of kissing those slick, cherry-flavored lips filled his head. He was horny—that was the simplest explanation— and he'd take care of that soon enough. But that didn't fully explain the flush of warmth that slid over him whenever he thought of the way Ryan had held him and stroked his back. Or how he secretly wanted it to happen again.

Knowing Ryan had a crush on him only made it worse. Except that most of the time Ryan didn't act like he had a crush and still seemed blissfully unaware of what had occurred that weekend. Archer was the only one disturbed by those events. He had thought the Vancouver trip would clear his head, remind him of who he was, but here he was, already tied up in knots once more.

He jumped up and began pacing, stopping in front of the patio doors to check that the kids were still playing in the backyard where he'd left them while Ryan ran errands. A collection of dolls and action figures lined the edge of the pool, and Emma and Dillon seemed absorbed in the story they were enacting. For a brief moment, time shifted and he saw himself and Margie, hiding beneath the covers, lost in their own fantasy world. Margie was the princess in need of rescue, and Archie was her knight.

Emma and Dillon were good kids. They had Marguerite's sweet nature, and it almost hurt to think that he'd miss seeing them grow up. His hand went to the ring he wore on a chain around his neck.

Ryan's parting shot echoed in his head. *"Your career is obviously far more important than the people in your life."*

Ryan didn't understand. He hadn't grown up with nothing. He hadn't lived on the streets or worried about his next meal. No one had spit in *his* face and told him he was shit. Now Archer was about to leave that behind for good.

And who said he had to miss out? He could visit the kids now and then, check up on them. He liked the idea of having ties somewhere. As long as they didn't become too cumbersome.

His thoughts heavy with Marguerite, Archer returned to the computer and sighed in defeat. The ideas weren't coming. The caustic voice in his head was unusually silent.

Where usually his fingers flew across the keyboard, unable to capture his thoughts fast enough, now those same thoughts were buried deep and couldn't be coaxed out. *So write something, anything.* It was a trick he had learned long ago to get through writer's block— keep typing, even if it's nonsense—but his fingers refused to obey.

He hopped over to his blog, which sat neglected. He hadn't posted anything since before Margie's death, not capitalizing on all the publicity generated by his stunt with Glenn Smith. God, that seemed so long ago. Twitter was the same: except for a short burst of activity back in July, his handle was dead. Shit. At least Kim was keeping his Facebook page and website up to date. He had spent years building his audience, and now he would lose all his followers if he wasn't careful.

He scoured the internet, hoping for some inspiration. Usually it didn't take much to get a good rant going: a report of stupid legislation, the antics of a closeted celebrity, a quote by a politically correct activist. But after an hour of trying, he was no further ahead.

It all seemed so pointless.

Hoping to spark that fire in his belly, Archer skimmed a few of the old posts on his website. But his words sounded hollow as he reread them, less ironic and witty, and more hateful. It wasn't that his views had suddenly changed—he still believed in most of what he had written—but he could see how he had straddled the line between opinion and intolerance.

He frowned. What if Emma and Dillon read this someday? They might not have discovered the internet yet, but it would happen eventually. What then? He wasn't as worried about the explicit content—yes, he'd posted the intimate details of some of his encounters—as he was about the opinion pieces. How would he explain the disdainful way he referred to straight couples as "breeders"? His assertion that anyone who believed in love was wasting their time? What would they think of him then? He was supposed to be a fucking role model. *Him*! Archer's fingers leaped to the mouse, ready to delete it all, but what would that solve—a click wouldn't really undo anything.

His head pounded.

He needed to give his readers *something*. A blogger without readers was nothing. At the very least he had to let them know he was still alive. So he settled in and started typing out a quick excuse for his absence, citing a death in the family. He doubted his readers cared much—they followed him for his sarcastic wit, his outrageous views, and his exciting, if somewhat exaggerated, lifestyle, not the mundane activities of his daily life. They wanted entertainment, not reality.

His thoughts turned to Marguerite again. His fingers paused, a memory of her wedding day taking shape, the small, simple ceremony at city hall so vivid in his mind that he could almost smell her perfume. It was the day he had finally believed she was safe. He hadn't known then that it wouldn't be for long.

But on that day anyway, he'd stopped worrying. Every trick he'd fucked, every wallet and purse he'd stolen as an angry young man had been worth it, even if they had cost him more than he'd bargained for. Jackson had been a good and kind man who would make her happy.

He wrote down every detail he remembered of that day. All the things he'd never said to Marguerite but wished now that he had. How proud he was, how much he loved her, how much he regretted not being involved in her life. The words suddenly seeped from his fingers and bled across the page. So many memories, so many regrets. When he was done, Archer had ten long paragraphs. It was raw and from the heart, unlike anything he had ever written, but he felt for the first time that it was actually him on the page. He hit the button to publish before he could change his mind.

In minutes the responses began coming in. More comments than he ever expected—there was nothing like the instant validation of the digital age. He was used to haters; in fact he sometimes encouraged them. Hate fueled publicity far better than love. But these comments were different: heartfelt condolences, readers sharing similar stories, words of encouragement. Archer didn't know what to make of it. His eyes began to sting.

"What are you working on?"

Archer slammed the laptop closed at the sound of Ryan's voice. He hadn't heard him come in. "Nothing."

He cursed the newfound awareness that made his heart beat faster every time the younger man got close.

"Where are the kids?" Ryan set down a couple of grocery bags on the kitchen counter.

"In the backyard."

Ryan spun around. "Archer! You can't leave them unattended."

"They're fine. I checked on them. Dillon is almost eight. Do you know what I was doing at eight?" Yes, he was deliberately provoking a fight, but damn, it felt good.

"He's not you."

"Thank God for that."

"Dillon!" Emma's piercing cry turned Archer's blood to ice. He jumped up a second too late—Ryan beat him to the patio doors.

All Archer saw was Dillon thrashing in the deep end of the swimming pool, and he froze.

After that everything happened in a horrific blur.

It was Ryan who ran outside and jumped in the pool. Ryan who pulled the struggling boy safely to the side where he clung, coughing. Only then was Archer released from his paralysis. He rushed to their side, grasped Dillon beneath the arms, and hauled him onto the warm stones. Ryan flopped down beside him.

Dillon retched as he gasped for breath. A trickle of water ran from his mouth when Archer pounded him on the back. "I'm okay," he croaked. "I swallowed some water."

"You know you're not supposed to be in the pool without an adult," Ryan scolded.

"I had to rescue the princess." He held up a plastic doll in a dripping-wet ball gown.

Archer watched, shaken, as Ryan pulled Dillon into his arms and held him tight. He thought Ryan might be crying, but it was difficult to tell as he was soaking wet.

Grabbing a towel from the nearby chair, he wrapped it around them both, feeling useless and worse. This was his fault for not paying attention. He'd just stood there frozen. If Ryan hadn't leapt into action . . .

Bile rose in his throat. Dillon could have died because of him.

"What were you thinking?" Ryan shrieked suddenly. "You're supposed to watch them. One afternoon, Archer . . . you can't even manage one afternoon. Why did I ever think you could do this?"

"Do you think I don't ask myself that question?" he roared back, so vehemently that Ryan flinched. "That I don't wonder that every fucking day?"

"Stop!" Dillon cried hoarsely, struggling from Ryan's hold. "Stop fighting!"

Emma had begun to cry. She moved to Ryan's side and clung to his neck protectively.

Archer's anger evaporated, replaced by a fear so intense he started to shake. His saliva turned to dust in his throat.

This was all him. Everything he touched, everything he cared about, turned bad in the end.

So he did the only thing he was good at.

He left.

"Fuck."

Archer knocked his companion's hand away from his limp cock and sat up in bed. The image of Dillon struggling in the pool haunted him. The fear in Emma's eyes when he'd yelled. He couldn't get them out of his mind no matter how hard he tried. His stomach turned over remembering the terror he'd felt. The terror he still felt.

"I said stop," he snapped when the guy reached for him again. "It's not going to happen."

He scrubbed a hand down his face. Sex had always been the one thing he could count on. And now even that had failed him.

His partner, a young, platinum-blond twink with a couple of bad tattoos across his chest, shrugged and rolled to the other side of the bed. He produced a baggie of weed and some papers from beneath the mattress and promptly began rolling a joint.

"You said you were drug-free," Archer accused.

"And you said you were a great fuck." His companion sneered, flicking Archer a derisive glance. "Besides, it's only weed. That doesn't count." He reminded Archer so much of himself at that age—hard and cynical and teetering on a precipice—that for a minute he couldn't breathe. For the first time since he'd stopped tricking, he felt dirty. Old and used and ashamed.

"What's your name, anyway?"

Suspicion flashed across the young man's face. "Joel. Why?" He exhaled a cloud of acrid smoke.

"Well, Joel, fuck me if I'm not as deluded as you." Archer glanced around the shabby room, only now seeing it clearly. Clothes were piled on the floor. An empty pizza box sat on the dresser. Jesus Christ. It looked like a fucking dorm room. What was he doing here? Joel had been the first to message him, so he'd gone with it. But shit. Was this what he'd come to? A hate fuck with a stranger? He laughed as he suddenly realized the person he hated most was himself.

"What the fuck, man?" Joel held the joint out to him. "Try this. It might help."

The skunk-stink crept up Archer's nostrils, beckoning. Why fight it anymore? Margie was gone; the kids had Ryan. He was tired. This crushing weight he'd carried on his chest—since the day he was born, it seemed sometimes seemed—would finally disappear. All he had to do was give in.

He took the slender joint and had it halfway to his lips before he stopped. His fingers trembled. In the back of his mind, Marguerite's face hovered.

That split-second hesitation was enough for the doubt to start creeping in—all the "what ifs." What if he liked it too much? What if he couldn't stop with just this? Wouldn't he only be trading one addiction for another? And sex *was* an addiction of sorts for him. Looking around, he had no choice but to admit that now. At the very least it was a compulsion. He bolted upright.

Archer handed the joint back and scrambled into his clothes before he changed his mind.

"Your loss, man," Joel said, stretching his naked body across the rumpled sheets.

"Can I give you some advice, Joel?" Archer turned back toward the bed. "Get your shit together before it's too late."

"Whatever," Joel muttered. He already had his cell phone in his other hand and didn't even look up.

Archer shook his head and left.

He drove aimlessly for a long time, until his nerves had calmed and the old itch subsided. When he returned home, the house was dark. Sighing in relief, he climbed the stairs and stood outside the open door of Dillon's bedroom, watching him sleep. This afternoon had scared him, more than Uncle Russ ever had, more than leaving Margie behind.

He stepped into the room and knelt before the bed. He'd thought he was being quiet, but Dillon raised his head sleepily. "Daddy?"

A sharp pain stabbed Archer between the ribs. "No," he said. "It's Uncle Archie."

Dillon rubbed his eyes. "Where did you go?"

"I had to go out for a little while."

"Because I made you mad?"

"Why would I be mad at you?"

"For causing trouble. Because I didn't listen."

Archer stroked Dillon's hair. "Oh, Dillon, you did nothing wrong. It was me."

"What did you do wrong?"

He forced a smile to his lips. "Nothing I can't fix."

Dillon yawned and snuggled back into his pillow. "But you're back now?"

"Yes, I'm back." *But not for long.* He wouldn't endanger the kids with his carelessness ever again. They deserved better. "So go to sleep."

As soon as Dillon's breathing deepened, Archer rose and went downstairs. He felt calmer. He knew what needed to be done. Flipping on the light in the basement office, he rummaged through the papers on Margie's cluttered desk. Where the hell was it?

"Archer?" He turned to find Ryan standing there in his pajamas, hair ruffled and a pillow crease across his cheek. "What are you doing?"

"Looking for the fucking custodial application forms. They're here somewhere." After his latest visit to the lawyer, he'd tossed the paperwork on the pile.

"Why?" Fear tinged Ryan's voice. "Archer, about this afternoon. I'm sorry for what I said. I didn't mean it. It was fear talking, and I overreacted. I know you would never—"

"It doesn't matter." Archer cursed as papers slid off the desk. He left them on the floor; they weren't what he was looking for. "We both know how this ends. Let's get it over with."

"Archer, no. You promised. Let's talk about it in the morning." He took a step closer and sniffed the air. "Where did you go?"

Archer's calm deserted him. He couldn't wait until morning. He needed to find those papers—now—before he started second-guessing himself. Before he started thinking about Marguerite again.

"Goddamn it," he roared. "Where is it?"

He knocked over another stack. This time, something heavier fell to the ground. When he looked down, he saw a thick, legal-sized envelope with his name on it. The address was crossed through and someone had scrawled *Return to sender*.

Something cold and oily slithered in his belly. "Get out," he rasped, lungs suddenly too tight, limbs frozen in place, unable to tear his eyes away from his name in black block letters.

"What is it?"

"Get. Out." He pushed Ryan bodily out of the room and slammed the door shut.

With his mouth dry, Archer spun around and crept toward the envelope, not understanding his reaction to it, but aware nonetheless of the hair on the back of his neck standing on end, and his heart racing like a motherfucker. Summoning all his courage, Archer crouched and reached for it.

It was from Marguerite, as he'd known it would be. The mailing address was one he'd used last year—no wonder it hadn't been delivered. How long had it sat here, buried beneath other papers? With trembling hands, he slit the seal and withdrew a file folder. Affixed to the front of the folder with a paperclip was a handwritten note. His vision blurred when he saw Marguerite's handwriting. The letter was dated last autumn.

When he flipped open the folder, the first thing he saw was a copy of Sonia's police file. He closed it quickly and set it aside, not quite ready for that yet. But the note he read.

My dear Archie,

I am such a coward. You don't know how many times I've started to tell you about this project of mine, but as soon as I mention her name, you shut me out. So I'm taking the easy way and sending this to you instead.

Please don't be angry with me. When Jackson died, it made me think about how short life is. How pointless anger and hate is. We never talk about the past, but I feel like it's always there. Holding on to it keeps us from living in the present. We need to let it go, and the only way to do that is to see it through. We could spend the rest of our lives assigning blame, but the fact is, what happened to us was no one's fault. It just was.

I forgive her, Archie. I hope, in time, you will too.

Everything I am, everything I have, is because of you, not her. You shouldered all the bad, even when you didn't have to. There are times I wonder if you hate her so easily, how can you not hate me a little bit too?

When I look at Emma and Dillon, I see us, the way it should have been, and my heart breaks. Loving them, loving Jackson, no matter how briefly, has been my greatest joy. I wish you could know what that's like because love is what really matters. So I choose to look forward, not back.

When you're ready, the truth about our mother (or as close as I could get to the truth) is here in this folder. She didn't forget about us. I hope you'll find the same peace I have.

Love always, your adoring sister,
Margie

The letter fell from Archer's numb fingers to the floor. A heartbeat passed. Then two. He was frozen in place, staring at the wall but not seeing anything. Margie's words echoed in his head. He could almost hear her voice, like she was right *there*. But she wasn't, and she never would be again.

Suddenly his entire body shuddered, as if someone had applied a defibrillator paddle to his chest. The first sob came out of nowhere, erupting from a place so deep inside him that Archer hadn't known it was there. It was loud and rusty and full of a lifetime's pain, and he tried to hold it back, but it was as if something inside him had broken. Once the flood began, he couldn't seem to make it stop.

Vaguely, from far away, he heard a tap on the door, but he couldn't answer. He shook with the effort to hold back the tears, shook so hard his teeth rattled and he thought he might shatter into little pieces. His heart thundered as panic flooded his body, beating so hard it was a wonder it didn't explode in his chest.

His lungs seized as if crushed in a phantom grip. He reached for the chair to support himself but didn't make it. He doubled over, gasping for breath, overturning the chair. Black dots swarmed in front of his eyes as the pain streaked across his chest and down his arm. Jesus. He was having a heart attack. He was going to die right here, right now.

He fell to the floor choking, trying to draw a breath into his useless lungs. Tears and snot ran down his face and into his mouth. *The kids*, he thought frantically, *who will look after the kids?*

Suddenly Ryan was there, crouched in front of him with his hair all stuck up in clumps and his eyes warm with understanding.

"Breathe," he ordered. His voice sounded faint, like he was speaking from miles away.

I can't, he wanted to rail. He fought off Ryan's touch, but the man was stronger than he appeared, and he gripped Archer's head between his hands, holding him steady. "Breathe damn it. You're having a panic attack."

Archer's vision dimmed, until all he could see were the flecks of gold in Ryan's hazel eyes. And then miraculously the hand squeezing his lungs let go and sweet, blessed air rushed into his lungs once more. His contorted muscles went limp. When Ryan pulled him into his arms, he went gratefully, weak and shaking like a child.

"It's okay," Ryan whispered against his ear. "You can let go now."

And Archer did just that, as if after twenty years or more, those simple words of permission were all it took.

"It's too late," he sobbed. "I didn't get to say good-bye." With each repeat of the refrain, it hurt even more. He clung to Ryan, cried until he lost track of time and place. The only things that kept him from shattering completely were the strong arms around his back and the lingering scent of vanilla on Ryan's skin. He turned his face into Ryan's neck and breathed it in.

Finally, slowly, Archer came back to himself. He became aware of outside things: the chair overturned beside him, the sound of his own raspy breath, Ryan's shoulder wet beneath his cheek, Ryan's fingers in his hair, on his neck. He soaked up the soothing touch, letting it seep through his clammy skin, too exhausted, too wrung dry to move. No one had ever touched him like that—without wanting something in return.

He hadn't cried like that since the day he left Marguerite behind, since he learned that tears were useless and brought nothing but more pain.

He waited for the shame and embarrassment at his vulnerability to creep in, but surprisingly it never came.

"I read what you wrote. On your blog," Ryan confessed softly. "It was beautiful, Archer. The best thing you've ever written. I felt like I was there with you."

"I was supposed to protect her," he whispered.

Ryan's fingers stilled on the back of his neck. "You did. She knew everything she had was because of you, trust me. She knew everything you did for her."

Something in Ryan's voice told Archer the man understood more than he let on. But how much? "Did you know about this? You read it?" Archer reached an arm out for the letter he had dropped on the floor, but he didn't leave Ryan's embrace.

"No, I've never seen that before," Ryan murmured. "But she talked about you a lot."

Archer tensed as the thought of Marguerite's betrayal cut deep. How much had she revealed to this man? He couldn't stand the thought of Ryan, of all people, pitying him. "God, she told you?"

"Only some of it. Other things I inferred. She didn't break your trust."

"I never blamed her for any of it," Archer insisted, recalling Margie's heartbreaking words. "I never hated her. Never."

"I know."

"She was the only good thing. The only reason I kept going. And now she's gone, and it's too late to tell her that." His voice cracked. "What was the fucking point of all that sacrifice? I'm alone now."

Ryan's fingers tightened in his hair. "No, you're not. Don't you see that? And maybe this was it—these kids, this moment—*this* was the point. They need you. And I think . . . you need them."

Archer closed his eyes, buried his face against Ryan's neck. Like this, all his fears seemed less scary. Now he knew why the kids clung to Ryan so happily—he was magical.

They stayed like that for a while, on their knees on the floor. It had to be as uncomfortable for Ryan as it was for him, but the younger man made no attempt to move and Archer had no desire to leave the blanket of peace that had settled over him. For the first time in a long time he didn't feel like running.

How could he ignore Marguerite's last wish? He'd been foolish to try. He couldn't let her down, and besides, the kids were all he had left of her now, his only connection to her. He *wanted* to see them grow up. Be happy. But . . . "What if they don't let me keep them?" he asked abruptly, as fear crept in again.

Ryan seemed to have been waiting for that question. "I don't think that will happen. The courts generally try to keep families together."

"You don't understand. I've done things . . ." He wished he could make Ryan understand, but he couldn't bear to see pity in the man's eyes. Or worse, disgust.

"Do you have a record?"

"No," Archer conceded. But only because of luck.

"Is there anyone who is likely to challenge your application?"

"Only you."

"I'm the one who's been pushing you together."

Archer hid his smile. "Yeah, you are."

"It should be fine. Trust me, no one wants to add two more children to an already overstressed system if they don't have to. Talk to the lawyer about this—he'll tell you."

"They'll look into the records. They'll find out about our mother."

Ryan pulled back so he could look Archer in the eye. "Archer, no one holds you responsible for what happened to you as a child. You're the only one doing that."

He shook his head. Ryan didn't understand. "They'd still be better off with you."

"No, I don't think they would be." Ryan's face softened, his eyes widening as if he was surprised by his own admission. He clasped

Archer's face in his hands. "You're not a bad man, no matter how much you want to believe you are."

Archer stared into the mossy-green depths of Ryan's irises. There was an unfettered honesty and goodness there that he'd only ever encountered in one other person: his sister. How could Ryan be so gentle but so strong at the same time? He craved both qualities with a suddenness that startled him. Needed it more in that moment than he'd ever needed anything.

Desire rushed in to fill the empty space inside him. In a bold move, he ground his mouth down on Ryan's, hard enough to unbalance him. He sent Ryan rocking backward, knocking his head against the wall. Ryan didn't seem to care. He didn't pause. His arms tightened around Archer's neck. His lips parted eagerly for Archer's invading tongue. And then Archer was in, past the cherry-flavored lip balm, and tasting a sweetness that was entirely Ryan.

Ryan let him take what he wanted, but not passively. He held Archer close, met every flick of his tongue with his own, countered every nip and taste. Archer wanted more.

He fumbled beneath Ryan's thin pajama pants and found him already getting hard. Archer squeezed him through the soft fabric and swallowed Ryan's muffled exclamation. Suddenly, Ryan turned his head to the side, and Archer moaned in protest at the loss of contact.

Ryan brought one hand up to Archer's lips, not pushing him away, but clearly putting an end to the kiss. With his other hand, he soothingly stroked Archer's nape. "Don't," he cautioned, breathing unsteadily. "Don't ruin the moment."

Archer debated ignoring Ryan's words. He was sure Ryan wouldn't complain if he kept going—his eyes were dazed and heavy-lidded—but even as Archer deliberated, the world outside the office began to intrude, and a thud at the office door made them both start guiltily. Emma's squeal of protest followed.

"Shh, I'm listening," he heard Dillon complain.

"I want to listen too," Emma whined.

Archer groaned and dropped his forehead onto Ryan's shoulder. "What do I tell them?"

"You don't have to tell them anything. Say you were feeling sad. They'll understand that."

The door latch clicked as the handle was turned and opened a crack. Emma's round face peered in. "We heard a noise. Why is everybody awake?"

Archer reluctantly pulled away from Ryan and sat back on his heels. Swiped his arm across his wet face. "Sorry, Monkey. We didn't mean to wake you up."

Emma crept over, her bare feet poking out from beneath her nightgown. "Are you sad? Do you need a hug? That always makes me feel better."

The lump in Archer's throat threatened to choke him. "I think I do," he managed. Suddenly serious, Emma wrapped her thin arms around his neck and leaned her small body against him.

Dillon lingered in the open doorway. Archer waved him in with his free hand. "C'mere. You too." And then Dillon slammed into his arms.

"I'm sorry, Uncle Archie. For making you mad today," he sobbed.

"You didn't," Archer whispered, his arms full of so much unconditional love he didn't think he could bear it. He hadn't done anything to deserve this. He knew in that moment he would do anything for these two. Not because he had to, or because it was his duty, but because he *wanted* to. Here was something worth protecting. And now he didn't understand why he had fought it for so long. "I'm sorry for yelling. I was—"

"Scared. I know. That's what Ryan said."

Ryan rose from the floor, pulling Archer's attention away from the children.

"Ryan was right," Archer agreed, looking directly at the man. Ryan's lips were pink and swollen as he ran his tongue over them, the color high in his cheeks. He looked deliciously ruffled and as unbalanced as Archer had ever seen him.

Even now, he was vividly aware of the electric current still flowing between them. Did Ryan feel it too? Judging by his inability to meet Archer's gaze before he darted from the room, the answer was a resounding yes.

Chapter 13

*B*y next Saturday night, Ryan was a wreck. Avoiding someone in a house this small was nearly impossible, even with the kids as a diversion. And when that someone was Archer, it was doubly difficult. That stupid kiss in the office had turned Ryan into a teenager again, blushing uncontrollably at nothing, losing his train of thought whenever the man walked into a room, remembering the way he tasted, felt: the possessive thrust of Archer's tongue in his mouth and how quickly he had submitted. It was embarrassing, especially since Archer was behaving as if none of it had ever happened. Ryan didn't know whether to be put out or relieved. Archer used sex the way other people used alcohol or drugs—to avoid their problems, to forget for a little while when things got to be too much—so Ryan wasn't fool enough to believe it actually meant something. It was simply the product of an emotionally charged moment. Still, it would have been nice if Archer had been a bit affected by it.

It was just as well since things with Kenny were finally turning around. They had talked a lot in the last week, and for the first time in a long time, he felt hopeful about the future. Maybe Kenny was right: they had needed some time apart. Now, if only this lingering attraction for Archer would stop getting in the way.

He'd never met anyone quite like Archer. Cold and arrogant one minute, sensitive and unexpectedly caring the next. At times he saw the brother Marguerite had adored: the boy who read her stories when she got scared, who paid for her college tuition while he scraped by. Against *that* man, he had no defenses.

He groaned as he caught the spiraling direction of his thoughts. He was doing it again—obsessing. Ryan couldn't wait for Archer to go out tonight so he could breathe for a bit. Tonight, of all nights, he needed some space. He'd thought he was over it—that today would be just another day—but Kenny had called him a few hours ago, and now all he could think of was the wedding that could have been. He'd rushed out and bought a bottle of wine to drown his sorrows with later, after the kids were asleep.

He was shoulder deep in the blanket fort he was constructing for the kids between the chair and the couch when Archer came down the basement stairs after dinner. "What are you guys up to?" he asked. Ryan tensed.

"We're going to watch a movie and have a pajama party," Dillon cried excitedly. "Ryan says we can sleep down here if we want."

"You sure have got enough blankets and pillows for it. If I go upstairs am I going to find any left on the beds?"

"Don't worry," Ryan replied from within the tented folds, thinking that maybe he could hide in here until the man left. "Yours are safe."

"Oh, I'm not worried." Archer's voice came from behind him this time, and Ryan had a sudden picture of himself, ass stuck in the air as he rearranged pillows. He resisted the urge to check if the waistband of his pajama pants was still in place. "But does that mean I'm not invited?"

Ryan wriggled out of the draped confines, tugging down the back of his T-shirt as he did so. He ventured a quick glance at Archer, who was watching him closely, his gorgeous chocolate-brown eyes inscrutable. Ryan cursed his fair skin as the heat bloomed uncontrollably in his cheeks. His stomach did an anxious flip-flop when he noticed Archer was still wearing the same casual shorts and T-shirt he'd sported all day.

"How about some popcorn?" Archer asked with a grin. "You can't have movie night without popcorn, right?"

"On the stove?" Dillon scrambled to his feet. "Can I help make it pop?"

"Me too," added Emma.

Ryan sat back on his heels and frowned. "But it's Saturday night."

"Yeah."

"Aren't you going out?"

Archer shrugged. "It's better if I don't. Besides, this looks like more fun."

Ryan blinked. It did? Since when was movie night more fun than cruising to a man like Archer Noble? "We're watching *Mary Poppins,*" he challenged. "There's singing."

A flash of white teeth cut across Archer's tanned face as he grinned. "A classic. I'm in. I've actually never seen it."

"You don't know *Mary Poppins*?" Dillon asked incredulously. "But it's old."

"What are you saying, kiddo? That I'm old?" Archer grasped Dillon in a playful headlock. "I know of it. But we didn't have a TV when I was a kid."

Dillon's eyes widened. "No TV? Why not? Were you poor? What did you do for fun?" He peppered Archer with questions all the way up the stairs, tripping once on the trailing edges of Marguerite's teal scarf, which Ryan had fashioned into a sarong and Dillon now proudly sported over his pajamas. Since retrieving the scarf from the giveaway bag, he hadn't let it out of his sight. As soon as they were gone, Ryan pushed his face into a pillow and screamed. It was like Archer was torturing him on purpose. Why did he have to be the good guy tonight of all nights? When Ryan was at his lowest point? Where was the arrogant jackass when he needed him?

He loaded the disc in the DVD player and sat down to wait. Then, thinking he might need an added layer of protection with Archer around, he slipped into his silk robe and tied the belt tight around his waist. When Archer and the kids returned with two bowls of only slightly burned popcorn, Archer took the spot next to him on the couch and set his bowl between them. Dillon and Emma crawled into the blanket fort with theirs.

"This is a pajama party, Uncle Archie," Emma proclaimed. "You have to put your pajamas on."

Archer's teeth flashed again. "Sorry, kiddo, don't own any."

Heat rushed to Ryan's cheeks once more, and he was grateful they had turned out the lights. Like he needed that image in his head right now. He couldn't remember the last time he'd been so sexually aware of another man—maybe back in the early days with Kenny—and it was getting all mixed up with the other emotions churning inside him tonight. Did Archer have any idea of the effect he had on Ryan?

Of course he did, Ryan decided a few minutes later when Archer nudged him with the bowl. "Popcorn?" he asked.

In the flickering glow of the television, his expression was innocent, but Ryan was beginning to feel like the proverbial mouse being stalked by the cat. Archer wasn't turning over a new leaf; he was only changing his game. *He* was the evening's entertainment.

Would he stop if he knew how susceptible Ryan was tonight? Did he want him to?

Absently Ryan reached for the popcorn. So did Archer. Electric tingles raced up his arm when their fingers brushed. His groin tightened. He didn't hear a word Julie Andrews was saying.

How many times had he dreamed of this? Cuddling on the couch with his significant other, and a kid or two beside them: family night. Only this wasn't *his* family. He kept forgetting that. The wave of bittersweet sadness threatened to choke him, and Ryan had to close his eyes for a minute until the urge to cry passed. He just needed to get through tonight and he'd be okay.

When he opened his eyes again, he found Archer watching him carefully. Ryan quickly looked away, grabbed a handful of popcorn, and stuffed it in his mouth. A dry kernel lodged in his throat, and he stifled a cough.

Archer's cell phone buzzed intermittently for the first half of the movie until he finally switched it off with a disgusted sigh.

"You're awfully popular tonight," Ryan observed. *Had that been Max texting him? Or one of Archer's other nameless dates?*

"It's my publicist. She's been sending me marketing ideas all day. I think she's worried about losing her job. Pretty soon she'll be booking me for birthday parties."

"I thought you were a writer, not a talking head for hire."

Archer shrugged, but the lines bracketing his mouth deepened. "I've done a lot worse to earn a buck."

"But don't you ever want to do something . . . I don't know—meaningful?"

"Meaningful doesn't pay the bills."

"Have you heard anything more from the network about your show?" Archer hadn't said a word about it since he'd returned, and Ryan had to wonder if his trip hadn't gone well.

"Nothing final," Archer said after a brief hesitation. Was he holding something back? Ryan frowned.

"There are lots of other options out there, you know," he offered. "Options that don't include pimping yourself to a network like PROUDtv."

"Yeah? Guess I'm not seeing them right now." Archer folded his arms across his chest. "And they're not *that* bad."

Ryan snorted. "They call themselves a queer-centric network, but they only perpetuate stereotypes."

"Are you guys going to talk *all* the way through the movie?" Dillon demanded, clearly unimpressed, from inside the fort.

"Yeah," added Emma. "We're trying to watch."

Archer turned to him with an impish grin. "Way to go, Ryan. You got me in trouble."

Ryan narrowed his eyes, but his lips curled in an answering smile.

They hadn't discussed it, but he knew Archer had come to a decision about the kids. He hadn't missed the look of acceptance on Archer's face when they hugged him after his breakdown in the office. How that would work with his career, he didn't know—that was up to Archer to figure out. Ryan had spent the past few days on tenterhooks, waiting to be told to pack his bags. But Archer hadn't actually brought it up, which was fine by him. September was only a couple of weeks away. As long as they didn't discuss it, he could still pretend he had a family.

Ryan had trouble focusing on the movie: the bright colors and cheerful animation flickered by without him noticing. He'd seen it a million times anyway. But as the film neared its conclusion, as the beloved nanny brought the Banks family together and Mary Poppins had to leave, Ryan couldn't stop the tears leaking from his eyes. Wishing he'd picked something lighter, something not quite so close to home, he quickly brushed them away. Fortunately Emma's and Dillon's attention was on the movie. And Archer? Archer, too, was staring at the screen, his brow wrinkled in thought.

"Can we watch another one," Dillon begged as soon as the credits began to roll.

"Not tonight. It's late." Ryan turned off the television. The sooner he got them to sleep, the soon he could be alone.

"Can we have a story, then?"

Ryan suppressed a groan and was about to decline when Emma spoke. "Uncle Archie can do it," she said, moving to make room inside the fort. "C'mon, Uncle Archie."

A sudden pang of jealousy caught Ryan off guard. He forced it back. This was the way it was supposed to be. There was no reason for him to feel jealous.

Archer gave him a concerned look. Ryan plastered a fake smile on his lips and shrugged as if he didn't care, then watched as Archer Noble, the man who swore up and down that parenting was the realm of straight people, dropped to his knees and crawled inside the makeshift fort.

No longer needed, Ryan slipped away.

Upstairs, he poured himself a big glass of wine and stepped out onto the back patio. He left the lights off, preferring to sit in the dark and let the night sounds wash over him.

The Leblancs' leafy, overgrown backyard shut out the noise of the city. There was only the water in the pool lapping at the filters. Crickets chirping. The temperature was still summer-warm, with the barest hint of autumn-chill around the corner. The two-seater swing gave a rusty squeak as Ryan pushed off with his feet, seeking comfort in the soothing motion. In no time at all he would be back in the classroom, with a fresh crop of eager young minds waiting to be challenged. He wished he felt more excited.

The sky was remarkably clear for the city—he could even see stars. It would have been the perfect night for a wedding. *His* wedding. The old hurt warred with his eagerness to try again with Kenny, and he didn't know which to heed. What he wouldn't give to be able to turn to Marguerite right now and ask her opinion. Jill was blinded by her loyalty to him. He needed Marguerite's objectivity and forgiving heart. Only Marguerite was gone. He let the tears come this time, let them run unchecked down his cheeks in the dark.

Sometime later, when his glass was nearly empty, he heard the patio door slide open.

"Ryan?" Archer asked quietly.

Ryan stopped the swing, debated staying silent until Archer left. But he didn't want to be alone. "Out here."

"Mind if I join you?"

"It's your house."

Archer moved cautiously as he navigated his way. "Why don't you turn on a light?"

"It's nice like this. Your eyes will adjust soon."

Archer swore as he walked into the edge of the swing. "Not soon enough." He sat down beside Ryan on the narrow seat. It was a tight fit, and Archer's thigh pressed against Ryan's. "The kids are asleep in your blanket fort. Everything okay?"

"Yeah." Ryan took another sip of crisp chardonnay. Tried to ignore the heat spreading over his skin from the simple contact with Archer's leg. Checked his cheeks to make sure they weren't still wet.

"Try again."

"I was thinking about Marguerite."

"Ah." Archer paused, drew a breath. "Ryan, I've been—"

"Don't," he interrupted. Archer was going to tell him he wasn't needed anymore, and he couldn't bear to hear it now. "In the morning, okay? Not tonight."

"Why? What's tonight?"

"You're going to make fun of me."

"I won't."

"I was supposed to get married today."

"Oh," he said flatly. "Kenny."

"Yeah. I mean it's been months since we broke up, but still . . ."

Archer stretched one arm out along the back of the seat cushion right behind Ryan's head. "What happened? Did he cheat?"

"No. Sometimes I wish it was that simple." Ryan circled the lip of his wineglass with his index finger. He felt Archer's attention, tangible as any touch. "I think it was too much at once, with the wedding and then the adoption." For the longest time afterward, Ryan had blamed himself for the breakup, for not being exciting enough, sexy enough. For not being what Kenny wanted. For putting too much pressure on the relationship. But now he saw it took two people to build a relationship, and two to end it as well. They were both at fault to some degree.

"Adoption. Wow, you don't waste any time do you? You're young. Why the rush?"

"Yeah, that's what Kenny says. I guess I didn't want the chance to slip by. I've always wanted kids of my own." Ryan took a shaky breath. "And then Kenny decided it was too much and he wanted out."

A tremor ran through Ryan's hand, and he set down his glass. "Kenny was right. I got carried away. Too wrapped up in what I wanted to see how it was affecting him."

A warm, rough palm landed on Ryan's thigh. The heat of it seeped through the thin cotton of his sleep pants. "I'm sorry. It doesn't mean much, but I think you'll be an amazing father—or mother," he teased. "Whatever you want to be."

"Really?" Ryan turned to look at Archer, but in the shadows he could only make out the man's silhouette, not his expression.

"Yes, really."

"Even though Archer Noble is totally against heterosexual trappings?"

"Archer Noble doesn't know what he's talking about anymore. He's a bit of a dick."

Ryan found himself smiling. "Sometimes. Sometimes he's actually very nice."

"Well, don't let that get around. You'll ruin my reputation."

"It'll be our secret." Ryan leaned his head back on Archer's arm and stared up at the stars. If he moved slightly, his head would rest on Archer's shoulder. "I don't know. Maybe you're right. Maybe we're not meant for things like marriage. My parents aren't married and it's worked out for them more or less."

"Not married? You continue to shock me."

Ryan smiled in the dark. "Yeah. I'm a great disappointment to them."

"I find that hard to believe. Because you're gay?"

"Because I'm boring. Conventional. They're artistic and creative. It's all about freedom and expression for them. Karen's always asking me why I want to be so normal. But I can't help it. Maybe it's because growing up I always felt so insecure about them not being married. I wanted a nice, normal family." He forced another laugh. "I should tell her it's all their fault." He paused. "Do you think if our parents knew how much they screwed us up they would have done things differently?"

"Wow, if that's not a ringing endorsement for parenthood I don't know what is," Archer quipped drily.

"I didn't mean it that way. Besides, for me it's not only about having kids—I want everything that goes along with it. A man who loves me, a home. Maybe that *is* a fairy tale, but I love the idea of a big family. I always have. I know I work with kids every day, but it's not the same thing. I don't get to see them grow up."

"Doesn't it scare you? It's such a big responsibility." This time Archer's tone was deadly serious.

"Of course it scares me. But not enough to not want to try." Ryan wound the belt of his robe around his finger. "Jill gives me hell for it, but I think I was meant to take care of people. It's what I do best."

"But who takes care of Ryan?"

Ryan sighed. He hoped it didn't sound as sad to Archer as it did to him. "No one, right now. Maybe someday."

To Ryan's surprise, Archer tugged him closer. He went willingly, resting his cheek on Archer's shoulder, breathing in the clean, masculine smell of the man.

"Think you'll take Kenny back?"

"I want to," he admitted out loud. "We've been talking it over. He wants to try again and it almost seems wrong not to, after five years together. I still have feelings for him."

"*Feelings*? That sounds pretty wishy-washy to me."

"Yeah? What's the longest relationship you've had?" When Archer didn't respond, Ryan snorted. "That's what I thought. You're hardly in a position to judge me." He'd been ready to spend his life with Kenny once. He loved Kenny, and tonight only underscored his longing for a family of his own. But he also finally understood what Kenny had meant about chemistry, and he wasn't sure if he was willing to go back to a one-sided relationship. Why did things have to be so confusing? "He asked if we're sleeping together by the way."

"Who? Kenny?"

"Yeah." Ryan grinned at the memory of their last conversation. Kenny hadn't exactly been jealous, but it had been flattering that he'd thought Ryan stood a chance. "I mean, that's crazy, right?" When Archer didn't immediately answer, Ryan repeated the question. "Right?"

"Yeah. Crazy."

"I mean we're complete opposites."

Archer's arm tensed, and then his fingers were combing through Ryan's hair. It was a gentle touch, comforting, one he hadn't thought a man like Archer was capable of. Did he realize what he was doing? Ryan wasn't about to stop him.

They sat in easy silence for a long while. Finally Archer spoke. "I don't know what I would have done without you."

"You would have managed."

"I doubt it. There definitely would have been a lot more yelling and screaming. From the kids too." Ryan laughed at Archer's lame joke. "I think I might have kept on running."

"I guess we all have to stop some time."

"Stop interrupting. I need to say this. I completely misjudged you," Archer said. "When I first met you, I thought nobody could be that selfless. You were either an idiot or up to something. I thought you were fragile and soft. Weak—and growing up I learned being weak was the worst thing you could possibly be."

"A doormat." Jill had practically said the same thing.

"But you're not weak. Hell, you're stronger than any of us. No matter what we throw at you, you don't break."

Ryan tilted his head back, grateful for the darkness, glad that Archer couldn't see how his words affected him. "That's probably the most romantic thing anyone's ever said to me. Careful, you might end up likable after all"

"Not a chance," Archer quipped. His breath feathered Ryan's cheek when he spoke.

Ryan trembled. "Arch—" He felt Archer shift, the arm muscles bunching beneath his head, and then a pair of warm lips brushed his temple, skimmed across his cheek when he turned ever so slightly toward them.

And then he was kissing Archer Noble, sliding his hand into the man's thick hair, parting his lips when Archer's tongue probed for entrance. Excitement zipped along his spine. The heat from before was still there, but building slowly this time instead of in one fiery explosion. Archer groaned, the sound muffled by their mouths. "You're wearing that lip balm again. Fucking cherries."

Ryan tried to assemble his thoughts, but he couldn't concentrate on anything but the slow slide of their lips and tongues and the little flames flaring to life all over his skin.

Was Archer using him? Ryan wasn't sure he cared when Archer took his earlobe between his teeth and lightly bit down. His hand fisted in the folds of Archer's T-shirt. He didn't want to be alone tonight. He wanted to feel loved, even if it was all part of a fantasy that could never last.

Archer's hot palm slid along Ryan's thigh, brushing aside his robe and burning a trail through the thin cotton of his pajamas as they kissed. Up and down he rubbed, slowly massaging, making Ryan's cock stiffen and throb in anticipation with each stroke. He raked his nails over the sensitive skin of Ryan's inner thigh, and Ryan held his breath as his muscles twitched in response. He was hard and aching, and all without his cock even being touched.

In seconds Archer had undone the drawstring of his pants and wedged his hand inside, giving Ryan's erection a squeeze that made his eyes roll back in his head and a moan escape his lips.

"A little excited, eh?" Archer teased before taking his mouth again. *If he only knew*, Ryan thought before his brain dissolved into mush. His skin was on fire, and he loved it. Maybe it was the wine, maybe it was the moonlight, but he didn't feel like himself.

Mouths locked, Ryan delved beneath Archer's well-worn T-shirt and let his hand wander over the smooth planes of his chest. His fingers stilled briefly on the ring Archer wore on a chain around his neck before moving on. He plucked a hard nipple, felt Archer's shudder, and smiled. He did it again, this time drawing a groan from Archer's throat.

Archer continued to jack him slowly, his grip loose enough to be considered torture. Distracted, Ryan fumbled with Archer's fly, gave up and thrust his hand under the loose-fitting waistband, eager to get to what lay beneath. He inhaled sharply when he encountered only bare skin—Archer was commando—and the discovery fired his blood. He curled his fingers tight around Archer's erection, delighted when the flesh swelled further.

"Christ that feels good," Archer murmured against his mouth. Ryan moaned his agreement. Archer's dick filled his palm, thicker in the middle and narrower near the tip. The skin slid easily with each stroke. Archer's breath came in short bursts.

"How much have you had to drink?" he demanded roughly.

"Why?"

"Because I want to know if I can take advantage of you or not."

"That's so honorable of you."

"It is, isn't it?"

Ryan chuckled. "Only one glass. And yes."

"Yes?"

"Yes, you can take advantage. But not yet." With a final, lingering squeeze to Archer's cock, Ryan pulled away from the kiss and rose to his feet. This might be the only chance he got with a man like Archer Noble—he didn't want it to be over too quickly.

"What are you doing?" Archer asked, his voice thick with what might be desire.

Ryan let his robe slide to the ground, then drew his shirt over his head and tossed it in Archer's direction. With a tug on the drawstring, his pajama pants dropped to his ankles. Free at last, his cock sprang up in the warm night air, and he gave it a quick stroke. He was a different person tonight. Reckless. Exciting. "Skinny-dipping. Want to join me?"

"I can't swim, remember?" Archer replied, clearly amused.

"It's barely four feet deep in the shallow end. About time you learned, isn't it?" Could Archer see him in the dark as he stood there naked? The stars were bright and his pale, Scandinavian skin must stand out a little bit.

"What about the neighbors?" The swing squeaked as Archer stood. Ryan heard the rustle of clothes being discarded and wished he could see more than Archer's outline in the darkness.

"It's a high fence. And if I can barely see you, they won't be able to," he replied.

"Ah, but I can see *you*."

"You can?"

"Mmm, you're sort of glowing."

The thought sent a surge of excitement racing through Ryan's veins. He walked away, putting an extra flounce in his step, knowing that Archer followed somewhere behind him. As he descended the four stairs into the shallow end of the pool, the water slid over his skin like silk, lapping at his thighs and caressing his sensitive dick. Ryan hummed in appreciation.

"Enjoying yourself?" Archer asked, close by.

"Yeah. Feels good. I wish I'd thought of this before." He slipped beneath the cool water, swam out to the middle of the pool where he fanned his arms and watched Archer's silhouette cautiously descend the stairs. When Archer was waist-deep, Ryan submerged, using his hands to guide himself along the pool floor until he popped up directly in front of Archer. The other man started.

Ryan's buoyant cock knocked against Archer's. "Ever had sex in a pool?"

"Does a hot tub count?"

"Oh." Ryan bit his lip. Of course he had. There probably wasn't any place he hadn't had sex. Compared to Archer he might as well be a virgin.

"It's overrated," Archer continued. "Chlorine is hell on rubbers. But a handjob is good. Everything feels slower under water."

"Yeah? Like this?" Ryan found Archer's cock and jacked it slowly. The contrast of Archer's hot pulsing flesh in his hand and the coolness of the water was one more stimulation. He leaned down for a kiss, distracting Archer long enough to ease them both into deeper water.

Archer tensed when it covered his shoulders. "That was a dirty trick."

"Don't worry, I've got you. Turn around," Ryan instructed, keeping a steadying hand on Archer's back. He stiffened, but after a brief moment of hesitation, Archer complied. Ryan's cock snugged the curve of his ass, making them both shiver. He couldn't help wondering what it would be like to top him. It probably didn't happen very often if the man's blog was any indication. "Now, lean back against me and let your legs come up. Let yourself float."

"I'll sink."

"No, you won't. Trust me."

And surprisingly Archer did. He let Ryan take his weight by increments, until he was lying prone on the surface.

"There you go. Now relax your body."

Still in the shallow end, Ryan stood at Archer's head, resting his hands beneath Archer's shoulders although they were in fact, doing almost nothing. He used the lightest of touches to float Archer across the pool. In this position he could stare all he wanted at Archer's smooth body. Archer had almost no body hair, only a scattering around his groin, and when the clouds thinned, unveiling a nearly full moon, the silver light cascaded over his skin and made him shine. Unable to help himself, Ryan freed one hand to stroke his chest, whereupon Archer jerked in surprise and sank like a stone. Ryan hauled him upright, trying not to laugh as he spat out a mouthful of water.

"Sorry, I got carried away. Do you need mouth-to-mouth?"

Ryan was grasped tightly around the waist, an arm anchoring him to Archer. He immediately grew hard again, and harder still when one of Archer's hands went wandering and delved between his ass cheeks. He squeaked.

"You're a bit of a tease, aren't you?" Archer asked on a chuckle, his breath hot on Ryan's neck as he licked a trail up to Ryan's earlobe.

"Aren't you only a tease if you don't live up to your promises?" he rejoined before slipping out of Archer's hold and ducking back under the water. He swam to the far end of the pool and clung to the coping.

"And you plan on living up to your promises?"

"Come over here and find out," Ryan challenged. He bit his lip. Would Archer actually do it? There was only a yard or two separating them, but Archer would have to swim it.

"That's blackmail."

"It's called the reward system," he returned.

Archer grumbled something beneath his breath, and then he sent up a huge geyser as he splashed and kicked his way across the short distance, churning up so much water it was a wonder he didn't rouse the neighbors. When he arrived, sputtering and coughing, he grabbed the edge of the pool, trapping Ryan between his arms.

"Now, I believe there was something about a reward," he said archly.

Ryan drew in a breath to laugh, but it was cut short by Archer's demanding lips, and ended up being more of a sigh. Their bodies bobbed weightlessly, rubbing together, floating apart, connected only by their joined mouths. It was one of the most erotic experiences of Ryan's life.

At least until Ryan forgot where he was, wrapped his arms around Archer's neck, and they both went under. He pulled a gasping and spitting Archer up to the surface. "Enough of this shit," Archer croaked. "I'd like to make it through the night without drowning." With one hand on the coping, Archer guided himself back to the safety of shallower water, leaving Ryan to hang back, hoping he hadn't ruined the moment.

He didn't have long to wonder because Archer stopped at the stairs and sat down on the top step where the water pooled around his hips. There was enough moonlight now for Ryan to watch as Archer jacked himself leisurely. Ryan's dick throbbed in response, as if Archer had touched *him* instead. Mesmerized, he floated up to the stairs, crouched on the step below, his hand mirroring Archer's slow strokes on his own dick. When Archer parted his thighs, Ryan moved wordlessly between them and took over.

Archer's hand went to the back of Ryan's neck, guiding him closer, leaving no doubt as to what he expected for his reward. "I'm clean," he said, when Ryan hesitated. Caution was tossed aside as Ryan's mouth flooded with saliva. He wanted this. With an eager grin he hoped Archer couldn't see, Ryan bent his head and licked up the underside of Archer's shaft from root to tip, where he paused to flick his tongue over the slit repeatedly until Archer hissed. The chemical taste of chlorine gave way to the salty, musky taste of Archer's skin. With a little groan, Ryan closed his lips over the head of Archer's cock, and his eyes slid shut in pleasure. Archer urged him to take more.

Ryan immediately bobbed and twisted the way Kenny had liked. Archer's hand fisted in his hair.

"Slow down, a bit," he chuckled. "Yeah, like that."

Ryan hummed in agreement. He liked slower better too.

"Are you guys swimming?" The sound of Dillon's voice split the quiet backyard. Archer pitched forward into deeper water, taking Ryan with him and sending up a splash.

"Holy shit," he hissed.

Ryan crouched low, knowing the darkness and the water must shield their nudity but still unable to control his racing heart. "Dillon, what are you doing up?"

"I wanted a drink of water, and I heard you out here." Dillon's slender frame was silhouetted in the doorway.

"Last time I checked the kitchen was inside," Archer grumbled.

"Can I swim too?" Dillon asked.

"No," Ryan cried.

"But it's hot—"

"Not tonight, Dillon," Archer instructed, his tone firm. "This is adult time. Go back to bed."

"I never get to have any fun," Dillon griped as he trooped inside.

"Oh my God," Ryan breathed as soon as the patio door slid closed. Behind him, Archer had begun to chuckle. He swung around. "It's not funny."

"It's a little bit funny. Cockblocked by a seven-year-old. I can honestly say that's a first for me."

The last thing Ryan needed was a reminder of Archer's exciting sex life. What had he been thinking? He wasn't someone else. He was boring vanilla Ryan Eriksson. And this was Archer Noble. If he wasn't careful, he would end up as fodder for tomorrow's blog post. He shot to his feet and climbed out of the pool.

Archer whispered a curse. "Oh, come on, Ryan, wait—"

But he didn't. He stalked toward the swing where he'd left his clothes, only to have the floodlights in Mrs. Benning's yard next door burst on, blinding him. He yelped and ran for the shadows, grabbing whatever was in reach and darting into the house. Fortunately, Dillon was nowhere to be seen.

Archer strolled in seconds later as Ryan was struggling into his robe—the silk clung to his wet skin and made things difficult. Archer, damn him, was still nude, his cock not entirely soft either. He grinned. "I am so glad I didn't go out tonight."

"Put something on," Ryan snapped, thrusting his own pajama pants at Archer. "There are kids in this house, remember?"

"How could I forget?" Archer held the pants in front of him but didn't put them on. "Relax, I don't think he saw anything. If he had, there'd have been a lot more questions."

Now that his heart rate had slowed, and he was decently covered, a nervous giggle tickled Ryan's throat. Archer was right. Unable to hold it back any longer, he grinned. "Okay, it's a *little* funny."

"Uh-huh. The risk of getting caught always spices things up."

And Archer would know all about that. This was a man who boasted about having sex on a New York City subway train. Ryan sobered. "What are we doing?"

"Having fun?" Archer took a step closer. He tugged the belt of Ryan's robe open, parted the sides, and pulled Ryan's nude body against his. Despite himself, Ryan's penis hardened at the skin to skin contact.

"This isn't a good idea," he protested.

"I think it's a fantastic idea." Archer put his mouth on Ryan's neck, licked a path up to his earlobe, and then sucked on it.

"Maybe you should use that app of yours. Order up some—"

"Shut up, Ryan." Archer's hands slid into Ryan's hair, drawing his head down and cutting off his words with a kiss.

When he was released, Ryan could barely remember his name, let alone why he wouldn't want this. He sighed. "It's so much easier to resist you when you're being a dick."

"I know." Archer chuckled. Locking the sliding glass doors, he then raised a finger to his lips and tugged Ryan's hand, urging him to follow.

Once upstairs, Archer locked the bedroom door behind them. "Just in case," he said with a lopsided grin, advancing on Ryan whose skin prickled with electricity as he let the silk robe slide off his shoulders. He was probably about to make the stupidest mistake of his life, and he didn't even care.

Then his body was flush against Archer's in the dark, and Archer's mouth was on his. They fell onto the bed in tangle of limbs. Ryan didn't know what he'd expected from Archer as a lover, but it wasn't this: the slow kisses all over his body, the leisurely—almost reverent—touches, the way Archer patiently showed him exactly what he liked. Spurred on by Archer's murmured encouragement, Ryan's inhibitions slipped, and he let his desire to explore, to taste, take over.

And he quickly learned that yes, indeed, there was something to be said for chemistry after all.

Chapter 14

"What's wrong with Ryan today?"

Archer reluctantly tore his gaze from the hypnotizing sway of Ryan's ass up ahead and shut the door on memories of that pale skin shining in the moonlight; warm, vanilla-scented skin; the firm, rock-hard feel of that butt beneath his fingers when he'd squeezed; the way Ryan had held his breath when Archer had taken him right to the back of his throat. Fuck, he was doing it again.

It took remarkable effort, but Archer managed to focus on the boy beside him. They were on their way to the nearby park, Ryan and Emma walking several paces in front holding hands, and Dillon and Archer bringing up the rear.

Archer let his gaze dart back to Ryan. "What do you mean?"

"He put regular milk on my cereal this morning, and he knows I don't like it. And Emma's wearing two different socks."

Archer brightened. Considering he'd woken up horny and alone, and not entirely happy about it, only a few hours ago, the day suddenly seemed a whole lot better. It looked like he wasn't the only one distracted this morning. Was that a good thing? Frankly, he was a little confused. He'd pegged Ryan to be the dreamy, romantic sort, had half-expected to find the man snuggled up against him this morning—an early morning quickie wouldn't have been at all objectionable. But no, the bed had been empty except for the lingering scent of vanilla on the sheets. And other than a slight tensing of his shoulders at breakfast, Ryan hadn't acted any differently than usual.

Now Archer was left trying to figure out why it bothered him so much. They hadn't even fucked.

But if Dillon was right, maybe Ryan wasn't as unaffected as he pretended. "He must have something on his mind," he replied, doing his best to sound casual.

"Like what?"

"Uh. Like school?"

Dillon appeared to think that one over for a little while. "Does Ryan really have to leave?"

Archer tried to come up with an appropriate answer. He'd been wondering the same thing lately. Ever since his breakdown in the office. Maybe before that. Every time he thought of Ryan not being there, the tight feeling in his chest grew. It was because of Emma and Dillon he told himself. He'd accepted responsibility for the kids, but the thought of being entirely on his own terrified him. Sure he could hire a nanny or a babysitter, but it wouldn't be the same. He liked Ryan—he was the closest thing to a friend Archer could remember having. Things would be so much easier if he stuck around.

But in the back of his mind he knew it was more. There was an attraction there, different from what he was used to, but surprisingly strong and unsettling. Seeing Ryan hurting last night had brought out something in him he thought long gone. The need to comfort someone and make them happy.

He shook his head. What was happening to him? When had Ryan become so . . . essential? The sudden urge to run made his mouth go dry. His thoughts flickered back to the contract offer he'd received from the network on Friday—the one that said he needed to be in Vancouver by the middle of November—and his stomach squirmed.

"Uncle Archie, are you okay?"

Archer realized Dillon was waiting for his response. He tugged down the brim of Dillon's baseball cap. "He has a life to get back to, bud. He's already spent his whole summer with us. It's not fair to keep him all to ourselves."

"He might stay if we asked him too." Dillon turned his face to Archer, as if he expected him to do the asking. But Archer looked away. A minute later, Dillon spoke again. "Will you play soccer with me when we get to the park, Uncle Archie?"

"I can try. But I don't really know how."

"Didn't your dad teach you?"

Archer held back his snort. What dad? Growing up, he hadn't missed his unknown father one bit—he couldn't miss what he never had—but now he was aware of all the things he didn't know because no one had taught him. He couldn't ride a bike, or swim, or hit a baseball. How would he help Dillon grow up to be a man if he didn't know the first thing about it himself? He bet Ryan knew how to do those things.

But that was way too complicated to explain to a seven-year-old, so he settled for saying, "I didn't have a dad around."

"My dad didn't teach me either," Dillon said with a sad little shrug. "He didn't have time. He was always working."

Archer reeled. Was Ryan right? Was simply being there more important than being good at something?

"Sometimes I don't remember what Daddy looked like," Dillon confessed in a small voice. "I have to look at his picture."

"That's normal. You were very young."

"I don't want to forget Mommy too."

Archer's throat tightened. He wished he had something comforting to say to Dillon—Ryan would. For a man who made his living with words, he sure wasn't good at the important ones. "We'll make sure we don't forget her, okay?"

In response, Dillon slipped his hand into Archer's and an unexpected warmth filled his chest.

"I can teach you to play soccer," Dillon offered. "All you have to do is kick the ball." He was clearly trying to play it cool, like it didn't matter, but his eyes were filled with a hope Archer couldn't resist.

"I'd like that, bud," he replied and Dillon's excited grin made him chuckle.

Ryan and Emma arrived at the park first and went immediately to the swings. One of the boys on the jungle gym called to Dillon and waved.

"Oh, it's Tucker. Can I go play with him?" Dillon asked, thrusting the soccer ball into Archer's hands.

"Jeez, ditched already," Archer grumbled playfully. "What happened to soccer?"

"Oh." Dillon bit his lip.

"I'm kidding. You can teach me another time. Go play." Archer gave him a smile and a wave, and the kid was off. It was good to see him excited again.

Abandoned, Archer wandered toward the swings where Ryan pushed a giggling Emma. Ryan didn't say a word at his approach, but he tensed, and Archer had to hide another smile.

"Want to talk about last night?" he asked.

"Not really." Ryan was wearing that silly floppy hat of his, and the wide brim obscured most of his face. But when he turned his head, Archer's attention was caught by the sweep of color staining his neck and the visible flutter of his pulse beneath the open collar of his polo shirt. Instantly Archer was transported back to memories of that long, lean body sliding against his.

"Huh, I always thought you'd be the type to talk it to death," he managed to say, frowning a little at the depth of his attraction.

The push Ryan gave Emma was harder this time. She giggled as she flew higher. "I guess today's your lucky day, then."

"Does that mean we can do it again?"

The swing came back and caught Ryan in the chest. He staggered back. "Of course not. It was a one-time thing," he said. But the next push he missed entirely.

Archer grinned to see the man so rattled. "That's too bad. I thought we both had a good time." Good enough to know he didn't like the thought of it not happening anymore.

"It complicates things."

"It doesn't have to," Archer pointed out, although he wasn't so sure he believed that. At least Ryan wasn't denying that he'd enjoyed it.

"Yeah, for me I think it does." Ryan sighed. "Last night . . . we needed each other. That's all. It doesn't change anything. I'm trying to mend a relationship, remember?"

Kenny. Archer grimaced. He'd forgotten about the other man. He'd swear Ryan had too.

"I . . . uh . . . I'm going to check on Dillon. Will you take over?" Ryan walked away without waiting for a response.

Archer grinned as he stepped into place and gave Emma a push. Even with Ryan shooting him down, he felt good. Damn good, actually. And he had no idea why. Ryan had a point about things getting complicated. He was Mr. White-Picket-Fence. He wanted love and commitment and a family of his own, and those were things Archer wasn't prepared to offer. Ryan was partner material. *Permanent* partner material. And yet, that suddenly didn't seem as scary as it had earlier.

"Why are you smiling?" Emma asked over her shoulder. "Did Ryan make you happy?"

"I guess he did, Monkey." Archer's eyes tracked the younger man as he headed over to the play area. A little girl with pigtails ran up to him excitedly, and Ryan smiled and bent down to talk to her. She was soon joined by a woman who appeared to be the girl's mother.

"He makes me happy too. That's why I like him."

Archer paused. Could it really be that simple? He was starting to think these kids were smarter than he gave them credit for.

"But I like you too, Uncle Archie," Emma added almost guiltily. The burst of pleasure in his gut caught Archer by surprise, and he felt his lips stretch wide, unable to hold back his grin. "Do you like *me*?" she asked.

Archer caught the swing by the chains and brought it to a halt. Emma peered up at him expectantly. "No, Monkey." He forced the words past the thickness in his throat. "I *love* you." He glanced in Ryan's direction. "I've never said that to anyone except your mom. So let's keep that our secret for now, okay?"

Emma nodded with a wide smile. When Archer checked again, there were two more women hovering around Ryan and at least half a dozen kids of varying ages. They all seemed to know each other and were talking animatedly. "He *is* freaking Mary Poppins."

"No, he's not," Emma said with a frown. "He doesn't have an umbrella."

Archer's laugh burst from him before he could contain it. Ryan looked his way, and then seeing everything was fine, turned back to his fans. Jealousy stirred uncomfortably in Archer's belly. Ryan was *theirs*. He didn't want to share him.

Archer plucked Emma off the swing. "Let's go see what Ryan's up to, shall we?"

"But I'm not done. I want to swing some more."

"We'll come back later, okay?"

"Promise?"

"I promise." He tugged on her hand, but Emma refused to move.

"And you'll push me really high? As high as the big kids?"

Archer gaped at Emma. Blackmailed by a five-year-old. How far he had fallen. "That's not safe. I'll push you higher than Ryan. How's that?" Since Ryan hadn't let her go much above a gentle swing, his compromise wouldn't be too dangerous. At any rate, his answer seemed to appease Emma, and she let him lead her away.

He approached the circle with Emma in tow just in time to hear one of the women gushing over having her kid in Ryan's class this year.

"Hi," Archer said, coming up behind Ryan.

"Uncle Archie loves me," Emma proclaimed.

Archer squeezed her fingers. So much for secrets.

"I'm sure he does, Em," Ryan said patiently, his smile slipping a fraction when there was a quick, collective intake of breath as all eyes turned to Archer.

"Oh, is this your partner, Mr. Eriksson?" one of the mothers asked, her eyes wide as she looked him up and down.

"What? Oh, no."

Archer frowned at how swiftly Ryan shot down that presumption, and some perverse part of him wondered what it would be like to be at the side of a man whom everyone adored

"This is Archer. Archer Noble. He's Emma and Dillon's uncle." He fumbled with a round of introductions, the only sign he wasn't his usual implacable self.

The thing Archer liked most about large, cosmopolitan cities was that no one cared where he came from. Doors weren't slammed in his face because of the color of his skin or shape of his eyes. But he'd never been surrounded by a swarm of white, upper-middle-class mothers before, and the experience was more unnerving than standing naked at an orgy waiting to be judged. As the silence became uncomfortable and no one made eye contact, every insult he'd ever received flooded back in a tidal wave of insecurity. He was too poor, too dumb, too damn Cree to belong here. Archer steeled himself for hostility.

"We're . . . we're so sorry for your loss," stammered a tall, poised brunette with a razor-sharp bob. "If there's anything you need . . ."

The others nodded vigorously, clearly relieved she had taken charge. Ah, he got it now. They're weren't hostile, just struggling with an awkward situation.

"We'd love to have Dillon over," added another woman—this one wearing designer jeans that probably cost more than he earned in a month. "We're off to the lake again this week, but perhaps when we get back?"

A smart retort sprang to his lips, but Archer could hear Ryan's voice in his head warning him to be nice, so he smiled and said he'd have to check with Dillon. He may not have ever wanted kids of his own, but he knew how it worked. Stick with the popular kids and you'd be safe. For Emma and Dillon's sake, he had to get along with these women, make a good impression. He didn't want them to go through the same hell he had at school.

A second later an angry squeal from the direction of the jungle gym drew the group's attention. Archer's stomach lurched as he saw the familiar flash of Dillon's bright-red shirt through the haze of dirt being kicked up by the two fighting boys.

"Tucker!" one of the women cried.

"Is that Dillon?" Ryan asked, astonished.

Archer dropped Emma's hand and ran toward the skirmish. He reached the grappling boys before the others and pulled Dillon out from underneath the other kid, his arms and legs still flailing wildly. As his initial panic faded, Archer struggled to contain the anger flooding in to take its place. He wanted to get in there and pummel the bigger boy himself, teach the bully a lesson about picking on smaller kids.

"He started it," Tucker accused, pointing his stubby finger straight at Dillon as his mother—the tall brunette as it turned out—pulled him to his feet and brushed off his clothes.

Archer felt the fight go out of Dillon and loosened his hold a bit.

"Dillon?" Ryan scoffed. "I don't think—"

"Fuck you," Dillon yelled at Tucker. Jaws dropped as the epithet burst from his lips, even Ryan's.

"Dillon, apologize to Tucker," Ryan ordered, his voice tight, his face red.

"I won't." Dillon broke free from Archer, shoved Ryan aside, and ran. The look on Ryan's face was both heartbroken and dumbfounded, and for the first time since they'd met, Archer saw him at a loss.

"I'll go," he volunteered and jogged after Dillon. He could deal with angry little boys better than ruffled feathers. Several yards ahead, he saw Dillon dart through the park gates and out onto the street where he disappeared from view, blocked by an overgrown evergreen hedge. He shouted Dillon's name, but the kid ignored him. A fear unlike any he'd ever known clawed at his gut, and Archer quickened his pace.

Is this what he was getting into? A lifetime of emotional ups and downs? Worrying himself sick every time they were out of his sight? Was it worth it? It wasn't too late to change his mind.

What if Dillon ran away? What if some stranger plucked him off the street? Or he was hit by a speeding car? There were so many dangers out there, and Dillon was only a boy. *If you think this is bad,* his head counseled, *wait until they're teenagers.*

By the time Archer found Dillon sitting on the sidewalk curb outside the park gates, his heart was thundering and his stomach was somewhere up around his throat from imagining all sorts of horrible scenarios. Relief made his knees weak. Thank God Dillon had had enough sense not to run far.

He approached cautiously. Dillon didn't look up. "Care to explain what just happened?"

"No."

"The Dillon I know would never hurt someone. What would your mother say?"

"She's dead," he spat. "She can't say anything."

Archer sighed and sat on the curb next to Dillon. "Was he bullying you?" He knew firsthand how cruel kids could be. Dillon would have it doubly bad with his Native blood and Archer as his uncle. His throat closed up as he imagined all the taunts and insults headed their way.

"It was Sam. Sam made me do it."

Ah, yes. The imaginary friend reared his head again. "Why?"

Dillon's head hung so low it rested on his chest. He mumbled something Archer didn't quite catch. "Sorry, can you repeat that?"

"Tucker said we didn't have a mommy."

Archer blinked. Of all the things he'd been expecting, that hadn't been it. "Well, he's not entirely wrong. You have a mom—she's just not with us anymore."

Dillon dug the heel of his shoe into the crease of dirt where pavement met sidewalk. "Sam didn't mean to do it. But he got so mad," he whispered. "It's not fair."

"No, it's not." Archer tentatively touched the boy's small shoulder. Dillon was more like him than he'd first thought. "There's always going to be people who make you angry, Dillon. *Things* that make you angry. But you can't lash out at the world. Because then you hurt people you don't mean to hurt." Wow. Where had that come from?

Dillon regarded him with glistening eyes. "What do I do then?"

He couldn't help notice that Dillon hadn't brought up Sam's name this time. "When you get angry, simply walk away. Or better yet, come talk to me. Sam too."

Dillon jumped to his feet. "How can I?" he shouted. "You won't even be there."

"Of course—"

He burst into tears. "Ryan's leaving and you're leaving, and we have to go live with another family."

"Whoa, whoa, whoa. Where did you hear all this?"

"I *heard* you. You said you don't want us." Dillon's sobs wrenched Archer's heart. How long had Dillon kept this inside and worried over it? He felt like a monster.

"I'm so sorry, Dillon. I didn't know . . . I didn't mean any of that. I was scared."

"You?"

"Yes, me. I get scared too. But I'm not going anywhere, okay?" He had no idea how he was going to manage a career and a family, but somehow, he'd make it work. "Whatever happens, we're going to stick together—you, me, and Emma." Hearing the words out loud made Archer start. His decision had already been made weeks ago, but now it was real. He'd made a promise. And there was no breaking it.

"Really? You mean it?" The look on Dillon's face brought Archer dangerously close to tears.

"I mean it." He pulled Dillon into his arms and hugged him. "I might make mistakes sometimes," he warned. "But I'll try my best not to."

"It's okay to make mistakes," Dillon said, his face pressed to Archer's shirtfront. "Ryan says that's the best way to learn stuff."

Archer closed his eyes and held on tight. Damn kids, always saying things that choked him up. They sat like that for a few minutes longer before Dillon raised his head. "Do I still have to apologize?" The tears had left tracks on his dusty cheeks, and Archer wiped them away with the hem of his shirt.

"What do you think?"

Dillon made a face. "But it was Sam."

"Unless Sam can go over there and apologize to Tucker, you'll have to do it for him. Oh yeah, and maybe his mom too for that potty mouth of yours." Dillon groaned as Archer urged him to stand up. "Think about that next time you or Sam drop the f-bomb," he added.

"Am I going to be punished?"

Archer floundered. "We'll talk about it later, at home. Now, go."

As Dillon ran back to the playground, Archer kept an eye on him. That was it? That wasn't so bad. Hell, he'd passed the first test, and he was elated. He felt like a goddamned hero. Except for the little hitch in his chest when he caught sight of Ryan standing silently a few feet away. He'd been watching them.

As Archer narrowed the gap between them, he wanted to snatch off those mirrored sunglasses he could see Ryan's eyes and tell what he was thinking. Was he proud? Suddenly Ryan's praise was the most important thing in the world. And that worried him. "Okay, you can say it," he said.

"What?"

"I did good."

Ryan pursed his lips together. "I'm pretty sure I already told you that you would. Your ego doesn't need any more stroking."

"Maybe not my ego . . ." Archer winked. Ryan shook his head, but he was smiling as he walked away, and there was a new strut to his walk if Archer wasn't mistaken.

"Don't I get a hug? You always hug the kids when they do something good," Archer called after him. "Oh, come on. You want to hug me. You know you do."

Ryan turned around and gave him the finger.

Archer threw back his head and let out the laugh he'd been holding in.

Archer's good humor lasted until they reached home. Even Emma clinging to his back because she professed to be too tired to walk didn't dampen his mood. The car in the driveway did.

The shiny black Beemer was parked behind his rented compact sedan, inconsiderately hanging over the sidewalk. As they approached, the driver's-side door opened, and Kenny Lee stepped out. Beside Archer, Ryan stiffened.

"Well, shit," Archer muttered, slowing his steps enough to let Ryan go on ahead and enjoy a bit of privacy with his ex. "This guy doesn't give up, does he?"

Dillon turned to him. "That's a bad word. You're not supposed to say it."

"Okay, potty mouth," Archer retorted, his attention focused on the line of Ryan's back as he spoke to his ex. Did Ryan seem a bit tense or was that his imagination? He hoped Ryan kicked the guy to the curb. Anyone who would crush the dreams of a man as good and decent as Ryan deserved— Archer shut that thought down, not liking where it was headed.

As he watched, Kenny reached back into the car and withdrew a large bouquet of red roses.

Archer snorted. "Flowers? Like that's going to work."

"Ryan likes flowers," Emma chimed in his ear. Damn, she was right. Ryan was always bringing fresh-cut flowers home.

"But his favorites are daisies," added Dillon.

"That sounds like him. Roses are so pretentious."

"What's pretentious?"

"Showing off," Archer responded. His gut twisted as Ryan gave Kenny a long hug and a quick kiss on the lips, then took his arm and led him up the front steps. *No way.* Archer growled. What the hell did Ryan see in this guy? Had he forgotten all the things Kenny had said?

"It's okay, Uncle Archie," Dillon advised. "Me and Emma don't like him either."

"You don't?"

"He doesn't make Ryan smile."

"Yeah, well, neither do I, kiddo," Archer grumbled and then wanted to kick himself. When had that become important?

"Yes, you do."

"What?"

"Ryan smiles all the time." Dillon cocked his head, thinking. "Well, except when you make him mad."

"How come I've never seen it?"

"I don't know. Maybe you're not looking."

With his stomach knotting, Archer marched forward and up the steps. He sent the kids off to wash their hands before lunch and followed the hum of voices to the kitchen. He should probably warn Kenny about overhanging the sidewalk or he was likely to get a ticket. But then he found the two men in the kitchen, with Kenny's hand resting on the small of Ryan's back and any good intentions flew out the window.

"You remember Kenny, right?" Ryan asked. He sounded a bit breathless.

Archer smiled tightly. "Oh, I remember Kenny." Kenny shook his hand, obviously not catching the thinly veiled sarcasm, but Archer was sure Ryan did based on the way he eyed both of them nervously. "Ryan's told me a lot about you."

"I hope it wasn't all bad."

Archer shrugged one shoulder. "Not *all*." He grabbed a water bottle from the fridge and juice boxes for the kids. "Roses, huh?" he commented, peeking over Ryan's shoulder as he filled a vase with water and arranged the bouquet. "I'm partial to daisies myself."

Ryan dropped the vase in the sink with a clatter. When he turned around, his face was flushed. "Kenny's staying for lunch," he announced. It sounded like a challenge to Archer.

"Is he?"

"Actually, I was hoping I could take you out," Kenny interrupted.

Archer folded his arms across his chest and leaned back against the counter. Kenny shot him a glare, obviously hoping for a little more privacy. But this was Archer's house now. He wasn't going anywhere. "Ryan and I have an agreement about personal time. He's not free until next weekend."

Kenny's lips thinned. "He doesn't work for you, you know."

Ryan stepped smoothly between them. He narrowed his eyes at Archer. "Maybe you should check on the kids while I get things ready."

He was reluctant to leave them alone. He didn't like Kenny, and he especially didn't want the preppy, BMW-driving douche bag taking further advantage of Ryan. Exactly why he was so concerned was something Archer preferred not to think about. He was *not* jealous—after all, Kenny was an underperformer in the bedroom department. But someone needed to look out for Ryan's best interests.

"How much longer are you planning on being here?" he heard Kenny ask as he left the kitchen. Archer stopped and spun around. He wanted to hear this answer as well.

Ryan's eyes flew to his face, uncertain; he held his gaze for a second, as if asking a question, before dropping it. "I promised to stay until September."

Kenny groaned. "That's still two weeks away."

Archer's gaze bore holes into the long line of Ryan's back. There it was. Confirmed. No less than what he'd been expecting. Still, hearing Ryan say the words had wrenched something inside his chest. He turned and left.

As he neared the upstairs landing, he heard giggles coming from Emma's bedroom. When he poked his head in, he found Dillon and Emma huddled close together on the floor, whispering. "What are you up to?" he asked.

"Nothing," they both chorused, smiling back a little too innocently.

"Is lunch ready?" Dillon asked as he jumped to his feet.

"Almost. Go and help Ryan. And keep an eye on that Kenny character," he added.

Dillon grinned. "Don't worry, Uncle Archie."

"Yeah, don't worry," Emma chimed.

Archer winced as suspicion gnawed at his gut. They were definitely up to something. He knew trouble when he saw it.

Chapter 15

Ryan had no clue what was happening.

From his position at the head of the table on the patio, he watched in alarm as the usually polite kids devoured their hamburgers like animals, and Kenny and Archer patently ignored each other. The tension between the two men was so thick he could practically see it.

How had he ended up in this alternate universe where sweet and gentle Dillon got into fights on the playground and cursed like a sailor, where Archer Noble was a charming, considerate lover who acted an awful lot like a possessive boyfriend? He wondered if last night had completely addled his brain.

Last night. Ryan ruthlessly pushed the memory aside even as his eyes unwillingly drifted to Archer. Heat flashed below his skin and had to look away. He thought he'd been too smart to get all mushy-headed and goo-goo-eyed over a guy simply because the sex had been good.

Better than good.

Great.

Guilt cramped his stomach. He'd slept with Archer. Knowingly and willingly. He was a cheater. But then, he hadn't made Kenny any promises. They were only *talking* about getting back together. And he was sure Kenny hadn't exactly been lonely the past eight months. At least that's the way he'd rationalized it to himself this morning. And it wasn't like it was ever going to happen again.

That didn't make his lapse any easier to swallow, however. Maybe he'd made a mistake in inviting Kenny to lunch, but he'd been desperate to avoid spending more time alone with Archer.

"So, you're a lawyer, then, Ken?" Archer broke the strained silence.

"Yes. At Bingham, Bingham, and Bernstein." Kenny's voice crept up a notch.

"They snapped Kenny up as soon as he passed the bar," Ryan added with a touch of pride. "He finished top of his class at law school." Since Ryan's job had financially supported them both the last two years, allowing Kenny to concentrate full-time on his studies, he felt like he'd been part of his success. They had done it *together*. He smiled fondly, recalling all the nights they'd lain awake in bed, talking about the future and how Kenny would rise through the ranks. He remembered waiting anxiously by Kenny's side for his exam results and their private celebration when he landed the generous offer.

"What kind of bar?" Emma asked, drawing him back to the present.

"It's a test," Archer told her. "If you pass it, you can become a lawyer."

"I got perfect on my last spelling test," Dillon crowed, then scowled when he saw no one was paying attention.

"I'm the youngest lawyer on staff." Kenny slipped into the tone he used when he was trying to impress. Judging by Archer's raised eyebrows, he wasn't.

"You must put in a lot of hours, then. Pretty hard to have a personal life, start a family, that sort of thing."

Ryan frowned. What was Archer up to?

Kenny shrugged. "It is, but it's part of the sacrifice. Ryan is the most understanding person I know." Kenny took Ryan's hand and gave his fingers an affectionate squeeze. "It'll be worth it."

The table jerked beneath his elbow, snapping Ryan back to attention. His fork clattered to the ground, and when he bent to pick it up, he saw Dillon kick the table leg again.

"Dillon," he cautioned. "Stop it."

"It's not me. It's Sam."

They really were going to have to do something about this imaginary friend of Dillon's. Actually, it would be Archer's problem now. Ryan frowned again.

"Unless Sam wants to get sent to your room, he had better quit it," Archer warned. Dillon smiled gamely but stilled his foot, then glanced at his sister and then back down to his plate. Something was brewing, Ryan could feel it.

Archer leaned back in his chair, a tight smile playing on his lips as he stared at Kenny. "Ryan's definitely understanding," he agreed. "Maybe *too* understanding." His gaze locked on Ryan's and softened. "He's done so much around here. I could never have managed without him."

Ryan coughed as his last bite went down the wrong way. Would he ever figure this man out? The arrogant jerk who'd walked into this house nearly two months ago was easy to dislike. But the man who ran after Dillon today, the man who gave compliments and flirted and laughed and comforted him last night? That Archer Noble was dangerous. Which was the real one?

"Yeah, he's great that way." Kenny smiled at him too, but a hint of unease prickled the back of Ryan's neck.

He jumped when the table shuddered. "Dillon, I said stop kicking the table," he snapped, grabbing his fork before it skittered off the patio table once more.

"I'm not kicking the table," Dillon replied sullenly, his voice dripping with all the attitude a seven-year-old could muster. "I'm kicking the *umbrella*."

"Well, quit it," added Archer. Ryan didn't miss the glance he gave Dillon. He seemed to be trying to convey a message Ryan didn't understand. Maybe Archer would have more success with Dillon because Ryan appeared to have lost his touch.

"I just got this new case," Kenny announced with a visible burst of excitement, apparently heedless of the strange undercurrent gathering around the table. He paused to cut his hamburger into bite sized pieces, leaving the bun untouched on the side of his plate. "It could be a big one for me. Get me noticed."

"That's great, Kenny," Ryan enthused. Kenny looked so happy, he couldn't help but get caught up in the news too. "I know how hard you've worked for this."

"Bor-ing," Dillon muttered under his breath.

Archer choked on his iced tea. He carefully set the glass down. "Speaking of being noticed, you should have seen today at the park," he said with a wink. "I turned around and there's Ryan, surrounded by his mommy fan club. Seriously, it's like hanging out with a rock star. Too bad he's not into the ladies."

Heat rose to Ryan's face at the unexpected praise. He couldn't help feeling a bit like he was caught in a game of tug-of-war. If he wasn't so stressed out, if he didn't know these two men better, he would have been flattered by all the attention, but in reality, he didn't think they were fighting over him as much as they were marking territory.

"Yeah? Everyone adores Ryan," Kenny murmured. "Anyway, if all goes well, I think I can make associate by the time I'm thirty." He grinned at Ryan. "Do you remember how we used to scout out different neighborhoods on the weekends, and pick which house would be ours when we could afford it?"

"And crash open houses using fake names and pretend we were serious buyers," Ryan finished. "A fancy kitchen for me, and a home office for you."

"We wouldn't have to pretend much longer. And we'll be able to skip those 'fixers' and 'up-and-coming' neighborhoods too." Kenny's tone was serious. He meant it. "Actually, this area is hot right now, isn't it? If we lived around here, you would be close to work. And you could have that garden you always wanted."

The lump in his throat kept Ryan from speaking. Kenny hadn't forgotten.

"*We* have a garden," Dillon pointed out.

"And a swimming pool," chirped Emma.

Ryan ventured a glance at Archer and saw his lip curled into a sneer, his gaze turned sharp. He looked so pissed off that when he opened his mouth, Ryan knew whatever came out wasn't going to be good.

"Anyone for more salad?" he interrupted, wanting to keep the peace.

"Me." Emma waved a ketchup-stained hand. Kenny, sitting beside her, ducked and narrowly missed being spattered again. She'd already gotten him once with the ketchup bottle, and the pink stain on his crisp linen slacks still appeared damp.

Ryan jumped up from the table, grabbing a stack of napkins as he went. "Emma, honey, too much ketchup." He scrubbed at her face and hands until she no longer looked like she'd been bloodied in battle. "Now, finish up before your food gets cold."

She stuffed the remainder of the hamburger in her mouth until her cheeks bulged. She chewed noisily, with her mouth open. "All done," she said, showing everyone the ball of half-masticated food in her mouth. Kenny looked horrified.

Ryan sat back down, seeing his pleasant afternoon spiraling out of control.

"So are you gonna get married, or not?" Dillon asked.

Emma gasped, clearly delighted. "Oh, can I be a flower girl? Pleeeaaasse. Maddie was one and she got to wear a pretty dress."

"Guys," Ryan laughed. "That's enough."

Dillon frowned. "But—"

Archer gave Dillon's head a playful rub. "I'm sure Ken hears enough of this from his folks, right?"

The sudden silence was palpable.

"It's complicated," Kenny finally said, and Ryan's stomach knotted.

"Ah." Archer rested an elbow on the table and leaned forward. "And what about work? Are you not out there either?"

Ryan narrowed his eyes in warning. What was with the twenty questions all of a sudden?

Kenny's gaze flicked to Ryan and then back to Archer. "I'm not hiding it, but I don't go around advertising it either. Things are different in the corporate world—your personal life is separate from your work life. I doubt you'd understand since your personal life seems to be your work."

Ryan went cold at Kenny's confession. They hadn't discussed this since Kenny had started at the firm. He wondered if he'd be expected to stay in the background. Never invited to company functions. Kenny would be afraid he'd come off as too queer. It wouldn't be the first time. And what about Kenny's family? Would he be excluded there too?

He didn't have much time to wonder because a minute later Emma swung her arm around—"Shit" exclaimed Archer—and knocked over her full glass of iced tea. He jumped up from his chair but was too late. A river of tea, floating ice and all, cascaded off the table's edge and into Kenny's linen-covered lap. Kenny shrieked, leaped to his feet. As if in slow motion, Ryan saw Kenny's hand fly up . . .

Archer snatched Emma up under the arms so fast the chair tipped over. He hugged her protectively to his side. "Don't you ever touch my kids," he snarled.

"I—I wasn't going . . ." Kenny stammered, turning pale. "I swear . . ." He looked to Ryan for help and then down at his hands. "I would never . . . It was a reaction."

"I know," Ryan said, quickly moving to stand between the two men. Anger burned a hole in his gut. For all his faults, Kenny was not a violent person. Archer was out of line. He laid a reassuring hand on Kenny's arm and gently pushed him in the direction of the house. "Go treat that before it sets. I'll be right there."

When Ryan turned back to face Archer, the man was still frozen in place and clutching Emma. He blinked, the planes of his face slowly relaxing. He appeared shell-shocked, as surprised as any of them by his reaction. It was a heart-wrenching moment—what horrors he must have gone through to think Kenny would ever hit Emma. When threatened, his protective instincts had taken over, and Ryan couldn't help but be a little proud of him, even as he wanted to throttle him.

"You can put me down now, Uncle Archie," Emma announced, apparently unfazed by what had happened. Archer set her down.

"I—" he started. Embarrassment stained his features.

"Was this your idea?" Ryan demanded with a wave to their ruined lunch. "This little scene?"

"What?"

"Are you trying to wreck things for me?"

"You mean with Mr. Arrogant?" Archer smirked, but it quickly faded. "You can't seriously be into him—he's all wrong for you. What the hell do you see in him?"

"What do I see? I see a man who is willing to make a commitment. A man who's not afraid to admit when he's wrong and fix his mistakes. A man who loves me."

"All he cares about—"

"Who are you to judge?" Ryan cried, stabbing Archer's chest with his finger. "You don't know anything about him, how hard he's worked. Hell, you don't know the first thing about love. About what it takes to build a relationship."

"I know he's taking advantage of you."

Ryan snorted. "Oh, please. If anyone's a master at taking advantage, it's you." With that parting shot, he turned on his heel and went after Kenny.

"Ohmygawd, you did what?" Jill shrieked, trailing Ryan into his bedroom where he set down his load. He'd accumulated so much stuff during the summer that he'd decided to drop some of it off at the apartment now, while he was able to borrow the car, and after yesterday's poolside debacle, he needed a reality check from Jill.

"You heard me," he mumbled, too embarrassed to repeat the whole story again.

"Oh no I didn't. Because I *thought* I heard my best friend say he slept with Archer Noble. And that is impossible."

Ryan's face burned another degree hotter. Leave it to Jill to dwell on that one detail. He threw the duffel bag on the bed and looked around. Nothing had changed, but it seemed odd to be back in his room in the apartment. It didn't feel like he belonged here anymore.

Jill refused to be ignored. "Why am I only hearing about this now?"

"It's been a busy few days."

"I bet." She waggled her brows.

"Shut up."

"I hope it was worth it."

Ryan couldn't stop a sigh from escaping as he thought back to two nights ago. It was like Archer had lit a fire under his skin and the embers were still smoldering.

Jill's eyes grew big. "That good?"

Ryan fell back on his bed and pulled a pillow over his face. He'd always known that sex with Kenny was average. In the long run that was less important than being with someone he respected and trusted and had things in common with. Passion faded; compatibility didn't. And yes, they'd only made love once a week toward the end—they both had busy schedules. But Archer's hot skin under his hands, the taste of him on his tongue, had reminded him what he was missing. It threatened to change everything.

"Well at least you got something out of this arrangement," Jill muttered. "I guess experience has its rewards. Are you going to spill the juicy details? Was he all kinky and shit?"

"No." Ryan groaned. Jill would laugh if he told her there was only a blowjob. But Archer had used his hands and mouth like a master, teasing out erogenous zones Ryan hadn't known he possessed. Archer had kept him on edge so long that when he finally came, his orgasm had seemed to go on forever.

"What's happening?"

Ryan lifted the corner of his pillow and saw Alex, Jill's boyfriend, standing in the doorway. He was a good guy. After a string of losers, Jill had finally found one worth keeping. Ryan was happy for her but sad for himself.

"Our little boy's grown up," Jill replied. "He had his first one-night stand."

Alex appeared confused. "Congratulations?"

"Ryan is a serial monogamist. This is big news for him."

Ryan threw his pillow at them. "You guys suck."

"Does Kenny know?" Jill asked.

"Hell no."

"Maybe some competition would force him to step up and realize what he stands to lose. It worked with this one." Jill pointed a thumb in Alex's direction. Alex snorted.

"I already have a hard enough time looking in the mirror," Ryan grumbled. "I'm not playing games like that." Did he want Kenny to step up? Did he want to go back to the way things were? Ryan didn't know what he wanted anymore. As furious as he still was with Archer, he couldn't deny his feelings for the man.

"I've been thinking..." he began carefully. "Maybe I should stick around there a bit longer. Wait until Archer's custody application has been approved and help the kids get settled with school. It'll be Dillon's birthday next month—his first without his parents." He was grasping at straws now. Jill knew it too judging by her expression.

"Sweetie, Archer Noble is a grown man. If he needs help, he can hire a nanny like everyone else."

Ryan squirmed at the thought of someone else taking care of the kids, of Archer. It was irrational for sure, but they were *his* family. "I think I'm in trouble, Jill."

Jill shooed Alex out of the room, closed the door behind him, and sat down next to Ryan on the bed. "Okay, who exactly are you falling for? The kids or the man?"

Ryan shook his head. Tears threatened. "I don't know anymore. I don't know what's real. I don't know if I care. If he asked me to stay…"

The look on his face must have said it all. "Oh, Ryan!" she sighed.

"I think he needs me, Jill."

"Of course he needs you. The man's not stupid. With you he's got a housekeeper, a nanny, and now someone to keep his bed warm."

"He's not like that," Ryan insisted. Jill hadn't seen Archer like he had. "Not underneath all those hard layers. If you could see him—"

"What about Kenny?"

"I don't know. I love him too. Or at least I think I do." It was all so confusing. Kenny's ambition and drive had always been something he admired—he'd been happy to support that, thinking that as soon as Kenny was done with the pressures of law school things would be different. But he was starting to see things more clearly, and he worried Archer might be right.

"I've known you for six years, Ryan, and that whole time all I've heard about is how much you want to get married and start a family. It's what broke you and Kenny up, remember? You're the only guy I know who has a scrapbook of wedding ideas. What happened to the matching Tom Ford suits, and the platinum wedding bands, and the butterfly release? Are you seriously telling me you'd give up your own dreams to hang around at this guy's beck and call?"

"Maybe those things aren't important. They're . . . trappings. Maybe what's important is having someone who loves you."

"Love?" Jill croaked. "Time out. I think I need to implement emergency protocol."

"What's emergency protocol?"

She rummaged in his crowded bookcase and triumphantly held up a copy of Archer's last book. Ryan choked back his surprise. "What are you doing?"

"Just want to remind you of who you're dealing with here. The man might have done the responsible thing for a change, but that doesn't mean he's your prince charming."

"I know, Jill."

"Do you?" she asked pointedly, making a show of cracking the book's spine open. "'Chapter One,'" she read aloud. "'The Big Lie. The biggest lie a gay boy ever hears is that he is the same as everyone else.'"

Ryan's stomach churned. "Stop."

Jill licked her finger and flicked through the pages. "Oh, here's a good one. 'Love is a modern-day fairy tale best left to poorly written fiction and chick flicks. It's a man-made emotion that doesn't exist anywhere else in nature. When property, when paternity is not an issue, the idea of tying yourself to one person for life is absurd. I don't presume to be a biologist or a geneticist, but even our closest genetic relative, the chimpanzee, knows better than to stick to one partner. The bonobo, which shares nearly ninety-nine percent of its DNA with humans, is downright slutty. Can millions of years of evolution be wrong?'"

He cringed. "Okay. I get it. I get it."

"And my personal favorite: 'Parenthood is an unnatural state for any gay man.'"

"Put it away," Ryan whispered. "I don't need to hear any more." He had read the book cover to cover several times. He knew what it said. He had just conveniently forgotten for a while.

Jill closed the book with a resounding clap. "I'm sorry, sweetie. He's never going to change. You know that, right? Guys like him don't change. Maybe he actually cares about those kids. He might even care about you right now. But could you really be happy with someone who doesn't believe in monogamy? Be honest."

"Bitch." When Jill sat back down, he leaned into her hug and let her stroke his hair. "Thanks. I needed that."

"I know. What else are friends for?"

He sighed, knowing what he had to do. "Will you stock up on rocky road? I think I'm going to want it."

Chapter 16

"Uncle Archie, that lady is here," Emma called.

Archer emerged from the garage where he'd been re-sorting the giveaway bags—he still hadn't managed to actually give anything away yet—and trying not to dwell on how hot Ryan had looked in his bike shorts when he left for his morning ride. Bike shorts, for Chrissake. No one should look good in spandex.

A tense truce had reigned in the house since Kenny's visit last weekend, and Archer was content to let it be. Ryan stirred up far too many confusing emotions. That didn't mean he couldn't appreciate those incredible legs though.

He tensed when he saw Alyssa Sky crouch down and speak to Emma, who had been riding her bike in the driveway. As at Marguerite's service, the older woman wore a long, flowing skirt, but her only jewelry today was a large silver pendant around her neck. Her silver hair was plaited in a single braid. Emma was staring, apparently awestruck.

He approached in time to hear Emma say, "I like your necklace. It's pretty."

Alyssa held the carved pendant up so Emma could see better. "This is Hummingbird," she explained. "For my people the hummingbird is a symbol of peace and joy."

Archer gritted his teeth. The last thing he needed was this woman filling the kids' heads with nonsense. "Ms. Sky. What brings you here?"

Alyssa rose with a smile. "I thought I'd see how you were doing. You seem to be settling in." Her dark eyes bore into him. Archer couldn't shake the feeling she saw straight through him, saw every nasty secret and horrible thought he'd ever had. He almost hated her for that.

"And I wanted to drop off some reading material. About our organization. About the Native Centre." She thrust a thick packet of flyers and bound brochures at Archer before he could refuse.

Now Dillon rode up on his bike, breaking to a halt beside them. Marguerite's scarf was tied around his neck and hung down his back like a superhero's cape. "Do you have any books for kids?" he asked eagerly. "Me and Ryan couldn't find any at the library."

Archer tried to caution Dillon, but Alyssa ignored him. "What are you interested in?"

"Myths and legends."

"We have several books at the centre," she replied. "We're also planning to have a storytelling session soon."

Dillon's eyes widened, and Archer knew he was the victim of a well-orchestrated campaign. The woman played dirty, using the kids to recruit new members. He would look like the bad guy now when he said no.

She turned back to Archer. "But really I'm here to invite you to a children's powwow we're having next week at the centre. We're going to start holding them once a month. I thought the children might like to attend."

Dillon tugged at his arm. "Can we go, Uncle Archie? Can we go? What's a powwow?"

"It's a gathering where we dance and sing and drum," Alyssa replied with a crafty smile.

"I want to go too," added Emma.

Archer wanted to hit something. He didn't know what peace-loving, cultural utopia Alyssa had grown up in, but that hadn't been his experience. He'd spent his whole life trying to blend in and forget what it meant to be Aboriginal—he certainly didn't want to introduce the kids to that.

"I appreciate your interest, Ms. Sky, but I'm not an activist." He tried to hand back the material she had given him, but she refused to take it.

"I'm not asking you to be. The centre is not political."

"Well, I hardly think I'd be welcome."

She frowned. "Why wouldn't you be welcome?"

"I'm gay," Archer said bluntly.

"We have many two-spirited members, Mr. Noble."

Archer sneered. "Oh, is that what they're calling it these days?"

"Just come," she urged. "If only for the children's sake. It doesn't have to be the way it was for us growing up. You'll see."

Ryan's last week with them passed faster than Archer could have imagined; a flurry of back-to-school shopping and visits to the family lawyer handling his application for permanent custody. Now that things were in motion, he felt freer. Like he had a purpose.

And Ryan appeared to be moving on with his life as well, eager to get back to teaching, and to Kenny it seemed, judging by how glued to his phone he was lately. For the life of him, Archer couldn't understand why. He'd always thought Ryan had more sense than to be taken in by some slick promises, an expensive car, and a high-profile career like everyone else.

But it wasn't any of his business. Or so he told himself as he hid in the basement office trying to clear a spot on Marguerite's desk.

Still, the faint flutter of panic stirred in his chest again. In a few days, he would be completely on his own. And before long he'd be on the other side of the country—him and the kids.

The reality made his gut clench. It hit him suddenly how much he would miss having Ryan around, and not only because he cooked a mean roast chicken. He'd miss that warm smile—the one that always made him feel he'd done something amazing—the way Ryan didn't mince words, that aura of steady reassurance Archer was worried he couldn't do without. There was more too: like the scent of vanilla and taste of cherry lip balm, and the gentle touches he'd grown to crave.

He stopped his train of thought before he wandered into dangerous territory. Shit. He was taking this worse than the kids.

Archer Noble didn't have friends. Not real ones. He had lovers, fans and detractors, and people he knew in cities all over the world, but there wasn't a single person among them he would count as a friend. Except for Ryan. A new ache blossomed in his chest, and he was a little afraid of what it meant.

He was getting soft. *This is what happens when you start caring about other people. The pain gets in.* He'd gotten wrapped up in this cozy cocoon of domesticity, but now it was time to get back to the real world.

Archer turned his attention to the thick contract from the network that had been sitting on the desk for the last week. He'd already had his lawyer look it over and everything seemed in order. Donna had negotiated a nice signing bonus if the pilot got picked up too. He only had to sign. What was he waiting for? He'd spent the last decade working toward this—his name, his career was all he had. Sure this was a shitty network, and frankly a shittier show, but who knew where it could lead? It was a stepping stone.

Besides, there was nothing left for him here except memories. In Vancouver, he and the kids could start over

Before he could talk himself out of it, he grabbed a pen and signed. He'd courier it back to the network in the morning.

As he laid it to one side, his eye caught the file folder Marguerite had sent him. After Alyssa Sky's visit, thoughts of Margie and his family hadn't been far from his mind. Despite his best intentions, he'd read a bit of the material Alyssa left, and that had made him start leafing through the information Marguerite had gathered on Sonia. Some of it was difficult to read, but now that he'd started, he found it impossible to stop.

He perused the collection of police reports and stared at the broken, weary woman in the accompanying mug shot, searching for signs of remorse, of love—he would have settled for affection, but no matter how hard he looked, the eyes were always blank, the face hard. She might as well have been a stranger. *Who were you?* he wondered. *Why couldn't you love us?* He told himself he didn't care.

All his life he'd worried that he was like her. He knew now that he wasn't. He only had to look around to see that.

A tap on the door startled him out of his thoughts. Ryan stood there, a mug in each hand and a tentative smile on his lips. Archer did his best to ignore the way his heart leaped in response.

"Peace offering?" Ryan asked.

Archer nodded gratefully.

"How did it go today?" Ryan set one of the mugs down in front of Archer, and the aroma of chamomile tea wafted up.

"Good. The papers are all filed. It could take a couple of months to finalize, but the lawyer's certain there won't be an issue."

Ryan's lips twitched. He was polite enough to not say "I told you so," but Archer knew he was thinking it. "I'll give you a good reference, don't worry. And if they do a home visit, just be yourself."

"Myself?" Archer repeated, arching a brow. "Are you sure about that?"

"You can turn on the charm when you want to. I've seen it."

"It's a little rusty. It might not work."

Ryan's eyes slid sideways, avoiding Archer's. "Trust me, it works."

Archer grinned at the admission, but it faded fast at the thought of some stiff-faced, fat-assed social worker judging him. He shuddered. The ones who had shuffled him and Margie through the system had seemed like dull, vacant-eyed drones. All they'd ever cared about was passing the problem to someone else.

If Ryan was at his side, he would be so much more confident. A reference wasn't the same, although with his backing, how could he lose? No, there was more to it. For some reason Ryan never made him feel dirty and inferior. When he was with Ryan, he believed anything was possible.

He looked at him out of the corner of his eye. Couldn't Ryan see how much they needed him? He wanted a family—well he had one right here. But instead he was turning his back on them. Then again, Archer was used to people turning their backs and walking away.

He'd managed on his own before. He could do it again.

Ryan sipped his tea, his eyes glued to a framed family photograph on the wall. He appeared to be waiting for something, but Archer was afraid to speak, afraid to open his mouth in case the words lodged in his throat poured out. *Please stay*, he wanted to beg, but he'd never begged for anything in his life and he wouldn't start now.

After a few more seconds of strained silence, Ryan cleared his throat and picked up his mug. "Well, good night."

"Hey," Archer called, snatching at any excuse to keep Ryan in the room. He'd be alone soon enough. "Did Margie ever talk to you about this project she was working on?"

"What project?"

"She was trying to find out what happened to our mom."

"No, she never mentioned it. I swear," Ryan added when Archer narrowed his eyes. He moved closer. "Did she find something?"

"Maybe." Archer hesitated. He wasn't used to talking about Sonia, about the past, but Ryan had already seen him at his worst and hadn't judged him. For so long, he'd kept that part of himself walled off from everyone, including Marguerite, but now he found he *wanted* to let Ryan in.

So he swung back to the desk and pulled out the photocopy of Sonia's long rap sheet from the folder. Ryan drew up a stool from the corner and sat next to him.

"After she ditched us with Gran, she was arrested twice, once for shoplifting and then for solicitation. That last charge was in May 1989. She did some time, and then she seems to have disappeared. There's no further record of her in the system." Archer slid the grainy police photograph across the desk to Ryan without looking at it. While he didn't have any particular affection for the woman who had borne him, he hated that this image, the emaciated face with the slack mouth and vacant eyes, was his last reminder of her. "No one reported her missing. What was the point? All she ever wanted was money for drugs anyway. Friends, ex-boyfriends—if she knew you to say 'hi,' she'd be there with her hand out."

Ryan stroked Archer's back, the touch light but reassuring, and some of the weight lifted from his chest.

"You don't think maybe she cleaned up her act?" he asked. "Moved away?"

Archer hated to be the one to crush Ryan's optimism. He'd had hope too, the first time. "Nah. She'd been arrested before. Sure she would dry out in prison, but as soon as she was out, as soon as Family Services had handed us back over, she'd be right back at it. Plus, there's this.

"There are two Jane Doe cases still open with the RCMP in Winnipeg, both found in early 1990 that seem like promising leads. They were too badly decomposed for an ID, but they fit the basic description—First Nations female in her early twenties. Both showed signs of bearing children, though of course that could be anybody.

The statistics are pretty staggering. I looked it up. At last count there were 225 unsolved cases of missing or murdered Aboriginal women nationwide. Thirty-two in Manitoba alone. Those are only the reported ones. Sonia's not officially on that list."

Ryan sucked in a breath. "That seems high, doesn't it?"

Archer remembered having the same reaction when he first read the report. "Statistically, homicide rates for Aboriginal women are almost seven times higher than other women. The rates are only slightly lower among the missing."

"I think I've heard something like that on the news. That's horrendous. What happened to these two?"

"They're listed as homicides. Both blunt force trauma. They were found close to each other in the same wooded area, but months apart." Archer sorted through the scraps of paper and found the clipping he was searching for. "A whole series of prostitutes were beaten to death in the late eighties in Winnipeg. The police arrested a suspect in ninety-two, but he only copped to half the cases."

Ryan flipped through the police files. His hand stilled. When he looked up at Archer his eyes were wide. "Your mom was my age when she went missing."

"Sounds about right."

"How old was she when she had you?"

Archer did the mental calculations. "Fifteen."

"Fifteen and already on the streets with a kid?" Ryan gaped at him. To Archer, his reaction only further exemplified the divide between them. In his experience, Sonia's situation was nothing new.

"We weren't on the streets in the beginning. She was shacked up with some boyfriend in the north end—Margie's father probably. Not long after Margie was born, he left and somebody else moved in. That's when everything started to go to hell. By the time I was six, we were in and out of shelters." He grimaced. "Sonia could never manage to abide by the rules."

Ryan laid his head on his shoulder, and Archer breathed in the sweet vanilla and cherry scent of him. "That's so sad," Ryan murmured.

"Don't you dare pity me, Ryan Eriksson."

"I don't." Ryan pulled away. Archer felt the absence keenly. "What are you going to do?"

"About . . .?"

"About this." Ryan waved his hand at the mess of papers on the desk.

Archer shrugged. "Not much I can do. There's not enough there to identify her one way or the other. No fingerprints, no dental records."

"What about DNA testing? If they kept samples, then you could have them compared with yours."

"Why would I do that?"

"So you can finally know."

Archer closed the folder. "I've been fine for twenty-some-odd years. I don't need to know."

"But . . . she's your mother."

"She's not my mother. She just happened to give birth to me." Ryan's sigh was audible. "Look, I know it's hard for you to understand. But she didn't give a crap about us."

"Addiction—"

"Don't give me a lecture about addiction. I know all about addiction. She was weak," Archer spat.

"She was only a kid."

"So was I."

"Not everyone is as strong as you." Ryan's hazel eyes softened. "You and Marguerite had each other. You kept each other strong. Who did Sonia have?" He rubbed Archer's back the way he did Emma's when she couldn't sleep. And Archer, God help him, leaned into the touch. Ryan's words sank in, seeped past the barrier he'd erected as a child, and rekindled something he thought died long ago. "Don't you ever stop interfering? What more do you want from me?" he demanded hoarsely. "Last I heard you were leaving in a few days. What do you care about any of this?"

Archer's face was level with Ryan's, so he clearly saw the slash of hurt that crossed Ryan's fine features. "I care," Ryan said simply.

Archer didn't know who moved first. It didn't matter. Ryan was his drug—and it terrified Archer that he was already addicted to that quiet strength and gentleness, to his unflinching ability to see the good in everyone. When their mouths met, the kiss was hard, punishing—desperate. Ryan gripped his hair so tight it hurt, but it only stoked the fire in Archer's blood. Lips, tongues, hands grappled, and still he couldn't get enough.

Archer propelled Ryan out of the chair and back onto the desk. Papers skittered to the floor. He shoved Ryan's knees apart and stepped between them to get closer, but it still wasn't enough, not even when Ryan's long legs locked around his hips bringing their bodies flush together.

With a moan, Ryan broke the kiss, cupping Archer's face in his hands to hold him back. His pupils were dilated, his breathing choppy. "This is your answer for everything, isn't it? But sex doesn't really solve anything, Archer."

This is different, he wanted to shout. *With you everything is different.* He didn't only want Ryan in his bed; he wanted him in his life. But that wasn't what he said. Instead he fumbled with Ryan's zipper. Managed to draw it down. Found Ryan already hard, his briefs slightly damp. He rubbed the head of Ryan's erection through the cotton rough enough to make him shake.

"Are you sure about that? It seems to be working so far."

He leaned down and took Ryan's earlobe between his lips, making the man squirm. "Does Kenny do this to you?" he growled. "Get you so hot you're leaking?"

Ryan gasped. "That's not fair." He angled his head, and Archer licked his way down the curve of Ryan's neck to the spot where the scent of vanilla was strongest. "I want more than empty sex."

"There is no more, Ryan. This is what I have to offer."

Ryan's hand fluttered to his chest, stroking. "I don't believe that."

Then you're a fool. Archer paused, more torn up inside than he'd ever been. He felt tugged in a hundred directions at once and the only thing holding him together, the only thing that felt right, was here. His lips swept up Ryan's smooth cheek to take his mouth, gentler this time. Slower. He poured everything he was feeling into the kiss, everything he was too afraid to put into words.

Ryan whimpered his surrender. Archer snatched a quick breath before he was pulled back into another deep and electrifying kiss. Ryan's hand slid over his chest, squeezed his hardening cock though the denim of his jeans, before it slipped down the front without opening the button. He groaned into Ryan's open mouth at the contact.

A minute later Ryan's muscles tensed, but Archer ignored it. Then the tight hold on his cock was suddenly gone. He tried to put it back.

"Archer!" Ryan hissed, pushing at his shoulders.

Archer finally raised his head. "What?" he snapped.

"Emma."

Archer blinked. His brain refused to cooperate.

"Emma's here," Ryan repeated slowly and with emphasis, and this time his words sank in.

Without moving away, Archer turned his head and saw Emma standing in the open doorway in her ruffled nightgown. Mr. Snuggles dangled from one hand.

"I can't sleep, Uncle Archie," she said.

Archer's hard-on shrank, as if someone had doused him with a bucket of ice-cold water. "Fuck," he whispered. "Is this going to happen all the time?"

Ryan's lips twitched as he tried frantically to zip up his fly. Fortunately Archer's body shielded him from view, so Archer knew Emma hadn't seen much.

"What are you doing?" Emma asked. "Were you kissing?"

Having made sure Ryan was decently covered, Archer turned around. He ran an unsteady hand through his hair. "It's late, Monkey," he said, hoping to deflect the question. "You should be in bed." *Like me and Ryan.*

"But I'm not tired. Will you read me another story?"

Ryan hopped off the desk and scrambled to pick up some of the clutter they'd knocked to the floor. He stopped to read something. "What's this?" He held up Archer's new contract. "Why haven't you said anything?"

Archer winced. This looked bad.

Emma insinuated herself between them and tugged on Ryan's T-shirt. "If you're kissing, does that mean you're going to stay?"

Archer held his breath, his eyes locked on Ryan's face as he tried to judge his reaction. "Go and get into bed," he urged Emma with a little push. "I'll be up in a minute." He waited until Emma left the room before bursting out, "I can explain."

But Ryan surprised him. "Why didn't you mention this? This is great news, Archer. What's the show?"

Archer hesitated. He cringed every time he thought about it. "It's dumb hidden-camera stuff."

Ryan narrowed his eyes. "Why do you look like Dillon when he thinks he's going to get in trouble? I'm not going to like it, am I?" He glanced back at the contract and read out the title. "'*Till Death Do Us Part*'?"

"Probably not," Archer mumbled. "The tag line is 'Can your relationship survive the ultimate test?'"

Ryan grunted. "Well, knowing PROUDtv, I think I can guess the rest. I'm sure it involves half-naked men and lots of sex." He slapped the contract against Archer's chest. "I actually thought you'd changed. Guess I was wrong."

"That's not fair. I've done everything you ever asked of me. What more do you want?"

"What about the kids? How are you going to manage them and this?" His eyes widened. "Oh my God. Were you trying to seduce me into staying so you'd have a built-in babysitter?"

"What? No!" Archer suppressed a flicker of irritation. Hadn't he proven himself yet? Would Ryan always assume the worst of him? "They'll both be in school all day, and when we get to Vancouver I'll find someone to help out the rest of the time."

The color drained from Ryan's cheeks. "Vancouver? You're leaving?"

"I have to. If the pilot gets picked up, I'll be based on the West Coast." The prospect had never been as unappealing as it was right now. But he'd made his choice.

"How long have you known about this? Were you planning on disappearing without a word?" Ryan's hazel eyes glittered. "You're going to take them away from their friends? From this house? From m—?" His voice cracked. "From the memories of their parents? Just so you can become a . . . a reality-TV star?"

Archer shrugged off a twinge of guilt. "A fresh start might be what we need."

"What *you* need, you mean."

"Don't make me out to be the bad guy. You won't even be here. *I'm* the one who has to support this family."

"You said there was money—"

"There's enough to get by on for a little while, but most of it is tied up for their future. I'm not waiting until it runs out. I've been there."

"God, I've been so stupid." Ryan took a shaky breath and looked away. "Have you told them yet?"

"Not yet," he replied quietly. "There's still time. I have to wait for the guardianship to be granted before I can take them out of the province." He glanced around the cluttered office. "And then there's this place to take care of."

The broken look on Ryan's face turned Archer inside out. "I guess everything worked out for the best, then," he said in a voice Archer had never heard from him before. He sounded . . . defeated.

Archer took a step toward him. "Ryan—"

"I should go check on Emma." With a tight nod, Ryan practically ran from the room.

Chapter 17

"What do you mean you have to cancel?" Ryan asked dumbly with the phone pressed to his ear. It was the Friday before Labor Day, and he had spent the morning preparing his classroom for the first day of school, as he had the past two days. He had just said good-bye to Susan and unlocked his bike from the rack when he got the text from Kenny. "We made plans."

"I'm sorry." Kenny's voice held an edge of irritation. "It's work. I have to prepare for a last-minute deposition on Tuesday."

"But it's a holiday weekend. I rearranged everything." Ryan wanted to scream. He could have had an extra day with the kids, but Kenny had seemed so sincere about spending time together. "What happened to 'working on us'?"

"I can't say no, Ryan. Not if I want to get ahead here. I'll make it up to you. I promise."

Those words sounded eerily familiar. Ryan fought back the niggling sense of doubt. Relationships took work. "Okay," he sighed. "I understand."

"You're the best. I love you, babe."

He was slow to say the words back. But it didn't matter; Kenny had already hung up.

With a sigh, Ryan strapped on his helmet and turned his bike toward home. No, not home. Archer's house. He had to keep reminding himself of that.

His heart grew heavier the closer he got. Leaving was killing him.

The kids seemed to be handling his departure better than he was. Only he and Archer were quieter than usual. They spoke *through* the kids rather than to each other, like divorced parents forced to be civilized for the sake of the children.

It was easier this way. Now he wouldn't look back and wonder. But the thought of those three so far away, on the other side of the country, still made him want to cry.

Ryan locked his bicycle in the garage and strode in the front door—only to be greeted by Emma's squeal of pain. He ran downstairs in alarm and crashed to a halt at the sight of Archer Noble seated on the couch, an impatient Emma squirming between his legs as he braided her hair into two long plaits.

"Ow. You're hurting," she cried.

"Stay still, then," Archer barked.

Emma grinned when she saw Ryan. "Uncle Archie's doing my hair. And then he's going to take us out to dinner at a restaurant. I'm going to be an Indian princess, like Pocahontas."

Ryan bit his lip to keep from laughing. "Yes, I see that."

Archer narrowed his eyes at Ryan's amusement and flushed, as if he'd been caught doing something he shouldn't. "Pocahontas," he muttered under his breath in disgust.

Ryan approached, almost afraid to interrupt the rare moment. When he leaned over the back of the couch to take a peek, he saw that Emma's hair was equally sectioned in two halves with a perfect line of pink scalp down the middle. "That's pretty impressive. You missed your calling."

"Had a lot of practice," Archer grumbled. "On Margie," he amended when Ryan snickered. "She would wind up with a head full of tangles if it wasn't tied up. I'm a little rusty, but it's coming back to me."

"Marguerite was lucky to have you."

"We were lucky to have each other."

Emma twisted her head around. "Do I look like Mommy when she was a girl?"

Archer's fingers stilled. "Yeah," he replied roughly. He kept his head down.

"But Dillon doesn't look like Daddy," Emma mused. She cocked her head to one side, forcing Archer to straighten it. "He looks like Mommy too. And you." It was true. Both children took after Marguerite's side of the family. Their Cree heritage was especially apparent now after spending so much time outdoors; even with sunscreen slathered on, their skin had darkened to a creamy tan.

Archer's jaw tightened. His Adam's apple bobbed as he swallowed repeatedly, as though he was fighting to control some inner turmoil. Ryan's heart swelled with too many emotions to count, and his earlier anger dulled. He was about to lay his hand on Archer's shoulder when Dillon squeezed in between the couch and the coffee table, next to his sister, and splayed a large atlas out on the table.

"Is this your home, Uncle Archie?" he asked, his stubby finger almost entirely obscuring the province of Manitoba.

"It was never home, but yes, your mom and I grew up there." Archer leaned forward and tapped a spot on the map in the northern part of the province. "Right here."

"It's not marked," Dillon observed.

"No, it wouldn't be," Archer said with a sneer. He caught Ryan's eye and shrugged. "It's too small."

Dillon measured the distance with his thumb and forefinger. "That's so far away from here."

"It is." The hint of irony in Archer's voice told Ryan he was thinking that far more than distance separated his hometown.

"I didn't realize your band was so far north," Ryan murmured, as he sat down beside Archer. He wasn't ignorant of current events—every so often the state of the more remote reserves would pop up on a television newscast—but he'd had no idea that Marguerite had grown up in a place like that. She'd mentioned the reservation on occasion, but always in passing, and Ryan had never delved deeper. With all he knew now, and having done his own research, he felt slightly ashamed of that.

"Was it really cold there?" Emma asked.

"In the winter, yes. And there was lots of snow. The heater in the house never seemed to work very well, so sometimes your mom and I had to sleep in the same bed in order to keep warm."

"Did you have lots of friends there?" Dillon asked.

"No, not so many," Archer replied tightly. Tension radiated from his body, and this time, Ryan couldn't stop himself from laying a gentling hand on the man's arm. Archer's eyes snapped to his, full of surprise and confusion, as if no one had ever offered him a moment's comfort before.

"I can't wait to tell Amy," Dillon exclaimed excitedly. "It's so boring being from nowhere. Amy is from China. She did a speech about it in class. She takes Chinese classes after school."

"Cantonese," Ryan corrected.

"Do we speak anything, Uncle Archie?"

Archer's eyebrows lifted. "English. I know a few Cree words, but growing up it was mostly the Elders who spoke it."

"Why?" Dillon demanded.

"What are Elders?" Emma asked.

Archer floundered. Ryan supposed for a man so used to hiding his heritage, Dillon's interest must seem unusual, worrying even. No doubt he'd get used to the endless questions soon enough.

"Elders are like teachers," Ryan supplied. "They help pass on knowledge about their culture. Right?" Archer stared at him as if he'd lost his mind. Ryan blushed, feeling like he'd overstepped some boundary.

"You'll end up with lopsided braids if you don't let Uncle Archie concentrate," he teased in an effort to distract the kids from asking questions that Archer obviously didn't want to answer. "And then you'll have to walk around all day with your head cocked to one side." Emma giggled when Ryan did just that.

"I want lopsided braids, Uncle Archie," she immediately demanded.

"Now, look what you've done," Archer grumbled, but his face relaxed a bit. He shared a look with Ryan that was both curious and grateful, and Ryan found himself flushing under those dark, inscrutable eyes that were so much like Marguerite's.

As promised, Archer took them all out for a nice dinner at a family-friendly restaurant in the neighborhood. The kids were on their best behavior—Sam didn't make an appearance for once, which was heartening. Ryan drank two glasses of wine with his meal and tried to keep the smile on his face, while inside his heart was slowly breaking.

"Don't you have to go back to work too, Uncle Archie?" Dillon asked suddenly. "Like Ryan."

"Well, the things I do, I can do from almost anywhere," Archer replied with a quick guilt-laden glance at Ryan.

Dillon frowned. "How many books do you have to write to make money?"

Before Ryan could reassure him, Archer reached out and ruffled his hair. "Let *me* worry about that, kiddo. We'll be fine. Honest."

"Can I join soccer?"

"Well, sure."

Dillon grinned. "And powwow?"

"Me too," Emma chirped.

Once again Archer's gaze slid to Ryan's. "We'll see," he said thickly.

Back at home, they played a round of Emma's favorite board game, Chutes and Ladders, which she won handily. While Emma did a victory dance, Dillon disappeared for several minutes, and then returned bearing a clumsily gift-wrapped parcel which he shyly handed to Ryan.

"What's this?" Ryan felt the hard edges of a picture frame beneath the shiny paper.

"Open it," Emma cried, plopping down in his lap.

With trembling fingers, he slit the tape and revealed a framed drawing. His eyes burned.

"It's us," Dillon explained, as if the gift had needed any explanation. "Me and Emma did it. There's you." He pointed to an absurdly tall stick figure. "And there's Uncle Archie. And me and Em. And Mommy and Daddy." Marguerite and Jackson had been drawn over to one side, not quite angels but hovering above them all. Scrawled across the bottom in crayon were the words *Our family*.

Ryan struggled to draw air into his suddenly tight lungs. "Thank you," he whispered hoarsely, staring directly at Archer when he said it.

Archer shrugged carelessly, not meeting his eyes. "It was their idea. I just bought the frame." He jumped to his feet. "It's bedtime, you two."

Emma and Dillon groaned.

"Will you read to us, Ryan?" Emma implored.

Ryan smiled and wiped his eyes. "Yeah. I . . . need a minute though."

The look Archer sent him then stayed with him long after Archer left the room with the kids. If he didn't know better, he would have said it was almost as pleading as Emma's.

Ryan finished packing up the board game, and when he had his rioting emotions firmly under control, he went upstairs. Emma and Dillon were both already washed up and in pajamas. The three of them squished into Emma's bed as he finished the last chapter of *Charlotte's Web*. Ryan wished he had picked something happier, but sandwiched between them, he still relished every second. However, when Archer silently appeared in the doorway, Ryan stumbled on the words and lost his place.

Archer's expression was cautious, as if he didn't quite know if he'd be welcome so Ryan wordlessly drew his legs up to make room and Archer sprawled across the foot of the bed.

The words blurred on the page. How he would miss this.

By the time he reached the end, Emma was asleep and Dillon's eyelids were drooping. Even Archer's eyes were closed as he listened. Or maybe he was bored. When Ryan gently closed the book, Dillon struggled awake. "Don't stop," he murmured.

Ryan hid a smile against the top of the boy's head. He understood Dillon's objection; if he kept reading, he wouldn't be able to leave. "We're done."

"We are? I missed it."

"Uncle Archie can read it again tomorrow."

"Emma snored through the last chapter anyhow," Archer teased as he sat up and stretched. "C'mon, bud, into your own bed."

Dillon looked to Ryan, who quickly assured him he would follow shortly, and then let Archer lead him from the room.

Ryan stayed in Emma's bed a few more minutes, knowing this was the last time he would get to hold her like this. Once they were at school, he wouldn't be able to hug or cuddle them at all. Finally, he rose, kissed Emma's smooth cheek, pulled the thumb from her mouth, and turned out the light.

Dillon was sitting up in bed alone waiting for him. "Okay, little man. Time for lights-out." Ryan tucked the sheets tight around him the way he liked.

"Will you forget about us when you go back to your house?" Dillon asked, brown eyes wide and serious.

A lump of pure emotion lodged in Ryan's throat. He sat down on the edge of the mattress. "I will never forget you, Dillon. I promise. We're friends, remember? And I'll see you at school next week."

"Will you come to my birthday party? It's in October."

"We'll see," Ryan hedged. Would they even be here then? He couldn't bear to say no, but he couldn't lie to Dillon either.

"Is it wrong to have a party without Mom?"

"No, sweetie, it's not."

"I miss her. And Dad."

"I know. And you probably always will. But they're still with you." He tapped Dillon's chest. "In here."

"Uncle Archie's not so bad," Dillon added.

"No, he's not," Ryan managed to choke out. The words tore at his throat like a piece of glass.

"Sam likes him too."

He smiled through the tears. "That's good. Your uncle might need a little help though. So be good, and take care of your sister. And don't let me hear anything bad about you from Miss Bogie," he teased. "No more fighting. The same goes for Sam, okay?"

Dillon nodded. "Are you going to marry that man, Kenny?"

"I don't know, Dillon. I'd like to."

"If he doesn't marry you, I will."

Ryan held his breath until the urge to cry passed. "Let's give that a few more years," he finally managed to say.

"Or, Uncle Arch—"

Ryan laid his fingers over Dillon's lips. "We talked about this remember?"

"But you kissed Uncle Archie. That means you like him."

"How did—? Emma," he sighed. She must have told Dillon what she'd seen the other night in the office. "Your uncle's a good man, Dillon. I like him a lot. But we're very different. When you're older you'll understand."

"Why does everybody say that?"

"Because it's true. There's a lot of stuff you don't need to worry about right now. It gets complicated when you grow up."

"Then I don't want to grow up."

"Unfortunately we don't have much of a choice in the matter. It happens to everybody eventually." Ryan leaned down and kissed his cheek. He savored the moment when Dillon's thin arms encircled his neck. "I'm going to miss you, silly Dilly," he whispered before forcibly tearing himself away. If he didn't leave now, he never would. "Sleep tight," he called from the doorway.

"Don't let the bedbugs bite," Dillon returned.

Ryan closed the door and leaned his head against the jamb until his heart stopped feeling like it was being ripped out of his chest. It hadn't hurt this much when Kenny had left. But then he'd only been in love with one person, not three. He took a couple of deep breaths to steady himself. All he had to do was make it downstairs. He could fall apart once he reached his room.

Archer's bedroom was situated directly across the hall from Dillon's. When Ryan turned around, he found the door open and Archer seated on the edge of the bed, clearly dejected. Because of him? It was so wrong of him to wish it, but he hoped Archer would miss him just a bit.

Ryan hesitated on the threshold. "I'll leave first thing in the morning," he said softly. "Before they're up. I think it's best that way. You still have my number, right?"

Archer sneered. "Aren't you going to tuck me in too?"

His dark eyes challenged Ryan, but something in his icy tone made Ryan look closer, beneath the hard veneer Archer wore. Clarity came so quickly, he wondered why he hadn't seen it before. Archer and Dillon were so much alike. Both frightened little boys trying their best to put on a brave front. His heart turned over, and despite everything, hope flared in his chest. Archer *cared*.

"Well?" he snapped.

The seconds ticked by as Ryan warred within himself. He wanted to believe so badly that Archer could be *that* man. The man he knew was buried in there somewhere. Despite everything, he loved Archer. But he wasn't strong enough to risk his hopes and dreams on someone so determined to avoid that love.

As he stood there, the air seemed to thicken. Without thinking, he stepped into the room and closed the door behind him. When he engaged the lock, Archer rose slowly to his feet, the question in his eyes turning to surprise and then understanding.

With three quick strides, Archer was in front of him, on him, clutching him so tightly Ryan could barely breathe.

He cradled the back of Archer's head, threading his fingers through that silky, black hair. He loved their height difference—the way Archer's head rested perfectly on his shoulder, the whisper of Archer's breath on his neck.

"Why do you have to be so damned stubborn?" Archer asked raggedly, sounding both amazed and angry at the same time.

"Because you'd break my heart and not notice. I can't risk that." *Ask me to stay*, Ryan silently begged. *For the right reasons. Tell me you need me. Tell me you're ready to build something here.* Even now, not knowing what Archer really thought of him, knowing that he could be the doormat Jill always accused him of being, one small word from Archer is all it would take. But Archer remained silent, his mouth busy with other things, like kissing a path up Ryan's throat to his jaw and then finally to his mouth.

Archer kissed him urgently, his tongue sliding deep and scattering the last of Ryan's hesitation. He wanted this. He'd been attracted to the man from the very beginning; now that he actually *knew* Archer, faults and all, he wanted him even more.

Mouths locked, Ryan let Archer's weight press him back against the door. He savored the delicious hardness of Archer's body against his, his choppy breaths, the way his fingers clutched at him as if afraid he were going to disappear. It had been a long time since he felt so needed.

Ryan tugged up the back of Archer's shirt so he could get at that golden skin, and Archer drew it over his head and flung it aside. Then the rest of their clothes were stripped off quickly, in between frantic, stolen kisses. Somehow they made it to the bed. When they crashed onto the mattress, Archer on top, Ryan's breath caught at the contact. If he never had this again, he would always remember how perfect Archer felt covering him, skin against skin.

"This is how you like it, isn't it?" Archer asked. His teeth nipped at Ryan's neck. His fingers burrowed in Ryan's hair. He lined up their cocks and began grinding his hips so they rubbed together. Ryan raised both knees and locked his ankles behind Archer's back.

"Yes," he breathed. "God, yes."

Ryan's body was a riot of sensations. Insatiable. It didn't feel like it belonged to him anymore. His hands wandered freely, his mouth followed. And still Ryan couldn't get close enough. He bit back a moan when Archer stretched him with a spit-wet finger, setting his nerve endings on fire. But soon that wasn't enough either. He wanted more. Ryan rolled Archer over onto his back and straddled his hips. "Do you have condoms?" he demanded breathlessly.

"What?" Archer blinked up at him, his eyes wide and unfocused. Ryan didn't think he'd ever seen a sexier man.

He repeated the question. Archer pointed at the dresser. "Top drawer."

Before Archer even finished speaking, Ryan was up and rifling through the drawer. He found the box and grabbed a condom before crawling back on top of Archer. He blushed and laughed when Archer withdrew a bottle of lube from beneath the bed. It was a quarter empty. Seconds later Ryan had him sheathed, slicked up with lube, and positioned at his entrance.

"Hey, don't you want to slow down a bit?" Archer gasped. "We've got all, uh, night."

But Ryan worked himself down on Archer's cock, pausing after every inch to adjust to the size and feel of him, making Archer groan with the extended torture. Finally he bottomed out and they both moaned. He rocked slowly at first, getting used to the fullness again. It was good, but not nearly enough. Then, as if sensing what he needed, Archer dug his fingers into Ryan's hips and took over: slow, shallow upward thrusts until Ryan relaxed, and then he began to slam deeper.

Ryan splayed his hands on Archer's chest for support. He stroked the warm, golden skin lovingly. "Beautiful," he murmured, totally absorbed by the sight. Archer's heart pounded frantically beneath his palm, and Ryan gave up all control, let himself go in a way he hadn't truly ever done before.

And at the end he had to close his eyes because watching Archer come, having Archer watch him, seemed somehow too much, too intimate. As Archer tensed beneath him, Ryan's arms gave out. He fell forward onto Archer's heaving chest, memorizing the feel of the arms wrapped tightly around him.

With his heart thundering in his ears, he could almost convince himself he heard Archer whisper, "Please, don't go."

Chapter 18

On the first day of school, Emma decided to assert her independence by refusing to wear the new outfit they had picked out. Instead she was hell-bent of a pair of purple tights, a denim skirt, and rainbow-colored sweater.

"You'll be too hot," Archer warned.

"No, I won't," Emma stubbornly declared, darting out of his reach once again.

Dillon, who was already dressed and ready, danced impatiently. "We're going to be late, Uncle Archie."

"Tell that to your sister," Archer snapped. As if the last few days hadn't been stressful enough with Ryan sneaking out some time after he fell asleep, and the kids inconsolable the next morning when they found him gone, now Archer had a stubborn five-year-old on his hands. What a mess. If he had talked back as a kid, someone would have belted him.

How would Ryan handle the situation? Archer had his phone in hand and his thumb on the number before he realized it. Shit. He had to stop this—had to stop thinking Ryan would pop his head in the door any second now. As much as it hurt, as empty as the house felt, Ryan wasn't part of their life anymore. They were on their own. They would need to learn to do this together.

In the end, he gave up the fight. *Pick your battles,* Ryan had once told him. As long as Emma was covered, what did it matter? Still, at the last minute he tucked a T-shirt in her backpack just in case.

But because he'd wasted so much time arguing with Emma, he didn't have time to make a proper lunch. He ended up sticking last night's leftover pizza in their lunch bags with an apple before they rushed out the door. God, the people at the school would think he was a terrible parent.

They still arrived late, a fact which Dillon reminded him of repeatedly on the walk to school. Apparently he got a free pass on the first day, because Susan Taylor, the principal, smiled and greeted him and the kids warmly. She pointed him in the right direction and they hurried through the hallways searching for the classrooms. After dropping Dillon off at one end of the building, he rushed along the corridor with Emma in tow in search of her classroom, which he eventually found tucked away in the farthest corner of the first floor. Archer hadn't run into Ryan once; he didn't know whether to be grateful or disappointed.

"Running late?" asked a slightly rumpled blonde with whom he nearly collided. She looked as harried as he felt: her blouse was misbuttoned and there was a smudge of lipstick on her front teeth. The little boy next to her had a death grip on her leg and tears running down his face.

"Yeah," Archer grinned. "You?"

She nodded. "Alarm didn't go off."

Archer pointed at Emma. "Temper tantrum."

The blonde lady laughed. "I'm Sarah, by the way. And this is Mackenzie."

"Archer. And—"

"I'm Emma." Archer chuckled as Emma introduced herself. "Are you in this class? Why are you crying?" she asked Mackenzie. The boy shrunk back behind his mother.

"We're new to the area," Sarah explained. "Mac's shy, and he's afraid he won't make any friends."

"I'll be your friend," Emma chirped. "I know lots of people in this school. I even know a teacher. He's the best. Next year I'm going to be in his class."

Archer cringed. He hadn't yet told her she would never have the chance to be in Ryan's class. As he watched, she held out her hand to the boy. After a second, Mackenzie took it. He didn't look back at his mother as Emma led him into the noisy classroom.

"I'll pick you up after school, Emma," Archer called. He'd been so afraid she would make a fuss at being left alone, but instead she waved back cheerfully, already chattering to her new friend.

Archer's vision blurred. Except for the day Margie graduated college, he'd never been more proud of someone in his life. He only wished Marguerite could see this.

Guilt wrenched his heart. How could he take them away from this life? Force them to start over when they'd already lost so much? But what other choice did he have? They were young; they'd adapt and get over it.

"Well, that's just . . ." Sarah's voice cracked.

"Yeah," Archer agreed. "I should warn you though: she's a bit bossy."

Sarah laughed. "Mackenzie won't care. And neither do I. I was so worried he wouldn't fit in." She practically sagged in relief. "Hey, want to grab a coffee or something?"

Archer almost looked over his shoulder. This middle-class housewife wanted to hang out with him? He couldn't detect a hint of judgment or scorn or distaste in her welcoming smile. Of course she had no idea who he was. All she saw was someone in the same boat as her. He kind of liked that.

He grinned back. If Emma could make a new friend on the first day of school, maybe he could too. "That would be great."

"It's worth how much?" Archer gaped when the real estate agent repeated the figure. "You haven't even really looked around."

Chris Valenti was the top agent in the neighborhood, or so his card proclaimed in big, bold letters. The bastard must be salivating at the thought of a commission that big. The older man smiled at his astonishment. "Don't need to. This is a hot neighborhood. And you've got a great-sized lot here. You'll have no problem selling. It will go fast—probably multiple offers."

Lot? Archer frowned, thinking of the newly built McMansions popping up on the street. "Wait. You mean somebody would buy this place only to tear it down?"

"Buyers these days want new and modern, not these old, cut-up houses. Let's face it, this is a gut job. And it's easier to build new than add on."

His stomach soured at the thought of razing Marguerite's house. Sure it needed work, but it was the house where she'd loved her family, where the kids had grown up, where he and Ryan had skinny-dipped, where Ryan had changed their lives forever.

Suddenly Vancouver was the last place he wanted to be.

Archer swallowed hard. What choice did he have? He'd signed a contract and he couldn't back out, even if he wanted to. And they had to sell the house to afford the move; Vancouver was just as expensive, and they'd need every penny to get started there.

With a prickle of unease and a promise to get in touch as soon as his guardianship was legal, he showed the agent out. He leaned against the door and fought off the feeling he was letting everyone down: the kids, Marguerite, Ryan.

So far everything had been proceeding as planned. But with each day that passed, and as the move date inched closer, his anxiety only worsened until he had to wonder what was wrong with him.

He was becoming too sentimental, that's all.

Donna had jumped at his proposal for a new book—a memoir of all things—and so he had begun writing again, usually in the mornings after he dropped the kids at school. But working on it was dredging up the past, and more and more he found his thoughts wandering back to those early years. To Marguerite. And to Sonia.

It was making him reevaluate everything.

He hadn't said a word to the kids about moving yet but time was running out. He hadn't wanted to upset them and jeopardize the custody process, he told himself, but he needn't have worried. The home visit from the case worker had gone smoothly. So had their interview with the judge yesterday, even though Archer had been a nervous wreck the entire time. It had gone so well, he'd treated them all to hot chocolate afterward. Dillon had piled on the sprinkles and because Dillon's imaginary friend had been absent lately, Archer had asked, "Are those for Sam?"

Dillon had given him a strange look. "Sam isn't real, Uncle Archie," he'd explained patiently, as though Archer didn't know better. "He doesn't need sprinkles."

Archer had hugged Dillon despite his protests. The lady behind the counter had smiled. "Your kids are so polite," she said when Dillon and Emma thanked her for their drinks. He glowed with pride.

He'd gazed at Dillon, who had grinned back with his new gap-toothed smile, having recently lost a front tooth. "I think we're actually going to make it, bud." The only thing that would have made the moment better was having Ryan there to share it.

The thought sobered Archer. He wondered if he'd ever get over that hole in his life. He tried to keep busy and focused on the kids' homework or his book or their upcoming move, but every so often he'd catch himself about to say "Go ask Ryan" and that's when the loss hit him the hardest. Once or twice he'd considered hooking up while the kids were in school, but he always backed out at the last minute. It was no big deal. He was tired, and he had a lot on his plate. Once they were settled in Vancouver he'd have plenty of opportunities to wipe the scent of vanilla from his mind.

By the time the weekend rolled around, Archer decided he couldn't put it off any longer. His lawyer had told him it would be another week or two at the most, and then he'd be free to leave the province. Just in time too. The network wanted him there to film some promos and was becoming impatient with him dragging his feet. He'd have to start packing soon, and that meant Emma and Dillon had to be told about Vancouver. They would take only the essentials. Everything else he would sell or give away.

He assembled them in the living room, steeling himself for the tears that were bound to flow. Before he could break the news, Emma surprised him by asking if they could go to the cemetery.

Dread knotted his stomach. Any time the kids mentioned visiting their parents he had tried to change the subject, because the last place he wanted to be was *there*, but now he had no choice. He couldn't keep them away forever. And in a month or so they would be gone.

So he strapped them into his newly purchased SUV, and they drove to the cemetery. As soon as he got there, Archer realized he had no idea where to go. "It's over here, Uncle Archie," Dillon said, grabbing him by the hand and leading him down the winding path past the headstones to the Remembrance Garden. His heart thundered and his mouth went as dry as they rounded a bend and the kids left his side to run ahead. There beneath the drooping arms of an old fir tree, he found the granite boulder into which Marguerite's and Jackson's names had been etched. His eyes misted at the beauty of the spot.

"We forgot to bring flowers this time," Emma moaned.

"Look. Somebody already did." Sure enough, as Dillon had pointed out, someone had lovingly tucked a pot of cheerful brown-eyed Susans next to the rock. He knew without thinking that it had been Ryan. Ryan who had loved Margie almost as much as he had. The sight stirred an ache in his chest.

"Do you think they're watching us?" Emma asked suddenly, breaking the silence.

"I don't know," he answered after a brief pause.

"That's what Ryan says too. I think they are."

Ryan. Even here he couldn't escape the daily reminders of the man. He'd done his best to force Ryan from his mind, eliminate all traces of him, but his presence was everywhere. He'd invaded their lives, turned everything upside down, and now that he was gone, it fucking hurt, more than he thought anything could hurt him again. Archer couldn't shake the idea that a part of him was missing.

He crouched down to touch the stone. It was warm beneath his hand. In this beautiful, quiet spot he felt closer to Marguerite than he had in a long time. Not a day went by when he didn't see his sister in some little part of the kids: a laugh, a smile, the tilt of a head, the glint of mischief in Emma's eye. *What do I do?* he silently asked, as if she really were watching over them and would somehow give him the answer he needed. Except of course she wasn't, and no divine response was forthcoming. He didn't want it anyway. Everything was arranged, and they were leaving in another month. Sooner, if the house sold quickly. If he stayed, he'd be throwing away all his years of sacrifice and hard work. And for what? Ryan?

Ryan didn't want them anymore. He'd made that clear by running back to his successful boyfriend at the first opportunity. And who could blame him? Why would he want used goods like Archer?

That persistent ache in his chest gave a dull throb as if to remind him of its presence. Not that he'd ever forgotten. Was this what everyone meant when they talked about a broken heart? Archer snorted. That was crazy. That would mean he'd been in love to begin with.

Men like him didn't fall in love. Not like *that*. More importantly, men like him weren't loved by other people. And yet he couldn't get the thought out of his head. It clung stubbornly, forcing tendrils of hope beneath the wall around his heart.

Archer's hand crept to Marguerite's cheap rhinestone ring that he still wore around his neck. So many regrets.

He didn't realize he was crying until he felt Emma's arms around his neck.

"It's okay, Uncle Archie. Don't be sad."

He fell back on the ground with a sob and pulled her into his lap. Then he reached for Dillon, needing to hold them both close. Archer's tears ran freely as they clung to each other, and Dillon and Emma quietly sniffled against his chest. Their trusting hugs filled the empty spaces inside him with the warmth he'd been craving since he'd left Marguerite behind all those years ago.

Finally, when the damp grass began to seep through Archer's jeans, he drew back and wiped his face, before giving them a gentle nudge. "We should go, guys."

"Next time can we bring my art project and show Mom?" Dillon asked as he scrambled to his feet. "It's almost done, and she'd like that, right?"

Next time? Archer's stomach twisted. Oh God, he had to tell them now.

But as he studied Emma and Dillon's expectant, tearstained faces, the words deserted him. They needed this—needed to be here. Hell, *he* needed it too. And if he'd learned anything over the last few months, it was that love meant putting others ahead of yourself; it meant feeling stronger together than apart.

The way he did with Ryan.

Love.

Maybe it wasn't so far-fetched to think that Ryan had loved him. Hadn't Ryan spent the entire summer taking crap from Archer when he could easily have had everything he ever wanted? He'd believed in Archer from the start, shown them how to be a family, and never asked for a thing in return. If that wasn't love, what was?

The rest of Archer's life loomed in front of him: a new city, a new job, and a new family, but empty. Because without Ryan, there would always be a piece missing. How had he not seen that before? And now it was too late to do anything about it.

Or was it? When had Archer Noble ever given up on something he wanted?

Archer swallowed the lump in his throat and tugged Dillon to his side. "Yeah, kiddo," he croaked. "I think she'd like that. Now what do you say we go home?"

That night Archer sat down at his laptop after the kids were in bed and composed a post for his blog—the most important post he'd written in a long time. He knew what he wanted to say, but had to rewrite it three times before the words sounded right. Even then he wasn't sure it was enough. He chewed on his thumbnail as he read it over for the final time. *Will Ryan see this?* Archer certainly hoped so, but if he didn't, it still needed to be said.

> *Has Archer Noble Gone Soft?*
> *Fate is a fickle bitch, my friends.*
> *I'm not a man who admits he's wrong easily, and yet here I am, responsible now for two kids. Yes, there are days when I'm scared shitless—for them, for me. There are days I wish I could run away. But I don't. It's not a life I ever thought I'd have, not a life I wanted, but you know what? It's not too bad. In fact, sometimes it's pretty damned good.*
> *I've said repeatedly that gay men weren't meant to be parents. I'm guilty of calling monogamy unnatural more times than I can count. I've mocked those who believe in love and commitment. And all with the excuse that it's not in our nature.*
> *Like I said, fate's a bitch.*
> *What I forgot is that "nature" is always changing, and so are we. Am I a hypocrite? A liar?*
> *What I am is human, and the beauty of being human is that we can learn, we can change, and we get to make choices. Every day we make choices: to be good people or bad, to love, to hate, to forgive. Marriage,*

monogamy, parenthood—they're all choices. They're your choices. And no stranger, least of all me, should tell you they're wrong.

I guess I'm trying to say narrow-mindedness is not the purview of the Right. Don't listen to dicks like me who tell you how you should live your life. I'll tell you a secret: we don't know any more than you do. Find your own path. Be the person you want to be. And don't close your mind to the possibilities around you. You may be surprised.

Chapter 19

*I*t was after four o'clock when Ryan finally left school for the day. He had stayed behind to get some marking done—a new habit he had adopted in order to avoid accidentally encountering Archer in the school yard. He wasn't strong enough for that yet. But as it was, he heard everything from Dillon and Emma. They seemed to take great pleasure in tracking him down at lunch or recess and regaling him with the latest stories from home: how Uncle Archie tried to make cookies and set the fire alarm off; how they all ended up with pink underwear and socks when one of Emma's shirts got mixed in with the wash. He'd laughed at that. Outwardly, he pretended he didn't want to know any of it, but the truth was he savored every snippet of information.

The temptation to stalk Archer online beckoned, but except for that one cryptic, hope-inducing blog post, Archer had gone silent. Ryan must have read that post a dozen times searching for the hidden meaning. Had it been meant for him? He'd been certain it was, but when nothing else happened, he didn't know what to think.

Jill told him he should be grateful that Archer hadn't contacted him, but deep down inside he had to admit he was a bit hurt. It wasn't like he actually expected Archer to come chasing after him with declarations of undying love, but the occasional text message would have been nice. The kids were clearly thriving without him.

Every day he steeled himself to learn that Archer and the kids were packing up and heading across the country, but neither Emma nor Dillon mentioned it, and Ryan was afraid to bring it up. With each day that passed, his remaining hope dwindled a little more.

September had come and gone surprisingly quickly given how empty his life was now. He had managed one date with Kenny—postponed twice—before officially calling it quits. It wasn't so much a breakup this time as a mutual parting of ways. Their future as a couple was over and they both knew it, although he liked to think they had parted as friends this time. They were simply in different places. Kenny was focused on his career, and Ryan wasn't content to stay in the background. It wasn't enough for him anymore. He wanted to be an equal partner in a relationship. He wanted to be top of the list for once. Surely he deserved that.

Jill and Alex were talking marriage. She was careful about it, not rubbing it in his face, but Ryan knew it was in the works. She had already broached the topic of buying a house with Alex once, so it was only a matter of time before she moved out and Ryan was on his own again.

He tried not to dwell on that as he buckled his helmet under his chin and strode toward the bike rack. October had arrived, and the crisp autumn air was rolling in. He looped his scarf tighter about his neck and fastened the top button of his coat.

There was a familiar figure beside the bicycle rack. Ryan slowed, and his stomach clenched at the sight of Archer Noble. This was it. The moment he'd most dreaded. He would have turned and run, but Archer raised a hand in greeting.

"Hi," Archer said, when Ryan was close enough. He sounded nervous and looked nervous, with his hands tucked behind his back and the muscle in his jaw ticking like mad. Ryan had never imagined seeing him like this.

"Hi," he replied, hoping his voice didn't betray his own nerves. He glanced around for Emma and Dillon and saw them playing nearby on the slide. They waved.

"How have you been?" Archer asked.

Lonely. Sad. Wishing I never left. "Um, good. You?"

"Yeah. Good." Archer stared down at his feet. Ryan suppressed a nervous giggle. This was some conversation they were having. They sounded like a couple of teenagers.

"I, um, thought I should let you know things are working out with the custody situation," Archer blurted.

"I heard," Ryan said. "From those two. Congratulations."

"It's not final yet, but the lawyer says it should be any day now. Then we'll be official." Archer seemed to have run out of words because he stopped talking, looked over at the kids, then back at Ryan. "How's Kenny?"

Ryan shrugged. "Fine. I guess."

"You're not...?"

"No. It wasn't going to work out."

"Oh," Archer said. Ryan tried to convince himself Archer's eyes did not light up at the news. He didn't need any further heartbreak.

"Are you here to say good-bye?"

"Good-bye?" Archer frowned. "Oh, no. We're not moving."

"You're not?" A tidal wave of happiness flooded Ryan's chest. He forced it back down. "But you have a contract."

"For the pilot. Unfortunately I can't get out of that." Archer made a face. "I'll have to go to Vancouver for a couple of weeks to shoot, but once it's done, they're on their own."

Ryan's head spun. They were staying. *Archer* was staying. "But what will you do?"

"I've got some ideas. It might be tough for a little while, but that's not important."

"It's not?"

"No." Archer took a deep breath. "Everything we need is right here: school, friends, and ... you."

"Me?"

"Yeah, you." With a flourish, Archer produced a bouquet of daisies from behind his back and thrust them into Ryan's arms.

Ryan blinked. Archer Noble was giving him flowers? His heart pounded. He stared dumbly at the bouquet in his hand. The petals were browning around the edges, and a couple of stems were broken, but ... *Archer had brought him flowers.* He desperately tried not to read too much into it, but it didn't work—his eyes quickly filled. He *was* a doormat if this was all it took to lower his guard.

"What are these for?" he croaked.

"I lied." Archer's mouth twisted wryly. "I'm not good."

"You're not?" He couldn't hold back the rush of hope that time. *He hadn't been wrong. He hadn't.*

"And you like flowers."

"Yes, but—"

"These are your favorite, right?"

"Archer," Ryan cried in exasperation. It was a sweet gesture, but he needed to hear the words. He needed something more than bedraggled daisies before he took a leap this big.

Dillon ran up to them and grabbed his uncle by the arm. "Did you ask him yet?" he demanded.

"I'm getting to it," Archer snapped.

Dillon bounced on his toes, clearly unable to keep still. "We took a vote, Ryan."

"It was Uncle Archie's idea," added Emma who had somehow snuck up behind him. "And it was unamous."

"I think you mean unanimous," Archer corrected.

Ryan was totally lost. "I don't understand. What did you vote on?"

"We want you to be part of our family," Dillon said simply.

Ryan's knees threatened to buckle. He felt as if someone was reaching into his chest and tearing out his heart. "Oh, Dillon."

"A family is people who love each other. Isn't that what you said?"

The tears hit Ryan fast and hard. He clutched the bouquet to his chest. "I love you guys, but . . ." He looked at Archer through blurry eyes. "I don't want to be the nanny."

"I don't want that either," Archer rasped. He gave the kids a mock glare. "Could we get a little privacy here? I can handle the rest on my own, thank you."

Dillon's expression was doubtful, but he sauntered back to the slide with Emma in tow.

"Shit," Archer said. "I had this all planned out, and now I can't remember a single thing I was going to say." He took a deep breath. "Dillon's right. Somehow we're a family. The four of us. *You* make us a family."

Ryan's breath caught. He couldn't speak.

"I know you think I can't handle a committed relationship," Archer continued. "That I can't be exclusive—"

"I'm trying to be realistic. What happens when you get tired of the white picket fence and want something more exciting? Some*one* more exciting? I've read your blog, remember."

Archer exhaled. "Is *that* what you're worried about? Okay, yes, I admit it. If we'd met in a bar, I wouldn't have looked twice. But—" Archer grabbed him by the lapels of his peacoat when he tried to turn away. "But that would have been my loss. Because you, Ryan Eriksson, are the best person I've ever known. I never dreamed in a million years that someone like you would want someone like me. You believed in me when I didn't believe in myself."

"That's—"

"Finding sex partners has never been my problem, it's true. Finding someone I actually want to stick around afterward on the other hand doesn't happen very often. Never in fact. And I want you to stick around. I really do." He swallowed hard. "You have every right not to trust me. I don't exactly have the best track record. But I don't want to be that guy anymore. Because it's empty and lonely and . . . Fuck, if anyone should be able to tell the difference between sex and love, it's me."

Ryan's head snapped up. Love? His knees wobbled as he stared into Archer's oh-so-serious eyes.

"Yes, that's right. Love." Archer gripped him by the back of his neck, his face flushed. "You said I'd break your heart. But I won't. As long as you don't break mine either."

That was it. Ryan barreled into Archer, sending him careening a step backward before he caught himself. Ryan's bike helmet conked the side of Archer's head, and the daisies were crushed against his chest. They both laughed.

"Can we take this off?" Archer's fingers fumbled with the clasp beneath his chin.

Ryan held up the crumpled flowers as the helmet came off. "These poor daisies."

Archer chuckled. "And after I went to so much trouble finding them."

"Oh, now that's romantic," Ryan teased.

"In my defense, I've never done this before."

Ryan fought a smile. "You're not doing too badly."

"Are you sure you wouldn't prefer roses?"

Was there a hidden meaning in Archer's question? Either way, Ryan's answer was the same. He shook his head. "No."

Archer stroked his arm. "Does that mean you'll think about it?"

"Are you sure, Archer? You have to be sure about this."

"I'm sure."

With a sigh, Ryan burrowed closer, daisies and all.

"You didn't say good-bye when you left," Archer whispered against his neck.

"I couldn't. It hurt too much."

"Don't do it again," he ordered. "I hated waking up and finding you gone. It was like all the life went out of the house."

"Okay."

Archer pulled back slightly but didn't let go. "I think you deserve way better than me. And someday I'll tell you all the reasons why."

Ryan snorted, pressed his hand to the side of Archer's face. "And someday I'll tell you all the reasons why you're wrong."

"I can't promise you everything you want. At least not right now. Commitment, yes, but the other—"

"I know." Ryan felt his grin building. "You're not the only one who's been doing a lot of thinking. I was so fixated on making a family I didn't pay attention to who it was with. A marriage certificate is just a piece of paper without the trust and love and commitment behind it. Kenny showed me that. And that's what I want. The rest really isn't as important."

"It's important to *you*."

Ryan's eyes stung. After so many years together, Kenny still hadn't gotten that. But Archer did. That meant something. "Someone recently taught me not to close my mind to possibilities right in front of me. Yeah, I'd still like to be a father someday. But for now I'm happy to be an uncle. Or a friend. Whatever you, and they, need me to be."

"That, I think we can manage," Archer said with a smile as he pulled Ryan close again.

"Woooo. Are you going to kiss now?" Ryan looked down to find Emma at his side, regarding them with curious eyes. Dillon was right behind her. "Uncle Archie says you're going to be his boyfriend. And that we won't be able to sleep in his bed anymore."

Ryan shook with barely contained laughter. Archer sighed. "I forgot to warn you. You'll have to get used to the audience."

"You've already got me moved in?"

Archer Noble actually blushed. "Why don't we start with dinner first," he countered.

Ryan made a face. "I don't know. Are you cooking? I've heard all about your culinary experiments. Not sure I want to be a part of them."

"What a pair of snitches," Archer cried in mock outrage, twisting away to chase the two squealing children. A lump of emotion rose to Ryan's throat: hope, love, desire, and mixed with them all, a bittersweet happiness.

"Thank you, Marguerite," he whispered. "Thank you. You'd be so proud."

Archer returned to his side with a sheepish grin. "Did you say something?"

"No. Nothing."

"C'mon, then." He looped an arm around Ryan's waist. "Grab your bike. Let's go home."

Epilogue

Four Years Later

"*H*appy Birthday to you."
"You live in a zoo. You look like a monkey—"
"And smell like one too."

Archer pretend-scowled at the kids, but the other adults laughed and clapped as Dillon, Emma, and Mackenzie ad-libbed. Even Jill's two-year-old daughter tried to get in on the action but she was two beats behind the others and finished on a wobbly note. The flames on the wax numerals flickered in the mid-May breeze but didn't blow out as Ryan set the birthday cake down. 4-0.

He was aware of all eyes on him, and for a split second his eyes stung. He couldn't believe he'd actually made it to this milestone.

"Make a wish, Archie." Dillon clutched his arm and pulled him over to the table.

"That's *Uncle* Archie to you."

"Ryan calls *his* parents by their first name."

Archer looked up at Ryan, and they shared a commiserating look.

"Make your wish before the candles burn out," Ryan instructed with a grin.

He didn't care if the candles burned out. He didn't need to make wishes; he had everything he could ever want right here. Still, Archer leaned forward and blew the flames out with one breath.

More clapping. Ryan nudged him out of the way so he could begin slicing the cake.

"Forty is so old," Emma pronounced as she plucked the candles off the top and licked frosting from the pointed ends.

"Hey," he admonished. "Who're you calling old?"

"Don't worry," Ryan whispered in his ear. "I didn't think you were old last night. Or again this morning." He planted a peck on Archer's cheek before resuming cake-cutting duties.

Archer stood by and gazed out at the intimate group gathered in the backyard on this beautiful spring afternoon: Jill and Alex, Sarah and her husband Bruce, his producer Rahim and a couple of the guys from the weekly radio show he was now hosting. He spared a nod for Alyssa, who had gifted him with the braided leather bracelet he wore now. The kids adored her—no surprise since they spent so much time at the Native Centre these days—so he'd tried being less of a dick and wound up enrolled in a drum circle in return. She was as crafty as Ryan. And in her own way, almost as important to him.

All these people were here for him, he marveled.

He had friends.

Dillon was showing off his new beaded powwow outfit and demonstrating the latest dance he'd learned to Mackenzie. He had shot up like a weed this past year—all arms and legs, and they flailed about in tune to an imaginary drum. Now nearly twelve, he was still an affectionate and sensitive boy, too quiet and thoughtful sometimes, but overall, Archer couldn't have asked for a better kid. Emma on the other hand, was the one they had to watch out for. That girl was going to be a handful. It didn't help that she had him wrapped around her little finger.

He wouldn't pretend the past four years had all been easy. His memoir had cracked the best-seller lists for a few weeks—long enough to land him a weekly radio show and some freelance writing work— and he had turned that into a short documentary about his journey to find his roots. It had been well received, but his quest to put his mother to rest and his return to Manitoba had churned up a lot of dark memories. He might have given in to them if Ryan hadn't been there to pull him back from the brink. In the end, his efforts to give his mother's story a conclusion had proved fruitless. There had been no way to identify her remains. Why would the police keep the DNA of a dead Native hooker? They were a dime a dozen, and the case was twenty-seven years old. He'd left the province of his birth thinking that of all the tragedies Sonia Noblesse had suffered over her short, hard life, dying nameless was the worst.

No, these hadn't been easy years. But they had definitely been the happiest.

Jill sidled up to him with her four-month-old son, Daniel, strapped to her chest in some sort of harness that left his arms and legs bouncing free. Archer replenished her drink, which earned him a grateful smile. While they'd never be close friends, he liked to think he had finally convinced her he was in this to stay.

"So, Ryan says you're going to Ottawa next week," she said.

"Yep. For the opening of the inquiry." After years of public pressure, the federal government had set up a national inquiry into missing and murdered Aboriginal women. Archer was covering it for a national newspaper and also testifying on behalf of his family.

"That's great. You must be excited."

He grunted. The truth was, every time he went away, he couldn't wait to get back home again. *Home.* He shook his head in wonder. Sometimes when he looked at his life these days he didn't recognize it.

He held out his hand to the baby, and Daniel immediately grasped on to his finger with a gummy smile. Archer grinned back with an unmistakable tug at his heart. He'd deny it in a second if asked, but he missed that unconditional love. He missed the hugs. He missed bath time and bedtime. He missed Emma's hand in his and the way she used to let him braid her hair.

When he glanced up, Jill was watching him with a knowing smirk. "What?" he demanded.

She raised her eyebrows innocently. "Nothing. I'm just very familiar with that look."

The worst part was, he didn't need to ask what she meant.

A short while later, after the last guest had left and Emma and Dillon had been packed off to a sleepover at Mackenzie's house, Archer returned from taking out the trash and was struck by how quiet the house seemed. He found Ryan in their kitchen putting away the last of the dishes. "That was fun."

"Even without the strippers?"

Archer laughed. "Can you imagine?"

"Jill would have appreciated it."

Archer hopped up on the island counter. "Since we have the house to ourselves tonight, maybe you could give me a private show." He caught the damp washcloth Ryan threw at him before it hit him in the face. Grinning, he tossed it aside and captured Ryan between his feet as he passed. He drew him in closer, until they were nose to nose. "What? I've seen you and Dillon playing that dance game. You've got some moves. And a drawer full of sexy underwear."

Ryan shook his head, but he was smiling as he moved fully into Archer's arms. Archer closed his eyes and nuzzled the curve of Ryan's neck, sinking into the sweet vanilla scent.

"Thank you," he murmured.

"It was only a small party."

"Not for that."

"Ah," Ryan said. He stroked Archer's back.

"Thank you for being so strong. For loving me. I probably don't say that enough." There was a lot he didn't say often enough. "I love you."

"I know."

He pulled back, scrutinizing Ryan's face. "Things are good, right? With us?"

Ryan raised an eyebrow. "*I* thought so."

"Me too," Archer hurriedly assured him. He gave the back of Ryan's neck a quick, reassuring squeeze. "Things are great. It's just that . . . You're not sorry about not getting married?"

Ryan visibly relaxed. "I'm not sorry about anything, Archer. I love you. I love our life. Why? Are you proposing?" he teased.

"I might," Archer replied, enjoying the way Ryan's jaw dropped. He was slowly warming up to the idea. "One day." He turned serious. "What about kids? You don't ever bring it up anymore. Have you changed your mind?"

He shrugged. "No. But it's less important now. I have the three of you in my life."

"And you'd be happy with that?"

"I *could* be." That was Ryan's subtle way of saying it was his choice.

"I kind of miss it," Archer admitted. "Them being little. Needing me."

"They still need you. They'll always need you."

"It's not the same." He couldn't explain it. It wasn't that he thought of Emma and Dillon differently, or loved them any less than he would his own children, but lately he'd been picturing a towheaded baby in his arms. It was all he could think about some nights. A piece of Ryan to hold on to. Marriage could be undone, but parenthood was forever. He'd even gone so far as to start researching surrogacy on his own.

"What are you saying, Archer?" Ryan rasped. His eyes glistened with unshed tears.

Archer cupped the sides of his face. He'd never have enough words to tell Ryan how important he was. "I want to start a family with you."

"I thought we already did that."

"True. But this time it's by choice." A lone tear spilled from the corner of Ryan's eye, and Archer wiped it away with his thumb.

"Do you really mean it?" Ryan whispered.

"Yeah, I do."

"What about Emma and Dillon?"

"What about them?"

"We should see how they feel about it. They might think we don't love them anymore."

Archer frowned. *Why did things have to be so complicated?* "Okay, yes. But since Emma's practically told me she expects a baby sister, I don't think it will be a problem."

"Did she really say that?" Ryan turned his head and pressed a kiss into Archer's palm. He smiled tremulously. "You know there's a whole branch of Children's Aid dedicated to working with Native children, right?" he asked. "Finding Aboriginal families to place them with, especially in the city, can be challenging. And they have a very friendly LGBT policy."

Archer blinked at the change of topic. "Why—? You want to be a foster parent? I thought you wanted your own kids."

"I'm not sure it matters anymore. I keep thinking of how it was for you. Those kids could really use someone to look up to. A positive role model. You could be a good influence."

A good influence? Him? "I don't want to raise somebody else's kids," he protested even as something inside him latched on to the idea of making a difference. "I want to raise *ours*."

Ryan smirked. "Who's to say we can't do both?"

Archer shook his head in wonder. "You have the biggest heart of anyone I've ever met."

"Does that mean you'll think about it?" Ryan's hand slid suggestively up Archer's thigh, the backs of his fingers brushing Archer's crotch. "You know I'm going to get my way eventually. Why not save us some time and make it easy on yourself?"

He narrowed his eyes. "You don't ask for much, do you? Just where are we going to put all these kids of yours?"

"Ours," Ryan corrected, his eyes shining with a love Archer never imagined he'd be worthy of. "We'll make room."

Author's Note

Aboriginal affairs are complicated to most Canadians, never mind an international audience; Status versus non-Status Indians, reserve or non-reserve, band membership, Treaty Indians—it's a maze of legal definitions that confounds most people. Unfortunately stereotypes and misinformation abound.

Canada's Aboriginal, or Native, Peoples consist of First Nations (North American Indian), Métis, and Inuit; each have their own unique culture, history, and rights under the law. Even the terminology can be complex; the difference between a band and a reserve for example, or the use of "First Nations people" instead of the terms "Native American" or "Native Canadian." For the sake of an international audience, and because above all else, this is a romance novel, I have simplified some of the terminology and on occasion, generalized concepts. The Cree words used in the novel are spelled phonetically and are based on common usage. Any errors or misuse are entirely my own.

The Aboriginal experience in Canada tends to be portrayed as bleak. I didn't want that. I wanted to highlight the challenges but within a hopeful context. Archer's experiences may be distinctly Canadian, but they are entirely relatable by anyone who has ever felt disenfranchised because of their skin color or background. My intent was not to write a social commentary; however, I thought some readers might be interested in knowing more about the background and context of this novel. If that's you, read on.

For more than one hundred years, beginning in the late-nineteenth century, the government of Canada began a systematic campaign to "civilize" Native Peoples through the use of residential, or boarding, schools. An estimated 150,000 First Nations children were taken away from their families, deprived of their ancestral language, often abused (physically and sexually) and in some cases sterilized. The last residential school closed in 1996. The end result is generations of Aboriginal Peoples who were taught to be ashamed of their culture. Survivors of the residential system essentially grew up without parents, and so lacked models to follow when they came to have their own children. The full socioeconomic impact of this is only now being fully realized. In the province of Manitoba, where my character Archer grew up, recent statistics reveal upwards of eighty percent of children under the charge of the provincial government are Aboriginal. The problem is so severe that Aboriginal foster children with no placements fill entire hotels in Winnipeg.

In my novel, Archer alludes to many of the troubles plaguing the reservation system. The conditions on reservations vary widely depending on location, size, local government, and access to natural resources. While some are very prosperous, others do not even have fresh drinking water. The rates of substance abuse and suicide are far above the national average; solvent sniffing (glue, thinner, gasoline) is a real thing. Education levels are improving but still lag behind that of non-Aboriginals by a significant margin. Today many young Aboriginal Peoples are trying to reclaim their heritage and challenge stereotypes—topics like residential schools are now being taught as part of the regular curriculum—but there is still a long way to go as evidenced by the fact Winnipeg was recently (2015) named the most racist city in Canada ("Welcome to Winnipeg: Where Canada's racism problem is at its worst," *Maclean's*, January 22, 2015).

I rarely get political in my writing; in fact when I first came up with the idea for this story, Archer was not even Aboriginal. But a couple of things happened along the way. As I was writing, within the space of a few short months two shocking reports on the state of Aboriginal Peoples in Canada were released that made me impassioned.

When it comes to missing and murdered women, the statistics Alyssa Sky and Archer quote are all true. In 2014, the Royal Canadian Mounted Police released the official report on missing and murdered Aboriginal women in Canada. The total indicates that Aboriginal women are overrepresented among Canada's murdered and missing women. While the numbers may seem low compared to other countries, you have to remember Aboriginal women make up only 4.3 percent of females in Canada and yet account for 11.3 percent of reported-missing females and sixteen percent of female homicides. Repeated calls for a federal inquiry into missing and murdered Indigenous girls go unheard.

Shortly after the release of the RCMP report, the United Nations released a scathing report on the situation of Indigenous Peoples in Canada. In terms of socioeconomic conditions, heath, education, and justice, "the human rights problems faced by indigenous peoples in Canada [...] have reached crisis proportions in many respects."

Lastly, in August 2014 as I was preparing to submit this manuscript, the body of fifteen-year-old Tina Fontaine, a Native runaway whose own father had been beaten to death years before, was pulled out of the Red River near Winnipeg, Manitoba. She had been murdered and her body stuffed in a bag. The irony of it was that police found her only because they were searching for the corpse of a man, also Native, who drowned. In a shocking update, it was revealed that two Winnipeg police officers encountered Tina just days before her murder, *after* she had already been reported missing, but she was not taken into custody. Even now, as this manuscript prepares to go to print in late 2015, no suspects or leads in the case have been reported, and Tina Fontaine has sadly become another unfortunate statistic.

Chris Scully
Toronto, Canada
May 2014 – October 2015

Dear Reader,

Thank you for reading Chris Scully's *Until September*!

We know your time is precious and you have many, many entertainment options, so it means a lot that you've chosen to spend your time reading. We really hope you enjoyed it.

We'd be honored if you'd consider posting a review—good or bad—on sites like **Amazon, Barnes & Noble, Kobo, Goodreads, Twitter, Facebook, Tumblr,** and your blog or website. We'd also be honored if you told your friends and family about this book. Word of mouth is a book's lifeblood!

For more information on upcoming releases, author interviews, blog tours, contests, giveaways, and more, please sign up for our weekly, spam-free newsletter and visit us around the web:

    Newsletter: tinyurl.com/RiptideSignup
    Twitter: twitter.com/RiptideBooks
    Facebook: facebook.com/RiptidePublishing
    Goodreads: tinyurl.com/RiptideOnGoodreads
    Tumblr: riptidepublishing.tumblr.com

Thank you so much for Reading the Rainbow!

RiptidePublishing.com

Acknowledgments

This novel wouldn't have been possible without a number of people: firstly my wonderful beta readers and critique partners, Rob and Jamie, whose feedback, suggestions, and encouragement helped me immensely, and secondly, my editor at Riptide, Carole-ann Galloway, who pushed me (to the point of breaking sometimes) but was exactly the taskmistress I needed.

Finally, I'd like to highlight the work being done by Aboriginal and First Nations groups, commissions, and agencies across the country in an effort to bring attention to Aboriginal issues and give a voice to those who don't have one.

also by
Chris Scully

Fourth and Long
Inseparable
When Adam Kissed Me (sequel to Inseparable)
Nights Like These
Rebound
Snow on the Roof (anthology)
Touch Me

About the Author

Chris Scully lives in Toronto, Canada. She grew up spinning romantic stories in her head and always dreamed of one day being a writer even though life had other plans. Her characters have accompanied her through career turns as a librarian and an IT professional, until finally, to escape the tedium of a corporate day job, she took a chance and began putting her daydreams down on paper.

Tired of the same old boy-meets-girl stories, she found a home in M/M romance and strives to give her characters the happy endings they deserve. She divides her time between a mundane 9–5 cubicle job and a much more interesting fantasy life. When she's not working or writing (which isn't often these days), she loves puttering in the garden and traveling. She is an avid reader and tries to bring pieces of other genres and styles to her stories. While her head is crammed full of all the things she'd like to try writing, her focus is always on the characters first. She describes her characters as authentic, ordinary people—the kind of guy you might meet on the street, or the one who might be your best friend.

Although keeping up with social media is still a struggle given her schedule, she does love to hear from readers.

Website: chrisscullyblog.wordpress.com
Facebook: facebook.com/chris.scully.author
Goodreads: goodreads.com/author/show/6152322.Chris_Scully

Enjoy more stories like
Until September
at RiptidePublishing.com!

Blueberry Boys
ISBN: 978-1-62649-342-1

The Deep of the Sound
ISBN: 978-1-62649-276-9

Earn Bonus Bucks!

Earn 1 Bonus Buck for each dollar you spend. Find out how at
RiptidePublishing.com/news/bonus-bucks.

Win Free Ebooks for a Year!

Pre-order coming soon titles directly through our site and you'll
receive one entry into a drawing for a chance to win free books for
a year! Get the details at RiptidePublishing.com/contests.